PRAISE FOR

THE
SLEEPING
WORLD

"Restless, deeply imagined, and exhilarating, *The Sleeping World* is a lyrical novel about searching and loss and the essential urgency to live. Fuentes vividly evokes the yearning, churning rage of these students in tumultuous post-Franco Spain. A gorgeous and powerful debut."

—Kirstin Valdez Quade, author of *Night at the Fiestas*

"A bracing debut."

—*Atlanta Magazine*

"In *The Sleeping World*, Gabrielle Lucille Fuentes succeeds in capturing Spain's liminal period between dictatorship and democracy on an intimate, deeply personal level. The fever dream of Mosca's story, however, reaches beyond Spain's borders to confront universal questions of love and loss amidst the violent current of history. This is a novel that will stay with me."

—Gabriel Urza, author of *All That Followed*

"Fuentes's ambitious novel does succeed at creating a bleak and disturbing picture of post-Franco Spain."

—*Booklist*

"A stunning debut . . . beautifully written."

—Isthmus

"Full of ferocity, full of desire, full of sadness, full of love, The Sleeping World . . . is a marvelous novel. Fuentes goes all in here and the resilient people and damaged world of post-Franco Spain are conjured with bracing warmth and terrifying vividness . . . I was sweating when I put this novel down. That happens all too rarely."

—Laird Hunt, author of Ray of the Star and Neverhome

"A wonderful voice and a beautifully surprising third act."

—Kea Wilson, author of We Eat Our Own

"How do you have the energy to move forward when 2016 seems to have been designed to suck the life out of us? . . . You read Gabrielle Lucille Fuentes's The Sleeping World. It's a novel that thrums with revolution, with youth, and with longing. Set in 1970s post-Franco Spain, it's full of punks and students and siblings and activists and the possibilities of a world turned upside down."

—Kaitlyn Greenidge, author of We Love You,
Charlie Freeman, for The Fader

"The women in this novel are hard and sharp and searching, and the dirt and hunger and sorrow throughout get into your bloodstream fast, fastening you tightly to the narrative. It's both thoroughly engrossing and weird, that difficult-to-attain mix of skilled storytelling coupled with trust in the reader's ability to shift between modes and meet the story in its raw gut of feeling."

—Gina Abelkop, author of I Eat Cannibals,
for Lute & Drum

"Fuentes's heartbreaking story has Mosca mirror Spain's devastated society, but the saving grace is that Mosca also reflects her homeland's strength of character and the determination to survive."

—Rigoberto González, NBC Latino News

THE SLEEPING WORLD

GABRIELLE LUCILLE FUENTES

TOUCHSTONE

New York   London   Toronto   Sydney   New Delhi

Touchstone
An Imprint of Simon & Schuster, Inc.
1230 Avenue of the Americas
New York, NY 10020

First Touchstone trade paperback edition September 2017

TOUCHSTONE and colophon are registered trademarks of Simon & Schuster, Inc.

For information about special discounts for bulk purchases, please contact Simon & Schuster Special Sales at 1-866-506-1949 or business@simonandschuster.com.

The Simon & Schuster Speakers Bureau can bring authors to your live event. For more information or to book an event, contact the Simon & Schuster Speakers Bureau at 1-866-248-3049 or visit our website at www.simonspeakers.com.

Interior design by Kyle Kabel

Manufactured in the United States of America

10   9   8   7   6   5   4   3   2   1

The Library of Congress has cataloged the hardcover editions as follows:

Names: Fuentes, Gabrielle Lucille, author.
Title: The sleeping world : a novel / Gabrielle Lucille Fuentes.
Description: First Touchstone hardcover edition. | New York: Touchstone, 2016.
Identifiers: LCCN 2015039564
Subjects: LCSH: College student—Spain—Fiction. | Brothers and sisters—Fiction. | Missing persons—Fiction. | Protest movements—Fiction | Spain—Politics and government—1975–1982—Fiction. | BISAC: FICTION/Literary. | FICTION / Political. | FICTION | Coming of Age.
Classification: LCC PS3606.U37 S57 2016 | DDC 813/.6—dc23 LC record available at http://lccn.loc.gov/2015039564

ISBN 978-1-5011-3167-7
ISBN 978-1-5011-3168-4 (pbk)
ISBN 978-1-5011-3169-1 (ebook)

For my parents and for Thibault:
my rivers, my sea

In Spain, the dead are more alive than in any other country in the world—their profile cuts like the edge of a barber's razor.

—Federico García Lorca, 1933

Police and thieves in the street, oh yeah

—The Clash, 1977

PART I

AND BEST
PRESERVES
THE FIRE

One

Our final university exams were in two days. Grito would probably pass because despite everything, he'd been staying up and studying. La Canaria was sure to fail, and she'd get sent back to the Canary Islands, where they were rioting, and I'd have to deal with a blubbering Grito. As for myself, I just didn't know.

We'd spent all semester protesting, gathering in the plaza and marching for the Communist Party, for democracy, for the legalization of divorce and abortion, for jobs, for anarchy, for anything except what we'd always known. Our dictator general finally dead and there would be democratic elections soon, the first in more than forty years, but we didn't really know what they would mean. We'd stayed out all day, screaming and drinking, pinning the Communist Party's hammer and sickle to our bags and jackets. La Canaria walked around with safety pins she'd stolen from her part-time job at La Reina Tailoring, and a couple of potatoes cut in half, offering to pierce anybody and anything.

At night, fights would break out with the right wing, *facha* students whose fathers were all members of the old guard. We tried to stay clear of them because the *fachas* were armed and we were scared they'd use the guns they had sometime soon. So we'd go to El Bar Chico, where they played the newest bootleg copy of the Ramones on loop and set fire to pictures of our dictator general. The bar filled with smoke and ash fell on our hair. Everyone knew we'd grabbed the photos from the altars by our grandmothers' beds, but we acted like we hadn't. Like we'd sneaked into officers' houses and stolen them. Like we'd torn them down from municipal buildings. Like we were ridding the whole city of his face when it was really just our own apartments.

We couldn't be expected to go to class anymore. We had exams to take, but nobody knew what to write on them, which history, which present. Even at our *facha* university, some teachers were passing students for writing anything. Or they failed anyone who'd missed a day. Poor Marco tried to hang himself when he got his first exam back. He used a shoelace and it broke. But our courses were just another dream of that chimerical spring. They couldn't be real because nothing had been for months.

Dusk, and I was supposed to meet La Canaria and Grito under the big clock in the Plaza Mayor like always. I walked away from my abuela's apartment on Calle Grillo. The crowds grew thicker the closer I got to the plaza. Students who had already taken their last exams carried each other on their shoulders, cheap bottles of cava in their hands. They poured out the bottles on anyone passing by. Those who had just graduated lugged buckets of red paint for scrawling their initials on the university walls. They dipped their brushes into the paint and left trails of red across the plaza's stones. Someone had gotten into the Plaza Hotel and hung a big hand-painted flag of a crossed-out swastika from a balcony. The city had emptied out for the summer, all the officials safe in their country houses. We were the only ones left.

La Canaria and Grito detached themselves from a group under the clock and made their way toward me. Grito had on his backpack, but it wasn't full of just books anymore. Odd shapes pressed against the olive-green canvas. A crowbar stuck out the top.

La Canaria was wearing the top to a kid's Superman pajama set. Her jeans had started to split where her homemade bleach experiment had worn through the fabric. The night before she'd made me style her hair like Patti Smith's on the cover of *Horses,* but it coiled up as soon as I chopped any length off. "I'll shave it like a Tibetan monk," she said, but Grito bribed her out of it with some hash he'd been planning to give her anyway.

I tried not to look at Grito, ponytail getting greasier each week, pelvic bone pressed against his once-white T-shirt. On the front he'd written NO WORK, ALL DAY and freckled it, either accidentally or on purpose, with cigarette burns.

La Canaria hummed a song from a show last week, "Wha, wha I wanna wha—how's it go?" but Grito ignored her, walking and rolling a cigarette at the same time. "Wha, wha, bu, bada, ba!"

"Shut up," he said, "you don't even know the song." He flicked a speck of tobacco off his tongue.

"You're wrong, *tío.*"

"Then how come you don't know the words?"

"I do! It goes like this." La Canaria pulled on his ponytail and shouted in English, " 'Rot riot, I want that riot!' "

The crowd of students beneath the clock tower had started to thin, everyone choosing a favorite dive to start the night. The lights from the empty buildings winked down at us. Across the plaza at Café National, girls my age sat eating cream puffs and pulling at their pleated polyester skirts to be sure they completely covered their knees.

"Look at those virgins," La Canaria said. "They are in for a rude surprise."

"You going to El Chico tonight?" I asked Grito.

"Nah," Grito said. "I got something else to do."

We started at the bar under the philology library, with its low ceilings and cracked leather saddles for chairs. A leg of serrano ham, carved down to the bone, sat on the counter. It was the kind of place we would never go, old-fashioned food and paintings, except for what it had in back and who was always coming in and out because of it. A newspaper clipping of the dictator general's wife hung on the pig's hoof like a mortuary tag. Marco, in a turtleneck and scarf, was in the corner with a bunch of boring types I didn't recognize. We pushed through the crowd and found a table. Marco came over to us as soon as we sat down.

"Nice scarf," I said.

He sat down and, when we ignored him, pulled out a history textbook and started reading.

"You heard about that show tonight?"

"Yeah, Mosca, everyone's heard about it," Grito said.

"Is that where you're going?"

"Maybe."

"Let's go," La Canaria said. "Los Pasotas—I saw their flyer. They look hot."

"Where the hell did you see their flyer?" Grito said.

"Look at this *sapo*," La Canaria said, ignoring him and turning to Marco. She picked up her too-full beer and slammed it down on the open pages of Marco's textbook. The foam sloshed over the sides and pooled in the gutter. The muscles in Marco's arm shook, but he didn't wipe up the beer.

"That a Falange manual you reading?" La Canaria said. "How to suck *facha* head?"

Marco shook the beer off his pages. "Say it," he said. "I don't give a fuck. It doesn't make you a pig to study."

"No, my citizen," Grito said, and clapped Marco on the back. "The industrious Spanish male is the backbone of the fatherland." Grito had been studying, too, but he had the sense to do it in private.

The door to the print shop hidden in the back of the bar opened, and a young guy in a worn wool jacket hurried out. We pretended we didn't notice—we certainly weren't going to stare or say anything—but we sat quiet and important, like we breathed the same rare air, even though all we were doing was drinking beer close to where others risked their lives. He brushed his hair out of his eyes and I recognized him—Felipe, a doctoral student. He'd been friends with my brother. He spotted me and took a step toward us, but I looked away. Marco opened the textbook again and bent the spine completely backward, cracking the cheap glue binding. He skid the book across the table and onto the floor. The people behind us cheered.

"It's a pretty minor text anyway," I said.

"You would know, Mosca." Grito finished his beer and got up to leave.

Los Pasotas sounded the same as all the other bands who had started up in the cities and come out here at the end of their tours, but better, because they were in the ear-bleeding present.

"See those shirts they're selling?" La Canaria shouted at Grito at the bar. The band had made T-shirts with a photo of a dead rat belly-up in a gutter. They were to pay for the trip back. "Get me and Mosca one to share."

I pulled some coins out of my jeans and handed them to Grito. He came back wearing the shirt.

"*Pendejo,*" La Canaria shouted, and wrapped her arms

around him. She took the rubber band out of her ponytail, and her hair collapsed around her face, jagged and perfect somehow, just like the album cover. She must have ironed it straight. I was trying to dress like Patti Smith, too, in my black turtleneck and cheap rings. I liked the fact that she was ugly and looked like a boy and didn't give a fuck she couldn't sing—that was real punk. But La Canaria was going to steal her from me, too.

La Canaria broke away from Grito and pushed through the crowd to the bathroom. When she got back, she had on thick eyeliner and peacock-colored eye shadow, like the girl selling T-shirts, and her hair slicked back with someone's pomade. I wanted to get away from her, to get away from Grito slobbering all over her. I pushed closer to the band until I was right in front, in the shifting semicircle around them and their noise. Just a drummer and two electric guitars. They all had their shirts off, and sweat dripped down their chins and sprayed off their hair when they shook. At first they stuck to covers of the Clash that we'd heard when Samo snuck copies of the record back from London and fleeced them at El Chico. The records had disappeared immediately, gone before I could scrape together enough pesetas to buy one. Soon the band wasn't singing in bad English or Castilian or singing at all. That was fine. The crowd pressed tighter around me, the space between audience and sound shrinking. Pressed up against the speakers, the band's three chords churned my bones to paper, water, ash. We wanted to thrash to music that had no words, that had no music. There were no words for what we wanted, no sense to be made. We didn't want to build anything new. That was the general's line.

The band stopped playing and the crowd booed. We could finally stay out as late as we wanted—no law that closed the bars at ten—but our shit town was the end of the line, and the band wanted back on the road to Barcelona before the sun rose. Grito wanted to go with them.

"*Cabrón,* what are you going to do in Barcelona?" La Canaria teased. But the truth was we all wanted out.

On the street, Grito walked away with La Canaria.

I caught up to them. "Where are you going? To El Chico?"

"Actually, I've got an action tonight," Grito said. He wrapped his arms around La Canaria's torso, tucking his thumbs into the mounds of skin that eased over her jeans, looking at me the whole time. Oh yeah, Grito, I wanted to hiss. Be on your guard. Because at any moment I might start giving a rat's ass.

"Look at this big guy," La Canaria said, leaning back into Grito. "He thinks he's Che. You got an action tonight, Che?"

"Yeah, *chica,*" Grito crooned into her ear. "Tonight we are gonna fuck shit up. Wanna come?"

Under the railway bridge built to carry soldiers and equipment to the new U.S. military base, two punks tore up old shirts and handed them out to people who didn't have bandanas. A crowd of us waited in the dark, sticking to the shadows of the bridge's cement foundations, only a forearm or slice of neck visible when a train passed above. La Canaria pulled an old marmalade jar from her jean jacket. It was full of the liquor that Samo, who'd finally gotten fired from El Chico, had been making in his bathtub, though La Canaria said, "He doesn't have a bathtub, *idiota,* this is bidet brew." She gulped from the jar. It made her cough and sprayed out of her nose. She laughed and shot some at Grito through her teeth. The liquid sparked in a shaft of orange streetlight before it hit him. She passed me the jar. The liquor tasted like paint thinner, and the second I swallowed, I could feel it carving away at mucus and tissue, anything that was soft inside me.

When Grito finished the jar, tilting his head back and licking the rim, La Canaria pulled out another with the sardine label still on it. More students and punks pushed under the bridge, backing us against the damp foundations. We spit and swallowed, snorted and coughed. Grito passed the final jar La Canaria had brought. Felipe from the print shop, my brother's old friend, passed me a bottle and smiled. He moved to the front of the crowd, and someone handed me another unlabeled jar, and I drank the liquid along with the gob of spit floating on the surface. Grito jumped out from under the bridge and threw a jar at a passing train. It only hit the railing, but others followed him. We stood in the rainbows of glass shards that collapsed back on us.

We pulled our bandanas over our faces and moved out from under the bridge. We were out on the streets. The streets opened for us. "Like a *puta* parting her thighs," Grito said. No, I thought, like a river without sediment, like waking up in water and screaming to be carried downstream. We were carried, weightless, awake through empty streets. Bottles tossed at streetlights. Bring on the dark. Give us impediment. We frightened the city, emptied it of people. All that was left was their droppings. We broke windows, pulling kid leather gloves, feather hats, riding whips out onto the street.

"I wish Alexis were here," someone whispered in my ear, the voice impossibly clear and solid under our screams, and for a moment it was like I could see my brother standing beside Grito, a pile of stolen fedoras in his arms, neck arched back in a laugh, proud that we were doing something finally. I felt like I hadn't felt in years, like I was alive and awake, like he was smiling at me. Like he was all around me, though he could not be there, though only shadows danced behind Grito, and who could have even whispered his name? I reached through a broken store window and pulled out a toaster oven and threw it on the cobblestones. Give us impediment. Give us something to tear down. We turned onto Calle de la Gloria. We saw the parked government cars lining the street as we wanted to line it, filling space with black metal and shining chrome as we wanted to fill it. Why were all these cars parked outside municipal buildings late at night, at the beginning of summer? Why but for us? We surrounded the cars. Grito pulled the crowbar out of his backpack. We climbed the cars, made them sway under our weight. Grito stood on a hood, raised his crowbar, and crashed it into the windshield.

"What the hell are you doing?" A man in a suit broke through the crowd. He grabbed Grito's shoulder and tossed him off the car. The man was twice Grito's size, his hair cleanly clipped and his fingers thick from having been broken many times. He pinned Grito to the cement.

"Get off him," I shouted, and kicked the man in the back. He barely noticed.

"Get out of here, you fucking *facha*!" someone behind me shouted. We tugged and kicked at the man until he turned around to face us. Grito grabbed the crowbar that had fallen out of his hands and swung, cuffing the man's shoulder. He fell backward onto the pavement. We kicked him until he was still.

We could have kept going, but we didn't. A kind of pulse stopped us, a lack of inertia when our boots hit flesh that didn't resist. The man slowly pushed himself up onto his knees, one arm hanging limp. His face was bloody and his breathing whistled through broken ribs.

"*Idiotas*," Samo said beside me, "he's a police officer."

"You think I give a fuck?" Grito shouted through his bandana, still breathing heavily.

The man lifted his broken face to us and grinned, his teeth dripping red.

Grito dropped the crowbar. We turned and ran.

Two

My abuela didn't notice any change, or if she did, she herself did not change. She left the house only for Mass and to buy groceries. Her daily trips to the fruit seller, the bakery, the butcher used to last her all morning, but the old vendors had been replaced by their sons or nephews, and she had no one to talk to. They hurried her along, she said, like a log through a mill. She must have been happy in some way when the general died, but I think part of her didn't believe he could. She believed that he would rise from the dead or that it was a trick to draw out the seditious elements and slaughter them. The general had taken too much from her to be truly gone.

She set out my breakfast, a row of Maria cookies, even though it was almost midday by the time I stumbled into the kitchen. I turned on the burner to reheat the coffee. She snatched the moka pot out of my hands. "Don't touch that," she said. "That's disgusting." Her nails accidentally grazed the underside of my wrist, but they were too soft to make a mark.

She poured out the old coffee and started a new pot. It was just me and her left living in the apartment.

Last night's events surfaced hesitantly. It wasn't hard to push them back into the murky water. I wanted them to tunnel down the shower drain with the sweat and booze leaking out of me, but that was too much to ask. Everything was carried. After I toweled off and dressed, I found my abuela watching a television musical in the kitchen. Her posture was perfect despite her age, and she watched every commercial and news report as if it had the same importance. The song was a cover of a *ye-ye* hit that had been on the radio years ago. A woman singing about how content her heart was, the trumpets and violins rising to meet her upbeat soprano notes. The singer and her backups danced around a gas station in white go-go boots and bright yellow uniforms that showed their midriffs and upper thighs. An old officer with stacks of medals on his chest sat watching them and smiled. It was an old show, dated and safe.

"Can you believe this trash?" my abuela said. "Hardly any clothes at all."

She looked up at me from where she sat at the very edge of her gold-and-gray-brocade armchair, long fingers perched on the hand-knitted doilies that covered the almost half-century of wear. I was wearing a crumpled men's black button-down, the sleeves chopped short and layers of flea-market silver chains tucked under the collar like a tie, and the combat boots La Canaria and I found after months of digging in the trash. I hadn't let my abuela touch my jeans in weeks, and they were stiff with stains.

"Good," she said, and turned back to the television. "You stay serious." She'd supported my going to university, though when I'd started, her butcher said that only women who weren't going to be mothers went to university and women who weren't going to be mothers were going to be whores.

A glittering new kitchen appeared on the television screen, occupied by a housewife, one of those golden Spanish pillars, obedient and always pregnant, waxing her floors with orgasmic joy.

"Pathetic," my abuela said. She rapped out a counter-beat to the jingle on the armchair. Above the television was an altar with photos of my parents and saints. In a closed compartment under the altar, in a cupboard that blended with the wall, was my abuela's collection of novels, poetry, and history books from before the war. I never saw her open the compartment, but whenever I checked on it, each book was carefully dusted. The whole apartment was an altar to the dead, the disappeared, the lost, the gone. Nestled next to the faded photos of my parents was a new addition—a picture of me and my brother as kids.

"What's that doing there?" I said.

She didn't answer me.

I turned off the television, but my abuela didn't shift her eyes. She kept them pinned to the screen, as if scrutinizing the black glass and flecks of static for their weak moral fiber.

"What's that picture doing up there?"

Her lips were moving in prayer. The slow, precise shapes I knew so well, a track worn painfully over her false teeth. I kissed the top of her head where she'd gathered her soft white hair into a bun. She did her hair herself, kept it perfectly in place without lacquer. It smelled of baby powder and chamomile, a preserved scent, closed but clean.

"Study hard, *mija*," I heard her call as I left the apartment.

The university library was one of the oldest in Europe. It was empty except for a few nerds who still cared. My last chance to make up for a semester of not studying, but I just wandered the stacks, like I had before I was a student. I would walk through the library, trace with my fingers the worn stone seats of the ancient students, all men, all my size or smaller. See the medieval monks hunched over their books, the scribes copying the holy word, their industry fueled by devotion to the Savior, their devotion unshaken by doubt. Don't look too closely at what the scribes are actually studying—algebra from the Arabic, theology from the Talmud—ink out this act of translating. See them instead writing a new language made by a lisping king, its structures as narrow as the mind that sculpted it. There must have been pages that weren't burned, words not blotted out of recognition. I had searched for them. My murdered poets drew from deep wells, even if they were presently hidden from me. They spoke the same words as the monks, as the conquistadores, as our dictator general, but coaxed a language anew from the charred bones they'd been tossed. I had taken comfort that we had been lying for millennia, erasing whole races of writers, executing texts with aplomb. It wasn't new. And someone had always been pressing hidden words from quill to parchment backed by stone. Whispering them into someone's ear. Even if the parchment was burned and the hand chopped off and thrown into the same fire, the stone remained. Only there were the words legible.

Years ago, I'd decided to stay in the old library, chose philology over English for my major, because I thought there, among these old books, something must have slipped by. Some words that, despite their sedition, were too historically important to erase or too clever for the censors to detect. A couple of writers had done it right after the war. Their books were complicated, dense. The *fachas* never saw the crossbow pointed at their throats. You make a child hungry by denying her food. You turn hunger to anger when you rip pages from her schoolbooks. But I didn't find what I was looking for. In the bar underneath the philology library, the students didn't quote from the old books with their crumbling bindings. Instead, they growled and twitched in their seats, casting about for new words. Words shaped like handmade bombs and Molotov cocktails. Words that weren't words at all. Because there was nothing we could say that didn't have Indian, Moor, Republican blood dripping off it. Our tongue the tongue of murderers. The general didn't come from nowhere.

The bar underneath the library was empty. A few display plates sat next to the ham, but there was no bartender to swipe away the flies from the tortilla, and a hard skin had developed on the *membrillo*. The door that led to the print shop was locked and a heavy wooden bench pushed in front of it. Maybe everyone was in the plaza.

I smoked a cigarette under the tower and waited, but the plaza was empty, too. The huge black hands of the clock twitching slowly. Sometimes it looked like the clock was going backward, if you caught it right when the hour changed. The hands hovered for a moment, unable to decide whether to progress or regress. A man in a rumpled jacket, his hat pulled over his eyes, leaned against a stone pillar on the opposite side of the plaza. He was staring right at me. I stomped out my cigarette and hustled over to El Chico. There Grito and La Canaria were, sitting at the middle table, slugging big bottles of beer. They cheered when I walked in.

"Mosca! You found us!" La Canaria yelled. "We were hiding from you!"

"*Hijos de putas,*" I mumbled, and went up to the bar without kissing them hello. "I was standing at the clock for an hour. Why weren't you there?"

They looked at each other and then up at me. We didn't mention last night.

"Let me buy you a drink," Grito said, sliding up beside me. He was wearing his white T-shirt with the anarchy "A" drawn on it, the pits yellow from sweat. His arms were shaking a little and covered in bruises, either from fucking La Canaria or from last night. I didn't care.

"It's the least you can do," I said. Grito ordered us two pitchers to share because somehow La Canaria had finished both of their bottles in the time it took him to walk up to the bar. Under the table I saw his bag, full of books again. Maybe he'd had the chance to study earlier.

"I need to piss," La Canaria said before I could sit down. She grabbed my arm, blowing kisses to Grito when we squeezed by him. The bar was full of punks and their dogs. Greasy paper napkins and layers of sticky sawdust covered the floor. Newspaper blotted out the windows. La Canaria kicked the dogs we passed but moved by too fast for anyone to notice that she was the one who'd done it. The dogs strained at their rope and chain-link leashes, blaming their owners, blaming the other dogs.

In the bathroom, La Canaria jumped up on the sink, her back to the mirror. "You do me and I'll do you." She handed me a stick of black eyeliner. I leaned in close to her face and layered more makeup beneath her lashes and in thick lines on her eyelids. She turned to the mirror to see how I'd done and smudged the black with her thumb. It looked like she'd gone to bed without washing her face. "Nice. Your turn." La Canaria wrapped her legs around my torso, bringing me in close to her body. I could feel the zipper of her jeans pressed against my own.

"I don't want any," I told her.

"You never have enough on."

I could smell Grito on her, his acrid communion-wine cologne, his hash cigarettes, the powdery baby scent of the detergent his abuela used to clean his sheets. I could feel how those sheets used to press down on me. The sound of the novice Carmelites chanting in the abbey across the street. The sense of suffocating when the air under the sheets grew hot from our breath.

"That's enough," I said to La Canaria, trying to squirm away from her. She had me locked between her legs. She wrapped a thick arm around my neck and twisted my ear so I wouldn't move.

"I'm trying to make you look good, Mosquita."

A roll of skin escaped from underneath her black tank top. I could see ridges of flesh between her pits and her push-up bra, soft spaces prickled with three-day-old black hairs. Grito teased her about being chubby, but we all knew he loved it. Her skin was darker than the rest of ours. Not dark enough to articulate what it meant but dark enough to notice.

Somebody pounded on the bathroom door.

"Oh, Mosca, *chica*!" La Canaria cried out. "Right there, that's how I like it!"

I pinched her right where I guessed her nipple was, and though I got mostly bra, she was surprised enough to let me go. Grito was hanging outside when I opened the door, smirking. I pushed by him and he went into the bathroom. He scraped the trash can across the floor to keep the door shut.

There were only a couple of people I knew in the bar that I could talk to. I mean, I knew everybody, but I didn't want to talk to everybody. Stupid Marco was there, his neck still bruised from his attempted suicide by shoelace, and he was laughing because some girl was sitting on his lap, kissing the purple splotches. I grabbed one of the pitchers Grito had bought and sat down by them. The girl poured herself a drink from it, as did everybody else at the table.

"See this?" Marco asked, fingering his neck. I didn't know what made him decide to stop hiding the bruises and show them off, except maybe he'd run out of turtlenecks.

"Everybody sees it, Marco," I said. "And everybody wishes you'd done it with your abuelita's pantyhose, like you were planning, so it worked." I heard his scores weren't even that bad.

"You're just jealous, Mosca," the girl on his lap said. Some girl who hung around him sometimes, I could never remember her name, but I was sick of Marco grinning at me because of her. I threw my drink in her face. She got up, her white shirt soaked through. Instead of hitting me herself, she pushed Marco in front of her.

"I'm not going to fight Mosca," Marco said, putting me in a headlock. "I love her too fucking much." He started messing up my hair, and his forearm grazed my breast.

"Don't touch me!" I said.

His hands flew up in the air. "I'm sorry, Mosca. I really didn't mean to."

"If this bar weren't so full of wimps, I'd be happy," I said.

The girl walked over to the bathroom to clean up. She opened the door and faked a scream when she saw La Canaria and Grito in there.

"I heard if La Canaria fails, she's getting sent back to the Islands," Samo, who didn't really care that he'd been fired, said from a couple tables over.

"Mosca would love that, wouldn't you?" Marco sat back down and folded his arms tightly around his torso. "Have Grito all to yourself again?"

"They can get married and spend their honeymoon picking sugarcane for all I care," I said. I turned to Marco. "Buy me another beer."

He jumped up, which made me feel good. That girl was still standing by the bathroom door, shivering from the drink I'd thrown on her.

When La Canaria and Grito got back, they stank of salt and

plastic. Everyone howled at them and slapped Grito on the shoulder. La Canaria shouted and slammed her head up and down in the air to the music. She pretended she'd tripped over a dog and stuffed her tits in Marco's face. Marco high-fived Grito once La Canaria stood up and let him breathe again.

At Samo's table they were talking about the Madrid protests.

"Those fuckers don't stop," Samo said. "And I don't mean just marching or breaking shit, like here. I mean they are planning for armed resistance."

"Then they have very short memories," Marco said.

"Those *fachas* who killed the Communist lawyers in Madrid in January?" Samo said. "They didn't even think they'd get arrested."

"And they still didn't get the people who were really behind it," Grito said. "Yeah, Madrid, that's where the real action is."

The door swung open, and a group of punks with their faces covered by black bandanas rushed in. They pushed a table against the door of the bar. The dogs barked at them and their sweaty, shaky fear.

"*¿Qué coño?*" the bartender yelled. "What's going on?" The punks pulled off their bandanas as if we didn't already recognize them. They'd been the ones tearing up shirts and handing out hooch last night. Felipe was with them, still in his worn brown jacket, though his hair was dripping with sweat.

"It's cool," one of them said. "We're just going to chill here." Felipe sat down at the bar and counted his coins to see how many beers he could cover. Then he walked over to our table. I ignored him, but he leaned over us and spoke in a whisper. "Mosca, you should get out of here."

"Why?" Grito said.

It wasn't that we had forgotten last night, it just hadn't mattered. There was no firm ground. There was no past or future.

You could dream up a night like that and ride the reputation for months. Or you could dream and not wake up.

"That pig from last night? They're looking for you," Felipe said.

"There was a huge crowd," Marco said, "and we had bandanas on."

"You weren't even there," I said.

"I was," he said. "I was there."

"Look, I don't know why," Felipe said, "but the word is they're looking for you three." He pointed at Grito, La Canaria, and me.

"*Coño, coño,*" Grito mumbled. "How do they know who we are?"

"No one saw any of us," I said.

"I just wanted to tell you, Mosca," Felipe said.

The dogs started whining, their barks mixing with the police's German shepherds outside. Felipe had a handgun tucked in back of his black jeans. We glanced up at the photo of the general with a noose drawn around his neck. Underneath it someone had written our favorite epithet: *el Cabronísimo*. The hash in our pockets felt heavy. The police pounded at the door. The dogs inside went wild.

"I'm outta here," La Canaria said. We rushed out the back door, spilling our beers. Marco dropped some pesetas on the table for the bartender. "Such a gentleman," she called after him.

The streets were full of students partying, and the punks lost themselves in the crowds, dragging their dogs with them. We pushed a path away from the bar, and the barking faded.

"How do you know that guy?" Grito asked me over the crowds.

"Who?" I said.

"The punk with the gun."

"I don't know him."

"Yeah, you do. He wasn't gonna tell us except he knew you. Wasn't he friends with your brother—"

"Shut the fuck up," I said.

"Do you think he's right?" Grito said.

A couple of *fachas* pushed between us, spilling beer on my jeans and combat boots.

"You want to fight, Commie?" One of them threw a drunken punch at Grito, which he dodged.

"I want out of this Nazi city," Grito said. He held La Canaria tight around the waist. He looked skinny up against her, like a little girl with a long greasy ponytail.

"No one saw you," I repeated, but I was scared, too.

"Let's get out of town for the night," Grito shouted. "Find a little countryside hostel." He raised his eyebrows at La Canaria. Real subtle, that *tío*.

"Good idea," La Canaria said, tugging on his ear.

"We'll just hide out for the night," Grito said. "We'll be back in time for our exams."

La Canaria pushed Marco over to me. "Here, Mosca, you can bring this along for company."

Marco's face crisped in that pathetic way it did every time I looked at him.

"He's not the one they're looking for," I said.

"Maybe he's the one who ratted us out," Grito said.

"Fuck you," Marco said. "I was there, same as you. But maybe Felipe's right. We'll get out of town, just for a night."

It had been years since I'd left Casasrojas, even just for an afternoon. I had to be near for Alexis, just in case, but there was a pulling away, too. I needed only the softest words to wake it. The night before, I'd felt something—something dragging me awake—felt near to him somehow. I wanted that again. I thought of the calls he would make from phone booths, my abuela forced to accept the charge so she could hear his voice crackling back to us from wherever he'd disappeared to for the night. And the cities he'd describe to me when he returned— Madrid, Granada, San Sebastián, Barcelona—perfect for having held him.

"I'm coming," I said. "But I'm not coming with Marco."

"We'll be back before you know who you're coming with," La Canaria said. She tugged Grito behind her, deeper into the crowd.

The train station was full of grandmothers dressed in black who scattered like pigeons when we came onto the platform. The next train out of town was in fifteen minutes. Grito crumbled some hash into his cigarette while we waited. Since we didn't pay any attention to them, the grandmothers regrouped, edging closer to us and cooing about bad habits.

La Canaria jumped up on Grito's shoulders. "I'm hungry, *cariño*," she said, and slunk her tongue into his ear. "Get me something to eat." She nibbled on his neck, her teeth moving up and down like fingers doing piano scales.

He tried to shrug her off of him. "You want a sandwich?"

"I'm too starving to walk," she said. "You better carry me."

Grito stumbled off the platform with La Canaria on his back. Marco followed them.

"You look like a circus act," I said. "A clown following a fucking elephant on a beach ball that's about to pop!" They didn't turn around. Once Grito was out of sight, I walked to the phone booth and called my abuela.

"I'm gonna stay at my girlfriend's tonight." I spoke with the receiver close to my mouth, despite the film that had formed on it. "Yeah, Susanna—she lives next to the library." I hung up and heard the last of my coins clunk into the phone. "You're fucking kidding me."

"Hush," whispered one of the grandmothers. She could have been my abuela. I swear, the second they turn sixty, every widow in Castile-León goes through this ceremony where they get dropped into a vat of olives and wrapped in serrano ham, and by the time they're pulled out, they all look the same. "Don't talk like that," she told me.

"*Vale*, Señora. I'm sorry."

She offered me a hard anise candy. The other widows stepped closer to me. "Where are you going, *chica*?" one of them asked.

"To Madrid," I said, making up a lie. "To join the protests."

"What protests?" the little widow asked.

"For the Communist Party," I told her, wondering how many rosaries she'd had her head under and for how long.

"Why would you want to do that?" one of them said. "Those protests are a disgrace."

"The general gave the king very clear directions about how to lead our country once God took him," the widow said, crossing herself. "This election goes against the will of God."

Grito, La Canaria, and Marco came back then, La Canaria still on Grito's back, Marco following them. La Canaria was holding on to Grito with one arm and biting into a huge tortilla sandwich. Bits of greasy potato and egg stuck to her chin. "What are you talking about to these *viejas*, Mosca?"

"Nothing," I said. "Let's get on the train." I didn't want Grito to try to fight these pigeon-ladies. Didn't want to watch them slam their heavy purses into his skull while La Canaria cheered him on. I'd seen it before.

"Here, take this," Grito said, handing me a bulging plastic bag full of wine boxes and Coca-Cola bottles. "You owe me."

"No, I got her covered," Marco said, and tried to put his arm around my shoulder. I bent down to tie my laces, and he stumbled instead. La Canaria, still on Grito's back, laughed.

The train edged out of Casasrojas. The sun hit the university buildings, turning the gold stones pink. For years I'd known exactly where I would paint my initials on those walls when I graduated. How I would write the extra symbol for honors on the top right corner. The students used to write their names in bull's blood. Now they used red paint. We crawled out of the city. I could still see the spot high above the street. The spot I showed my brother when we were so small, we could barely see it, and he laughed.

Leaving the city, I thought I'd see Alexis. It had been two years, but I still thought I'd see him in Casasrojas, his black hair cresting above the mass of wool hats the old men wore out walking after siesta. He'd started writing his name in spray paint on the city walls—first making fun of the students and then as something else. He wrote in black spray paint, making curved and delicate letters, spelling out *ALEXIS,* and later just *A L X S,* sometimes a meter long, sometimes smaller than an outstretched hand. I looked for the signatures throughout Casasrojas. Most of them had been painted over or bleached out, but he said he'd tagged every place he'd been. I'd go on walks before dawn in the tunnels that the new streets passed over. The fluorescents would flicker, a power outage or a surge. I'd think, he must be here, he must have scared the pigeons flying toward me, but the lights jerked back on and it was only me who scared them, the echo of my footsteps. Or someone else walking in the dark before dawn.

The train was mostly empty. The cars smelled of smoke

and ham sandwiches, the windows yellow and smudged with kids' handprints. We opened the boxes of wine, chugged some, poured in the Coke, and swirled it around.

Even in our abuela's apartment on Calle Grillo, I'd turn my back to the front door and know he was coming in. I could feel him, not his breath but his whole body, his whole life, pressed down on the back of my neck. Soft as the place in a baby's skull before it's formed, heavy as that, too. And I would wait, wanting to hear his keys in the door even after my abuela changed the lock. I'd wait for his steps, the pattern I'd know anywhere, because if he made it to the door, he might be too weak or frightened to knock. It had to be me who let him in. I was the reason he wasn't coming back.

I'd stand there until my abuela called out, "What are you doing, *mija*?"

"Nothing," I'd say. But she knew what I was doing. I was never sure what I could hide from her. That I knew I couldn't.

The train jerked to a stop several meters from the platform outside a speck-dust town two hours from Casasrojas. After a few minutes when the doors didn't open and we didn't keep moving, Grito walked to the front to ask about what had happened.

"The tracks are blocked. It's the strikes, I guess," he said when he got back. He opened another box of wine. "They say we could be here all night."

"*Coño.*" La Canaria grabbed the box from Grito's hand. "I'm not staying here all night." She slugged the wine and Coke and pulled me out of my seat. "Come on, Mosca, let's find something to do." Marco and Grito pried the doors open and we jumped out onto the tracks.

The town was one of those dumps with one bread shop,

one café, and one ugly church butting up against scraggly foot-hills. No countryside hostel. The streets were full of widows again. La Canaria ran at them cawing, but they refused to scatter; instead, they shook their crooked fingers at her. The café owner saw our clothes and wouldn't even let us sit down, let alone sleep above his shop. The town ended at the foot of a steep hill, and we climbed it, La Canaria and Grito swaying arm in arm. Marco walked in front of me, carrying the wine and smoking. We turned off on a shepherd's trail and kept climbing, the scent of pine heavy in the air. Pollen glowed in the twilight.

We climbed higher, and the ground got soggier until the pines finally stopped and there was only grass. Wild daffodils covered the hills, their spiky yellow buds reaching up to us. The earth was soaked with snowmelt that trickled down in hundreds of slender streams. Sheep shit was everywhere, but the air smelled of grass and sun and water. La Canaria bent down to drink from one of the streams.

"Are you crazy?" I said, kicking a dried lump of manure at her. She just laughed and crouched down, lapping up the water.

"So we'll camp up here and catch the earliest train back in the morning?" Marco said. "Is that the plan?"

"You and your fucking plans," Grito said. He pounced on La Canaria and wrestled her to the wet grass.

"Why do you need to go back in the morning?" La Canaria teased. "Got something important scheduled?" She rolled on top of Grito. Marco had set himself up for their taunting.

"Mosca told those old ladies we're going to Madrid," Grito said. "Is that the plan, Mosca?"

"Nobody said anything to me about Madrid," Marco said. "I still have one more exam to take, and I need to pass it to graduate."

"Don't listen to that *pendejo*," I said, and started climbing again.

"Where are you going?" Marco called after me. "There's nothing up there."

I didn't answer him. I wanted to see how far he'd follow me.

The air changed quickly as soon as the sun went down. The scent of hot pine lingered, but with no moisture in the air, it suddenly turned cold. We noticed it slowly, our skin adjusting until it couldn't and we were shivering.

"*Joder*, I'm freezing," Grito said. "Let's find somewhere dry to make a fire."

We found a tiny circle of sand dug into the hill either by sheep or shepherds, and set down our backpacks. Grito and Marco walked back to the pines to try to find some wood to burn. We could see them in the distance, Grito hanging on a thin branch, trying to break it off.

"*Qué idiota*," La Canaria said.

They came back with sappy branches and a bunch of pinecones. We emptied the bags of wine and soda and used the receipts to start a smoky fire. Then we drank the wine to keep warm. La Canaria howled at the fire. Grito tried to get his hand up her shirt, but she swatted it away. Marco sat kind of close to me. He was still trying to figure out what to do next. I mean, he knew what he wanted to do, he wanted to touch me, he'd wanted to for years, but he couldn't. First Alexis was stopping him, then—then it was still Alexis. How to live with that want and do nothing. Part of me loved watching it run him ragged.

"Leave us alone," La Canaria said to them. "Mosca and I need some girl time." She leaned against my shoulder and soon fell asleep.

The few lights of the towns and shepherds' houses on the hills flickered like the piles of gold left on the shores of the river in Casasrojas. Saints' medallions, a spread-open wallet, sometimes a broken watch or a torn chain; the piles were never touched by anyone but the police. The money you could get from the pawnshop wasn't worth it. When the medallions and wallets were found, the person they belonged to could be identified and the family would know who had killed them. The secret police all killed the same way. Left the same mark. The body gone but the victim's saint medallion and wallet in the sand. They left the medallions because the people they took weren't human anymore. They didn't have names. They didn't have saints. God no longer knew them or never did.

I remembered standing with Alexis on the broken railway bridge when we were kids. Sticking our feet into the lumps of sand and spiky grass growing through the old railroad ties, daring each other to go farther out on the bridge, our hands red from the rusted rails we'd climbed to get there. We were young when we first saw the piles catch the sun on the sand. Ten of them all in a row. We jumped off the bridge to see what they were, Alexis running before me. A man stepped out of the tall grass and placed his hand on Alexis's shoulder. The man was smiling. I felt guilty—I'd seen the man just before he touched Alexis, and I hadn't said anything. Hadn't stopped him before he reached Alexis. The man was probably just walking home and saw some kids playing where they shouldn't be, but he scared me. He looked perfectly harmless.

"Stay away from here," was all he said. "This isn't for you."

As soon as the man stepped out of the grass, I realized what the piles were. I knew they weren't for us. It didn't need repeating. He stepped out of the grass, and I remembered when Mamá and Papá dropped us off at our abuela's and didn't come back.

The month of waiting that ended not with our parents walking through Abuela's door but with two policemen politely knocking. They handed Abuela my father's worn leather wallet and my mother's necklace—a gold medallion for St. Julia of Mérida and a small fist carved from *azabache*. My abuela closed her hand around the necklace and wallet. I never saw them again.

I didn't know how long it took Alexis to figure out what the piles meant. Whether he remembered the police coming to the door with our mother's necklace. How long it took him to connect our parents not coming back to the knock on the door, to the others who didn't come back, to the warnings in gold on the sand. I tried to keep him away from the piles, but if I lost him in a game of chase, I would find him there, crouched in the sand. Don't touch them, I'd say, and he wouldn't, he was still too afraid, but he stepped closer, the older he got. They were pulling him in and I couldn't stop it.

When I woke up a few hours later, the moon was bright above us, and La Canaria had wrapped herself around me so tight I could hardly breathe. Marco lay with his back against me, close enough that I could feel his heat. His jean jacket was pulled over his thick dark curls. Grito was by the fire, crouched near the dead coals and shivering.

"What are you doing, Grito?" I whispered, not wanting to wake La Canaria or Marco.

"I'm trying to get this fire going again."

"Leave it and go to sleep," I told him.

"I can't sleep. I'm too cold." He poked a stick at the coals and blew on them. They started glowing.

"Where'd you get that?" I asked, pointing to a pile of neatly chopped wood by his feet.

"I found it by an empty shepherd's shack over there."

He started throwing the wood into the fire. It was getting bigger. He looked unfamiliar, a weird elf backlit by the moon, his ponytail bouncing in the wind. He wouldn't turn toward me, and I could see only the outline of his face, but I knew what emotions it held.

"We're not going back in time for our exams, are we?" I said.

"*Joder*, Mosca. Did you think we were gonna make it back in time?"

"No."

He was surprised at that and laughed. "Me, neither," he said. "You'll have to tell your abuela you'll be late." He'd seen me then or knew that I had to tell her what I was up to. He refused to call his abuela. Like mine, she was his only family member left, but all that weight focused on him wasn't enough to make him tell her where he was going. He wanted to be like a scream, alone and jutting out, ungraspable. That's why his nickname stuck.

Alexis would always call. Whether he was gone a night or three or a whole week, the phone in the hall would rattle— the only time it ever did. He wouldn't tell me over the phone what he was doing. He'd return, worn and jittering, his hands swollen, a new grin smacked over the face he'd had when he left. And he'd say just enough that I could piece together the rest. He'd met a group of militants who were resisting the general's regime. He was gaining their trust. Small jobs, nothing dangerous, Mosquita. Just finding a few names, he said, a few locations. I scanned the papers, trying to link his clues to the codes hidden in the articles, but they never said anything. All I had were the few words he gave me, and he muttered them so carelessly, I wanted to hit him. Because whatever he was doing, it wasn't nothing, and it wasn't safe. People never came back home for less. He hinted that he'd crossed the border into France—hitchhiked through the mountains without a visa—and bragged that he'd seen the famous woman with a painted half-smile. He wasn't impressed. Not half as mysterious as you. Not a dying firefly to my girl.

Grito turned to me. His face was lit up in pieces by the flames. "Why'd you come along, anyway?" he said. "You can't stand Marco."

I pressed my hands into the scorched grass around the fire. Whether Alexis had ever gotten to Paris, I didn't know, but I'd added his words to the ballast sentences that sustained me. He left. He came back. He can leave. I can leave. I listed the cities he said he'd been—Madrid, Granada, San Sebastián, Barcelona, Paris, even. Their order was confused, but their names made a map of lights in my mind. A constellation leading not back but far. Each a whole world I'd never been, swallowing him up and spewing him back, crustaceans in his pocket and seaweed in his hair, on the shores of our prison town. I considered the cities he talked about not destinations but destructions. A chosen wreckage. Different only in that way from the one handed us.

The sound of sap popping woke La Canaria. Her makeup was smudged all over her face. She'd left a black pool of it on my shoulder. "*Coño,* Grito," she whispered groggily. "That's a really good fire."

She nudged Marco, who shot up in the air as if he'd been bitten. Grito didn't say anything; he just kept throwing logs on the blaze. I stood and did the same. The embers flew at our faces each time we threw more wood in. When we'd used all the wood Grito had carried, we stumbled in the dark to the shack and brought more over.

The heat batted our faces, drying our mouths, pulling our skin tight across our noses. I don't know who did it first. If it was

Grito who refused to say a word, La Canaria who kept running around the fire and threatening to jump in, or if it was me. We had climbed the cars together in Casasrojas. No one knew who had broken the first store window or who had tilted his head in such a way to give permission. Grito had hit the police officer with the crowbar, but who had made his lips bleed, who had broken his ribs. That wasn't the point. There were no government cars or police officers to wreck on the hillside in the dark. There were only our books and our clothes and our bodies. Our books first into the fire, a few pages, a corner of the binding to start. Our shirts next. Grito's glowing for a second like a moth before it burst like a moth. The flames high from the burning paper. My backpack and then La Canaria's. Marco stripped off his jacket and shirt, threw them in. La Canaria guzzled the last of the wine and tossed in the empty soda bottles and wine boxes. The wax and nylon made the fire shoot neon. We coughed at the smoke but kept breathing it in, hard and deep. We didn't speak. Our words were clear. I dare you. I dare you to retreat and attack in one moment. To make that one movement. Our jeans and our combat boots. Threw them in and stood with our toes digging into the cold sand. Staring ahead, watching the fire spark red and green and purple into the sky. I dare you to wreck it all. I dare you. La Canaria wrapped her arm around my stomach, and I could feel her sticky flesh press against mine. Marco edged in next to us. This time I relaxed into him. I waited until Grito stepped close to me. I took his hand. Felt that pocket of damp air between our palms shape and disappear.

Three

I'd known Grito the longest. He lived in the same apartment building as Alexis, my abuela, and me on Calle Grillo. I'd see him through the elevator gates when we were kids, holding on to his mother's skirt, coming back from the market. I'd press the close button so they couldn't get in and watch him disappear between the floors, only his brown hair and white hand on his mother's black skirt visible. Alexis would laugh, even though he wasn't ever mean to kids because they were skinny and still hanging on to their mothers. He was just following me. And I was mad that Grito still had a mother, though she died soon after, giving birth to what would have been his sister.

The first time Grito and I fucked, we were seventeen. He brought a black-market copy of *Sticky Fingers* with the songs that had been censored off the Spanish version and put it on the record player in my room. My abuela had saved up to buy the record player so I could listen to English lessons on it. She wanted me to learn English because it would open doors—she must have read that in one of her magazines. She was in the apartment, but she was watching her telenovela, and it only took a minute. Grito was on top of me with his shirt still on, and I reached underneath the collar to feel his sticky skin—a fine layer of pimples beneath downy hair refusing to turn thick and black. He didn't say any-thing when he came, softly above me, just put his slightly wet cheek on my chest when it was over. He left me the record and said he'd see me in English.

That spring, we read bootleg copies of our favorite murdered poet's books in whispers over the English-language records and wrote the best lines on each other's limbs to remember them. He wrote Lorca's words about the curve of a scream in the moun-tains on the inside of my right thigh, and that was the first time I called him Grito. I didn't know if he remembered, because we didn't read that poetry anymore. He told me he lent the book to somebody and that they lost it, but he wouldn't tell me who.

At dawn we rose from the grass but couldn't feel the cold. Our bodies were somewhere else. We started moving once we could see, keeping close, the dew between our toes. Grito and Marco walked ahead of La Canaria and me, their white asses glowing slightly in the dawn. The cottage where Grito had found the firewood was only a hill away. He stopped before the shut-tered window and plunged his hand into the wet, soft planks. Climbed inside the hole he'd made.

"There's a key on the door frame, *idiota*," La Canaria said when he opened the door. Blood dripped down his arm, and bits of wood and lichen stuck to his wet skin.

"There's nothing in here," Grito said.

"*Pendejo*," I said.

When my abuelo was young, he had sheep in La Mancha, and he always kept clothes in his shepherd's cottage if he came in from the rain and didn't want to freeze to death. I looked around the cottage and found it—an old army chest made of cardboard.

"What, have you done this before?" Marco asked, still standing in the doorway like a stupid stray cat who thinks someone's going to beg it to come in and eat from their hand. Inside the chest were army blankets, a sleeping bag, a pair of worn green trousers, and a torn wool sweater.

I tossed the clothes on the cot. "Put these on, Grito," I said. "Go get us some clothes."

"How do you know I won't leave you here?" he asked, grinning.

La Canaria walked up behind him, wrapped herself around his wet back, her breasts pressed against the grass caked to his skin.

"You better come back for us, *cielo*," she whispered into his ear. "Because if you don't, I swear by the Virgin and my dead abuela, I'll find you and chop off your balls. And Mosca will eat your dick. I mean cut up, chew, and swallow." She pushed him toward me and I handed him the clothes, letting my fingers linger on his.

"Don't think we won't, *cielo*," I said.

Marco was turned away from us, toward the window. He kept touching the bruise around his neck and looking at his fingers, as if the mark were paint that could rub off. The pants I'd handed Grito were too small and bunched up around his crotch. He had to stoop to walk. The sweater's sleeves were short, too, and they showed where the shutter had torn up his arm.

We wrapped ourselves in the blankets and walked back to the fire with him. It was only embers. We used the remainders of our boots and the green branches that hadn't burned to poke through it. Our coins had burned through the cloth and sat glowing on the coals. Marco scorched his hand trying to pick them up. Our clothes were destroyed. I took a piece of what had been La Canaria's shirt, picked up the coins, and dumped them in the wet grass. The dew sizzled and pulsed around them.

La Canaria kept off to the side, crouched down, her blanket folded around her. I knew she'd found what she was looking for, what only she and I knew existed. La Canaria always made a big show about not paying for anything. Not just around Grito—with anybody. I had to buy her stuff all the time. But I knew she carried a small cricket box everywhere she went. It was brass with tiny triangles stamped through the metal and had a miniature handle on top like a suitcase. Fit in the palm of her hand. Not much money in it but more than you would have thought she'd have. I stepped over to her. She was looking at Grito and Marco, trying to count the hot coins. She slipped two bills out from under her blanket, and I pretended to have found them in the bottom of my ruined backpack.

"Nothing fancy." I handed the bills to Grito. "No fucking around."

He bobbed down the mountain, the old clothes swirling around him. Marco kicked around the embers but couldn't find anything else. He ran back to the cottage to get warm.

Marco had been Alexis's closest friend. When they started hanging out, it made me feel better. Marco was kind of a geek, like me—he acted tough but no one believed it. I liked Alexis hanging out with him instead of the runaways who slept on the street, or people like Felipe, whose names I could hardly remember, they disappeared so often.

My abuela had managed to keep her apartment through the years, a lucky chance here and there, the money from the sale of my abuelo's farm placed in the right hands. Alexis would bring Marco over, and they'd sit in the kitchen and drink. Everyone else I knew lived in boardinghouses and shared a kitchen with five other families—you didn't exactly invite anyone over. That was what the parks were for, the tiny cafés where you didn't have to buy anything, the tracks of cement and stone in between buildings always covered by furtive knees, hands flicking cigarettes and cupping a mouth to say the same hidden thing. I didn't know where Marco lived, but he always brought a nice bottle of brandy, and then they'd split the bottle. My abuela would hum loudly the whole time because she didn't allow liquor in her house. But she'd stopped trying to say no to Alexis. My abuelo had been the only person who could do that. Perhaps my father would have been able to, but he never had the chance.

Marco was the only friend Alexis brought home, though he had many. For a while, Marco was in the kitchen every night, and I ignored him then like I did the table's chipped legs, different from how I ignored him after Alexis disappeared.

The night he first appeared in our kitchen, I'd just come home from trying to study for my university entrance exams in the bar under the philology library. I sat close by the door to the hidden print shop because I liked the sound of the machines, the whir of paper, the idea of the same secret stories and photos printed over and over, carpeting the room. It was the distraction necessary to exist in a world where my words were not my own. It worked for a time, anyway. I'd spent most of the afternoon crouched on one of the bar's leather seats. I tipped back against the damp wall, trying not to spill my *caña,* trying not to be noticed, eavesdropping on a group of young professors beside me.

"He's going to die," one of the men said, looking over his shoulder, then making the gesture of combing a perfect part in his hair with the exactitude of slitting someone's throat. When he was alive, no one used el Cabronísimo's name out loud. The gesture to signal who it was you were talking about changed regularly and could be disguised easily as a tic or normal movement. "He has to sometime."

I couldn't hear what his companions said in response because all I could hear were those reverberating words. The general had been alive all my life, all my parents' brief lives. The only person who knew of a time before him was my abuela. She wouldn't mention it or the war that had brought him to power, just as she wouldn't speak the devil's name.

I drank my flat *caña* and chewed my greasy tortilla. After lightning there is the sky, black as before but jittering. There was me, slightly drunk, tired, not having memorized any of the English vocabulary I'd brought but with the knowledge inside me that the general could die. Someone, a professor, had said it out loud. I smoked all the way home and then bought marzipan from the nuns on the corner of Calle Grillo and La Libertad to hide the scent from my abuela.

Alexis's voice came out of the kitchen when I turned the lock to our apartment. He was in a good mood, laughing, and I could hear my abuela humming because of it. She always moved softly across our floors, attuned to Alexis, each of her gray hairs a taut wire listening.

Entering the kitchen, I saw Marco first. Like all the kitchens in the apartments I'd been in, ours was small, made for one woman to move in and maybe sit down for a second to take her espresso while the rice finished. But Alexis and I had always stayed in the kitchen. We needed to feel that sticky air filled with oil fried, poured into a jar that once held asparagus, and fried again. Being in that kitchen always felt like we were in that jar. Our words and movements the burnt flecks of potatoes and skirt steak that passed through the sieve, suspended, immobile, but contained in a way that felt safe. The kitchen was where we had last seen Mamá. She kissed us and handed us a box of crackers and said she'd be back soon. At least, I wanted to believe I remembered the last thing she said and not just standing waiting for her.

Alexis's back was to me, as I would never put my back to his. He was a year and a half younger than me but in the past few months he'd put on weight. He always used to thump me on the shoulder when he came in, but it had started to hurt. Or he'd shoot a rubber band at the back of my neck when I was reading, and I'd scream, Abuela rushing in because she thought one of us had been burned. He didn't do it to hurt me, just to say he was there, that he knew I was there. It was the only way he could. Once I grew breasts, he could barely kiss my cheek. Even though I knew what his actions meant, they still scared me. He wasn't always in control. To study, I sat at the far side of the kitchen table, where I could see him coming in. After he disappeared, I would sit there because if I didn't, I might confuse my heartbeat with his steps down the hall and his breath with my own.

Marco looked up at me.

"*Buenas,*" I said to Alexis, and leaned down to kiss him, ignoring his flinch when our cheeks touched. He grabbed my long braid, slung over my shoulder like a kid's, and twisted it around his hand so I couldn't stand up.

"I told you not to start smoking," Alexis said.

I stayed still until he let go of my braid. Even a year ago I would have bitten his hand, but I knew where that would get me.

"I've been studying," I said, and went to cut some bread and cheese on the counter.

"My sister's a geek," he said to Marco. "And it better stay that way. Don't hang out in that shithole under the library."

It was impossible to lie to him. Marco still hadn't spoken. He knew he couldn't. Alexis was skinnier than most of his friends, but they all listened to him. He could destroy you in one sentence, and Marco wasn't really cool enough to be hanging around him anyway. Every neutral word Alexis said to Marco was a gift.

"Do you know Marco?" Alexis said.

"Hey." I bent over and kissed Marco's cheek.

"Hey," he said quietly, not looking at me.

"He has a crush on you," Alexis said.

"*Carajo*," Marco whispered.

"Yeah, he thinks you're really cute. Can't stop talking about you." Alexis ripped off a tiny piece of his bread and flicked it at Marco. "But I told him you're dating that *comemierda* Grito."

"What's wrong with Grito?" I said.

"Besides that he's dating my sister?" He flicked a bread crumb at me. "Anyway, Marco knows I'll kill him if he touches you."

Alexis was smiling, teasing Marco, but he also meant it completely.

"You're such a *pendejo*," I told Alexis, and walked out of the kitchen.

Down the hall, I could hear them goading each other. Then popping a wine bottle, then laughing. My abuela turned up the volume of the TV, pretending she could hear nothing through our cardboard walls.

Through the crack Grito had made in the shutters, I could see the rainclouds easing over the mountains. I walked behind La Canaria where she stood watching the clouds crest slow and shy over the rocks. The sun wasn't fully up yet, and we were shivering in the army blankets.

La Canaria turned to me and touched my hair. "We should have sent Grito for a comb, at least," she said.

"Or a mirror," Marco said from the other side of the room.

A big brass key hung on a shoelace around his neck, the bits polished where they rubbed against his skin.

"Shut up," La Canaria whispered.

I faced out at the splintered wood and air turning to water. Marco looked the worst; at least he looked worse than I felt. I'd been needing less and less sleep, eating less, enjoying the feel of my bones brittle beneath my skin. La Canaria ran only on food. The closest I'd seen her to tired was being slightly quiet. But Marco slept like a British tourist. Eight hours and it had to be regular. His face cast off a certain light that made me cold, want coffee. Made waiting seem long and the room small. I didn't like waiting. It was impossible not to compare it to other times.

When Alexis had been gone for three days without calling, my abuela stopped pretending to do anything but wait.

She sat by the television and kept turning it on and off. We had this black-and-white thing she'd won in a church auction that took a long time to turn back on. It would buzz for a few moments and burp white static until the sobbing faces of the telenovela would fade slowly into view. When she thought she'd heard something, she would get up and turn it off, the faces collapsing into a white star that flashed and disappeared. She'd jump up at nothing and then not hear an actual knock on the door. I sat by the television so she wouldn't have to get up. I turned it off when she told me to. It was summer, I hadn't been able to find a job, and I had nothing to do but sit with her and wait. Either that or sit in my room not doing my summer reading and pretending I wasn't doing exactly what she was doing.

Marco kept coming by with a bottle of brandy to see if Alexis was there. I didn't want Marco to know we were worried. I said I didn't know where Alexis was. I didn't say he hadn't called.

One night Marco came by with nothing in his hands and his face wrung out. I hadn't seen or heard from Alexis in six days. I lied to Marco and said Alexis was inside sleeping and maybe Marco should call before coming over to someone's house late at night. Marco wanted to believe me. His body sank in the doorway. He'd been holding it tight and forgotten how much that hurt. But he came the next night and I told him the same thing. That time his body didn't sink; it just stayed how it was.

In the doorway, he tried to look around me. He was scared and that made me scared.

"Do you know what happened?" he said. "What did he tell you?"

"She's in there," I said.

The credits song for one of Abuela's shows blared behind me. I didn't want to talk about where Alexis could be or what part we'd played in it. If we'd be next to not come home. I knew if my abuela saw Marco, she'd want to ask him about Alexis.

"Do you know if he still has it?" he said.

"I don't know what you're talking about."

I closed the door in his face. I didn't want him in my house again.

Even though I ignored him, Marco kept hanging around me. He'd always be in the background, even if I was with a crowd he hated. He'd follow me home from the bars late at night. He said he wanted to make sure I made it there safe. One night I turned around in the doorway of my abuela's apartment building and waited until he was standing right in front of me. I eased close to him. I could smell his breath on me. I slid my hand under his shirt and he closed his eyes.

"I just want to protect you," he said.

That was the last thing I wanted. I wanted to be wrecked.

I deserved it after what I did. My hand under Marco's shirt, I opened my penknife. Waited until he felt the blade graze his skin. I didn't press down hard, but it was unmistakable. I hated Marco for every second he'd spent with Alexis. Every laugh and trust they'd shared that I hadn't been a part of. I turned around and opened the door. Left him standing there with his shirt up, searching for blood. I never caught him following me again, but I knew he still did.

Inside the shepherd's cottage, the rain was all around us. I could tell La Canaria wanted to go out, wanted to get wet and dive in. I could see her skin twitching the way it would before a touch or a cigarette. Suddenly, I needed to distract her and keep her dry as long as possible. But I didn't want to mention looking for food in the shack if there wasn't any to find.

Before anyone else woke up, I'd sat in the grass, numb and looking for the sun. Out on the mountain ridge where the clouds pinked, I could see the world opened by our exams. The safe government jobs, the chance to use my English and collect a modest salary each month until someone married me. This if I were very lucky. Most people I knew, even those with degrees, were unemployed. I'd have to be grateful for anything I got, a woman and with no ties to the state. If I got it—that jewel job tucked deep in a municipal building—the letterhead would no longer bear el Cabronísimo's name, but the ink would smell the same and the work would be the same. I would be couched inside the body of someone making the same movements, filling out the same forms, as they had done for decades in his honor. When I found an old pen underneath the radiator, would I wonder what it had signed away; would I pause before I added my teeth marks to the indentations in the blue plastic, the marks of someone who didn't have to know how to aim to carry out death sentences?

I watched, waiting for the sun to come up, but there were only dissipating clouds and me, a fast-retreating star pulling back into darkness.

Marco leaned over a pile of kindling in the fireplace. "If Grito comes back soon," he said, "we'll probably be able to catch a train and be back in time for our exams."

"We won't be back in time," I said, even though I'd been thinking the same thing. We'd all been trying to gauge the time by the height of the sun or guess the frequency of trains back from where we were.

I closed my eyes and breathed in deeply. I was exhausted. But instead of darkness behind my eyelids, I saw a constellation. A dim handful of city names flickering slowly into focus. The cities Alexis would call from. Solid as bricks stacking, they formed in the back of my throat. Madrid, Granada, San Sebastián, Barcelona, Paris. I tried to swallow, but there they stayed.

"We're not going back," I said.

"You weren't going to take the exams, were you?" Marco said.

I shook my head. I'd known all along I couldn't sit through them. I just couldn't admit it until that moment. I had my reasons for not taking those final exams, and I didn't need to explain them to Marco. He knew better than anyone.

We wouldn't mention it again. Even when Grito returned, he would be able to sense what I'd done with those words. We'd all been thinking them—maybe not Marco, he was always watching me too carefully to notice anything else—but we hadn't said them out loud.

The cathedral in Casasrojas: its open halls, stained glass windows smudged with dirt and light, pigeons passing through streaks of sun. The view of the cathedral's facade and the new students trying to find the good-luck frog hidden among the skulls carved into the yellow stone. The passageways behind the walls that led to the unimportant towers, the ones without gargoyles and panoramic views of the city. Grito and I used to spend hours there, in between the walls, bent over each other, the scent of incense filtering through the cracked oak doors. We climbed curved stone staircases that led to narrow doors and opened to keyholes of gray sky. The stairs were covered in dust, layers of forgotten years, walls wet from sweet-smelling mold. The cathedral shifted the first time we opened one of those forgotten doors. It didn't look the same afterward.

"*Vale*," La Canaria nodded.

There had never been any power in what I said, what I prayed at night—even as a kid, I could feel the weakness—but with those words, I lucked out. It was luck, nothing of mine. The final whirring in a lock I didn't know I had, and I'd opened up to a new raw space. A field made of strange, wet mud, low clouds on the horizon. The words pushed the door wide and dared us to step through. We did without even knowing it. The new space was real and nothing else. That was where we stood.

La Canaria started looking through the old shack. There were the cot with the army trunk under it and a table made of wooden wine boxes covered in a torn oilcloth. She took off the cloth and started going through the boxes.

"You're not going to steal anything else, are you?" I said.

She didn't answer, but she turned away from me, her hands searching. She kept opening boxes. When she turned back, she held a handful of bullets and the raw wool they'd been packed in. She dropped the bullets one by one from her hand onto the floor, letting them fall like water. They bounced in the dust and rolled across the floor until they hit the walls or a crack in the floorboards too large to pass over. Closing her finger over the last bullet, she walked across the room and reached for my hand. Pressed the bullet into my palm. "Just for you," she said.

She met my eyes and I didn't look away. It was Alexis who'd first brought her to El Chico, before the newspapers went up on the windows, and I could see them walking together, his arm wrapped around her. We'd seen her around, smoking under the juniper trees on campus and at bars. Alexis was crazy about her, and she seemed to care about him, too, though she didn't stop flirting with anyone who talked to her. They'd fight and break up, get back together again, fight again. When they were together, they ignored everyone else, and we would just stand and watch them, hypnotized by the way they'd hypnotized each other. Hoping to catch a little bit of the light bouncing off them.

The rumor was that she was the daughter of a plantation owner on the Canary Islands out of wedlock. Or she'd been kicked out of school there and sent here. Despite what we called her, some people said she was *dominicana* or from Cuba. The scent of a bribe somewhere, money, a secret, and she played that part up, probably even started it. No one had ever been to her place.

But I saw a bleakness, too. When she wasn't cursing at the bartender for a weak drink or slinging herself into a sweaty crowd, her face in repose looked like it had been recently smacked clean. I thought there must be some good reason she'd left. Her skin drew her to us, that pause where she couldn't quite be placed. She could have just been from the south, but in some lights her skin looked darker. It made us lean in closer. Anything different was to be coveted, anything that showed the lie of the pure world the *fachas* preached. Even if that thing was not a thing at all. Either way, if she was here on the condition of not fucking up, she wasn't holding up her end of the deal.

"We didn't ask Grito for any cigarettes," Marco said.

"You better start thinking on your feet," La Canaria said, turning away from me. "Or else we'll drop you like a fist of burnt corn."

"Whatever that means." Marco looked over at me, but I didn't share his sneer. I curled my fingers around the bullet.

La Canaria finished going through the boxes, mostly raw wool used to pack objects long since removed. She pulled out a few rusted tools and a small jar of rice. There was only about a handful left, and I saw her finger the grains slowly, then put the jar back underneath the wool.

"Marco," I said. "Start the fire again." Just to give him something to do and me something to watch. La Canaria sat down by me. We waited for Grito to come back with our clothes and a way out.

My abuela used to say that no matter how small a house was, its walls would swell to fit those in it. I would lie in bed and imagine her apartment expanding with each new intake and exhale. The shack on the mountain felt aware of us. It sucked in air, but its walls never lifted. The walls drew out our breath and contained it, growing thicker, the air more stale. La Canaria lay on the cot, asleep or staring an escape through the roof. The blanket had fallen down her chest, leaving one breast open to the shack's low ceiling.

I knew Marco was looking at me, but I could still feel him all over me from the night before, and his eyes were vinegar on stripped-off skin. I was being kind to him, though he didn't know it, by not looking at him, not slugging him, letting the light from where his skin had been on mine vibrate and reappear. Just allowing that was very kind.

When Grito finally got back, soaking wet from the rain and with a plastic bag under his arm, we'd been silent for hours.

The sun shone weakly but high in the sky. The clothes must have been an old woman's; they smelled quiet, furious, and of fried *bacalao*. La Canaria and I put on two identical floor-length black polyester skirts. Mine sagged around me, and hers was so tight she couldn't button it at the waist. Then more sweaters, moth-eaten and stale with sweat at the neck, a pair of too-long trousers for Marco, and a few cheap white undershirts.

"It's just until we get back to Casasrojas, then—" Grito stopped.

I was right. He'd read my words in the shack's thin air, read them because they were all that was left to read, our faces blank, our bodies limp to the scrape of someone else's clothes.

There was still time to go back. We could have made excuses— bandits, the strikes, a sudden rash of penitence. Days later we could have returned, heads down, lashing our backs with the remnants of our schoolbags, and taken the exams individually. Maybe Felipe was mistaken, maybe it had all passed over us and we wouldn't be caught. Of course we were afraid, terrified, of the police, of getting caught. But that wasn't why we didn't go back.

"Casasrojas?" I said. "What have we got there?"

The fire was a dare, and though it had seemed like the summit at the time, it was only a few dusty crags on the shore of what the real dare would become. It had not started when we put on the bandanas. We thought it had ended when we threw our clothes in the fire. But the breaking glass, the policeman, the burning backpacks were all symptoms. We had broken the things around us that we hated and then broken our own things. Finding the ground scorched for miles, we turned to what was left.

The real dare was not to go back, to keep messing up, to step deeper and deeper into the murk. We skidded our eyes over one another's faces, looking out for the weakling. Who's gonna be the one to turn tail? Not me, we each silently, separately vowed. Me, I'm going for the bottom.

La Canaria spoke from the corner. "I don't have any reason to go back. Do you, Grito?"

"I'm not going back," Grito said, smiling snidely. "I meant Madrid. Aren't we gonna join the protests?"

Now that he understood where we were, he wanted to be the one to do the daring. All utterances were fair game. Anything we'd said before or threatened to do, we had to make good. There had been no decision and yet there it was, lodged deep. In the fire we'd seen the others' hidden faces and realized they were all the same. That was no comfort. We were unrecognizable in the span of a morning. We didn't trust ourselves.

"Madrid's where all the action is," La Canaria said.

"Sure," I said. "Madrid. Or wherever." I traced the cities lodged in my throat. Madrid, as good a place to start as any.

The woman at the station said that the direct train to Madrid wouldn't come through the town at the base of the mountain for another week. We'd have to take a bunch of regionals to get there. Marco spoke to the teller and figured out a route that avoided most of the strikes. La Canaria handed him a few bills and said it was the last she had. We found four seats with a table between them and sat down. Grito and Marco tried to sleep, but the seats didn't go back. An old lady kept poking their legs with her umbrella whenever their feet slipped into the aisle. Outside the window the mountains rolled into swirls of hue. Tiny villages, stucco houses with dirt floors, shantytowns made of surprisingly bright plastics and tin. The whole country melting into a plaything of the train and time, showing it for what it really was: blurs of carbon.

"What are we gonna do there?" Marco asked hesitantly.

"Where?" Grito said.

"In Madrid, where are we gonna stay, how are we—"

"You want a timetable?"

"We'll start in Madrid," La Canaria said.

"I'm just saying, how are we—"

"Hey, Mosca." Grito leaned over Marco to me. "Where'd you pick up this *pendejo* with the suit and tie?"

I tucked my tongue in my mouth and silenced the voice begging we plan for food before we got too hungry to spit, demanding we seek out a place to sleep that wouldn't leave us dew-drenched in the morning. The cities swarmed in my throat. Madrid, Granada, San Sebastián, Barcelona, Paris.

"I didn't invite him," I said.

"It's not *facha* to want to know what's happening next," Marco said.

"Isn't it?" Grito drummed his fingers on the sticky table between us. After a pause he spoke again. "But that's not what's *facha* about you, Marco."

"Oh yeah?"

Grito looked over at me and then quickly away. He lowered his voice to a harsh whisper, as if I couldn't hear. "Yeah, Marco. I know what you are. Who you are."

"Will you two shut up?" La Canaria said. "I'm trying to sleep." She got up and moved to the back of the car.

"You have no idea what you're talking about," Marco said.

"Everyone knows, *tío*. Want a chance to prove them wrong?"

I stood up and followed La Canaria. She leaned her head against the yellow glass and closed her eyes. There was a certain comfort in her, and I edged as close as I could without touching.

"All I know is I'm not going back to that fucking island," La

Canaria whispered, her eyes still closed. "Nobody is dragging me back there."

We were silent for a while. I tried to sleep, but Marco sat down next to me and he sat too close. I could tell he wanted to talk, to figure out what I was thinking, but I kept my eyes closed tight and let the towns pass by.

"Time to switch trains," Marco said, shaking us awake. The train started to slow, and the blurs of color solidified into red dirt and brown grasses.

"No, it isn't," Grito shouted from the other end of the car.

"Let's move before we miss our stop." Marco pulled at my arm. I shrugged him off but stood up. I hadn't paid attention to the route we needed to take.

"Come on," Marco said, and we followed him off the train. Another train was pulling into the station. "This is ours, come on, we're gonna miss it!"

"*Vale, vale,*" La Canaria said, rubbing her eyes. "We're coming."

We got on the next train and Marco found us a seat. "Now you can all go back to sleep," he said. He sat down next to me and I turned to the window, watched the green mountains swirl to soft terraces of yellow dirt.

The night before, I'd managed to get between La Canaria and Grito. I'd pushed myself onto Grito and held him still beneath me. Each of our faces was just visible, lit by something other than the fire, other than the black sky. We looked like ghosts, burnt-wood white, the shape of the dots in your eyes after staring at a lamp too long. Marco had his eyes closed, touching La Canaria. Hers were open and looking right at me. I couldn't read her expression and that made my legs relax and give enough so Grito could push me off of him and pin La Canaria's face to the wet grass and come on her back, her skin brighter in the places his semen landed.

Grito shoved Marco into me and woke me up. His skin on mine was like an alarm. Fine that he wouldn't leave my side. Sitting down next to me whenever he could. But I didn't want him touching me.

"What's your problem, *maricón*?" Grito said, pointing to a list of stops above us. "You made us get on the wrong train."

"*Joder*," Marco said. "I'm sorry. I guess I misread the signs."

"*No me jodas.* You're the one who talked to the lady who said where to go."

"What happened?" La Canaria appeared above us with a can of orange soda in her hand. "Want some?" She handed me the can. "I made this kid in the dining car buy it for me. He's really cute, even though he's just a baby. I might have to wait for him." She flicked out her tongue at Grito.

"This *idiota* got us on the wrong train," Grito said, shoving Marco again.

"Shut up," Marco said. "I'll figure it out." He stood up and looked at the list of stops. "Let's get off here." He pointed to the next stop.

"Why?" I said. He usually had a good sense of direction. I didn't understand how he had gotten turned around.

"We can get back on in the morning. I've got a place we can stay around here." He said it flatly and wouldn't say anything else about it. We got off when the train stopped outside a town surrounded by olive groves. Across a dirt road loomed a billboard with the far-right candidate staring stoically into the distance. His face was painted over by graffiti that read simply, LEÓN SIN CASTILLA.

"We're in the fucking province of León?" Grito said.

We'd been going north all day instead of southeast, toward Madrid, and we'd been too exhausted to notice.

"Wait here," Marco said. He left us standing in the middle of the tiny station and came back in a couple of minutes. "The bank's closed," he said when he walked back to us.

"What do you need a bank for?" Grito asked. "How are we gonna buy the next ticket?"

Marco walked up to one of the old Renaults that served as taxis outside the station. He held the door open for us. The driver pulled his hat down at Marco, who climbed into the front seat. The three of us crammed in back. The driver didn't ask where we were going, he didn't even look at us, bulky in our long skirts and sweaters in the dry sun. He just drove down the dirt road lined with collapsing stucco houses. The town—dusty with flaking stone, skinny cats swaying sagging stomachs and swollen tits, dying vines hanging from balconies to graze the cars—didn't notice our arrival, didn't bend or breathe at all. We drove into the terraced hills of olives and grapes. We stayed silent, staring at the red ground between the olive rows, the leaves so dark they almost turned red, too, before our eyes. We passed old people walking along the road. The women in black, bent over, carrying huge bundles of wood or wheat on their shoulders. They stared at Marco, sucking him up with their eyes. They kept their faces as blank as the dirt.

The driver turned off on a gravel lane and stopped outside an iron gate lodged in a high stucco wall that curved around a large villa. A small hut leaned against the outside of the stucco wall, sharing one of its walls with the barrier. A *tío* who looked just our age sat outside the hut, drinking from an unlabeled green wine bottle. When he saw the car stop, he slowly stood up, placing his bottle in the dirt, stepped inside the hut, and closed the door. Something crashed inside and a speckled hen flapped out the window and down into the dirt yard. Marco reached into his pocket, but the driver shook his head—good thing, because I knew Marco had nothing left. The driver might have been upset that Marco didn't insist on tipping him at least, but his expression remained the same, shaded by a brown shepherd's cap, dry as the leaves on the olive trees and impassive as the sun. We got out and Marco opened the iron gate with the key around his neck I'd seen that morning.

The villa sprawled over the hard red dirt. Several stories with wrought-iron balconies, high windows, and paint peeling off in layers of pink and graying white. A chapel rose in the middle, its bell tower empty. The house sat close to the gate, only a narrow, dusty yard with a worn table and a cork tree between it and the stucco wall. Glasses filled with green slime and seedpods covered the table. Marco opened the door to a huge kitchen, dark and cool. He whistled and a dog came slowly out of the shadows toward him. A sleek bronze hunting dog, not one of the shabby mutts we'd seen on the side of the road following the farmers.

I could hear sounds throughout the house, but no one seemed to acknowledge our arrival, and I didn't know where in the house the sounds were coming from. Marco opened the icebox. He pulled out an unmarked wine bottle with pale, almost green liquid, some chorizo, and a hard cheese wrapped in brown paper, then grabbed bread from the low, long table. Then he led us silently through the dark house. The voices seemed to both follow and precede us, the words inaudible. The dog circled lazily, licking Marco's ankles when he could catch them, unbothered when he didn't. Marco's pace wasn't slow enough to acknowledge that he was making sure we followed him or fast enough to seem like he was hurrying. He touched a few things—a table, a low-slung curtain covering something on the wall—but his fingers didn't linger. The dog didn't bark or whine. He was as determined as Marco to keep the silence. We slunk through the long, high halls, easing through the scent of dust and closed rooms.

As we stepped out of the dark house, the sun hit our eyes, silent and lethal. I thought of the rebels who had hidden in these hills during the war, sucking on their fingers to drink their own sweat. Their bodies were found curled up like children baked in a witch's oven. Red dirt swirled, tossed up by chickens the dog ignored. The dirt ended abruptly at a tile-lined pool with leaves in the water.

Grito jumped messily into the pool and howled at the cold water. He stayed in the shallow end because he couldn't really swim. "*Cabrón,* what is this place?" he said.

Marco put the wine down on the side of the pool and dove in, parting the leaves with his body. The water didn't look very deep, but his form was perfect. He came up for air after making a full lap underwater and opened the bottle of wine. "It's my home," he said.

"The wrong train?" La Canaria said to Marco.

Grito pushed through the water to us and pulled himself half out of the pool. He pushed his wet hair back from his face. "This was your plan all along?"

"Now who's asking about plans?" Marco said, and dove back into the pool.

I got in slowly but didn't really notice the water. Marco had never mentioned his family, so I'd assumed they were gone like the rest of ours were, or an ocean away like La Canaria's. The shame of it: villa, land, pool, the sounds of what were proba-bly servants airing out embroidered linen above us. There was only one party that parents like this could belong to; there was only one side they could be on. I could see it on him in retrospect, in the way he blushed every time he offered to pay for anything or how he always bought something that was a little too nice. Those expensive bottles of brandy. I wondered if he'd kept the wealth a secret from Alexis, too.

I went deeper into the water, and it was cold, but all I really noticed was the sky—a blue that was closer to red, scorching our retinas, and silent, an echo of the peasants we passed who nodded at Marco though he didn't nod back. The water seemed to numb all that, to keep me separate. I was just looking at the sky that could kill, not at those people who surely wanted to. The wine tasted sharp—too fresh to be drinking. It made me sink to the bottom of the pool. The water kept me where I wanted to be until it didn't.

My abuela had been sitting with only her lips moving for six hours when the police came with Alexis's wallet, watch, and gold medallion—what they'd collected from the pile on the sand by the river. She took a handkerchief out of her sleeve, one of the white hankies that her sister had embroidered for her dowry, the lace edge pulled off and sewn onto new cloth many times. She was careful not to touch the policeman's hands but brandished the handkerchief in front of her and wrapped what he dropped into it with the same careful folds she used to cover a pastry or a piece of tortilla for our midmorning snack in grammar school.

"Thank you," she said to the policemen.

I held my breath, afraid they'd stick a foot in the door before she closed it. Afraid they weren't done with us. I knew we could be questioned and the house searched. Maybe I'd be dragged out with them, and a week later the same pair would bring her my medallion. I knew more than enough to justify this.

But the door closed and the policemen left. My abuela handed me her handkerchief and took off her apron. She placed her finest *mantilla* on her head and walked to our church to arrange the service. It would be the same Mass as all the other ones when they couldn't find a body. The same my parents got.

That week of waiting, I'd left the house only to fuck Grito in the alley behind our apartment, silent, my mouth closed. But when I told him about the police and Alexis's medallion, he didn't want to touch me. I was crying and screaming, I needed him to hold me down and fix me to the earth. He just walked away. I didn't see again him for months.

I traced the slime at the bottom of the pool with my fingers. Marco's and Grito's white legs moved through the cloudy water, interlocked by perspective. My arms pushed the water aside and my legs propelled me forward. I hadn't swum in years, but I remembered quickly. I could stay underwater for a long time.

Four

Out of the heat and the sun where we'd been drinking that fresh wine for hours, the Americans appeared. They were a mirage from one of their dubbed-over movies: blond women in bikinis carrying drinks in tall glasses, giggling and moving in a way that was not about getting anywhere faster but because they were aware of being watched. They were trying to activate every cell in their skin. They could feel it working in their movements and in the movements of the eyes behind them. But when they saw us, their movements stopped, all except for the liquid in their glasses, which was moving just as fast as their cells had been; it slung itself forward and fell into the dirt. La Canaria sat up when they stopped, her breasts swinging down and resting to point right at the American women, who stared, caught themselves, and looked away. Marco and Grito, who'd been splashing each other like a couple of twelve-year-old girls, stopped and stared at the American women.

"Who's that?" Grito whispered to Marco.

Marco paused. He knew but didn't want to say, was waiting for the men following the women to round the corner arched by grapevines. We could hear them laughing.

"The Americans," Marco said.

"I got that much," Grito said.

"Whoa! I'm sorry!" one of the American men said when he saw La Canaria. "Wait, what?" He was short with a belly and neatly layered hair and tight, bright green swim trunks. He carried a bottle of port.

"Who are they?" one of the women said, the one in the red bikini, backing up slowly to stand beside the man who had just spoken.

"Hey, we're renting this place," the man started to say to La Canaria. She tilted her head to the side, making her breasts shift, and smiled. "I don't know who you are, but—"

"Jaime," Marco interrupted him.

"Holy shit," the man said. "Dude! Marco! I didn't see you there!" He set his bottle of port down behind one of the loose stones and came over to the pool. "I didn't mean to be rude." He knelt beside the pool and shook Marco's hand. "I just didn't want anyone trespassing, you know."

"That is fine," Marco said. "I understand quite well." His English was strong though formal, and it made his body stiff to use it, his jaw overworking each syllable of the garbled sounds. I hadn't known he could speak English that well. The other men relaxed but stood close to the women, holding their beer cans, all in shorts and burned pink from the sun.

"But what are you doing here?" Jaime asked Marco, slowly letting go of his hand and passing it over his shorts, then through his hair to cover the movement. "I mean, I'm glad to see you, but I thought you weren't—"

"It is true what they say about American manners," Marco said, his smile tight and straight as a child's drawing.

"Oh, man, I'm sorry," Jaime said. "You're right, I'm glad to see you. No buts about it."

"Good!" Marco laughed, though his neck stayed straight. "And I you. Let them try to remove me if they wish."

Jaime smiled, not knowing whether he should or not. Started to say something, then didn't.

"Are these ladies and gentlemen the other members of your crew?" Marco asked, turning toward the rest of the Americans.

"Yeah, man," Jaime said, turning behind him. "This is Greg and Howie and their wives, Melanie and Lisa."

Marco pulled himself out of the pool, shook the men's hands, and kissed each of the women on the cheek, which made them giggle.

"This is Marco's place," Jaime said to the others. "He's Señor Lara's son." The men nodded but still looked wary, though Jaime had placed his arm around Marco's shoulders. "I've known Marco forever."

La Canaria leaned in close to me, and I could feel her wet hair landing on my shoulders, her hot arms brushing mine. "What's going on?" she whispered into my ear. She didn't speak English. I shrugged and swam over to the group. I pulled on Marco's undershirt and it stuck to my wet skin.

Marco introduced us all, and the Americans kept moving their faces in the wrong directions when we kissed hello, grazing our lips with theirs and turning red because they hadn't done it on purpose. They were a group from an American university on an archaeological dig who rented Marco's villa for the summers.

"But who are they?" La Canaria asked me after we were all sitting down by the pool. Jaime had opened the bottle of port—"I hope that's okay?" he asked, and Marco nodded with the smile of a dying abuelo giving a blessing to his favorite grandson. La Canaria kept asking me instead of Marco or Grito, and I realized she didn't want them to know she couldn't understand the conversation.

"Some Americans," I told her, which she probably already knew.

One of the men, Greg or Howie, kept tugging at his wife, Melanie's or Lisa's, bikini straps and jerking his head over at La Canaria and me. The woman finally slapped his hand away and came to sit by me. "Are you from around here?" she asked. I shook my head.

"No? You are from where?" she said, pointing first to me and then to the hills behind us, making a person with her fingers, and walking him across her hand.

"Casasrojas—it's in Castile. We are on holiday after university."

The woman's fingers kept climbing up her skin to her suit, tightening the knots, touching her bleached and feathered hair. "Do you have a place like this where you live?" she asked finally, curling her wrists in the air to gesture across the sky.

"No," I said.

"Me, neither." She seemed to relax. "Greg and I just live in a studio in Cambridge." I nodded and tried to remember that Greg was her husband, which made her Melanie. "I'm just glad he let me come. I mean, this is really the life, right?" She reached her arms into the sky.

La Canaria laughed at that. Then she walked over to the edge of the pool and dove in, surfacing right next to Jaime and Marco, flinging her hair back like a fucking mermaid. I watched Melanie and Lisa—who was now standing partially between us and her husband—attempt to divide, categorize, and make irrelevant each of La Canaria's movements. Place her skin on a shelf next to theirs and make sure theirs gleamed brighter. I laid my hand on the nape of Melanie's neck, and she flinched but tried to hide it and didn't shrug me off.

"I really like your bathing suit," I said. It was a bikini made of brightly colored geometric patterns with white fringe on the seams.

"What, this?" she said, not looking at me, still looking at La Canaria, but not really looking at her anymore.

"Yes, this," I said, touching the fringe around her neck. "You have the best clothes. We get nothing nice here. The styles take years to get here, and then it's only what you've decided to toss out."

"Oh," she said. They were older than us, I realized. The men almost or over thirty, the women approaching it.

I dropped my arm from her neck. "You are married to Greg?" The name caught in my mouth, such a stupid combination of sounds.

"Yeah, I am, but I'm getting my Ph.D. in literature."

"Why?" I asked her.

She blinked several times. "Because I want an education. I'm not just going to rely on Greg all my life."

"He does not make money?"

"No, it's not that—well, he doesn't make enough now, but we're hoping with this dig—"

"That you'll strike Incan gold?" Lisa said behind us. Both Greg and Howie were in the pool, swimming around La Canaria.

Melanie laughed, her disembodied wrists returning. "It's just a joke. We know the Incans aren't from here."

"You would have better luck over there," I said. "The bones are too recent here."

I was making a joke, but they both looked at me with their mouths open, turning from La Canaria and their husbands for the first time.

"That's just the thing," Melanie said. She leaned in to me. "They're Classicists, looking for Roman structures, but Greg— Howie, too—they found something recent. Really recent. And terrible."

"It was a mass burial," Lisa blurted out, then covered her mouth. She was a little buzzed. "But it wasn't even a burial. They just piled them in there. Fascist bastards."

"Now, we don't know for sure who it was. And there's loads of red tape. But it's terrible. No marker, nothing. In the middle of this hideous pine forest."

"Well, what did you expect?" I said, and dove into the pool.

The air and water and wine and Americans created their own air and language. We stumbled through the few words we shared, flipping more rapidly between them the darker it got. We didn't talk about what they'd found and couldn't talk about, we didn't talk about what we'd left. La Canaria kept getting closer and closer to Greg, making exaggerated gestures with her head at Howie, but the rest of her body a current focused on Greg. For a few hours I had my toe on the floor of the pool, but then the ground drifted away, the tiles sliding so far below me that it didn't matter if they'd melted or ever even existed. Which was what I realized about that new space I'd made in the mountain shack. No one had mentioned the exams since I'd said we were going to miss them. No allusions, no glances, and I believe no one had even thought of them. The perimeters of this space didn't matter. We were in the dare, fully and floating.

The story of the burial kept circulating in whispers until everyone had heard it, but everyone pretended it was still a secret. I wondered how close it was, if there were bones beneath us, pushing up through the cracked tiles in the pool. The discovered grave loomed larger, stretching and spreading like mycelium. We drank more and shouted more and dove into the pool to keep it and all the others away.

Late at night, Marco appeared from behind the cork trees

on a horse, its mane coiled in tiny knots on its neck like a row of marzipan. The horse reared up against the moon and Marco laughed. We were sitting in the dust by the pool, hair wet. Marco galloped the horse in a tight circle around us. Jaime cheered. For a second, Marco paused and leaned into the animal's neck. The yellowing bruise around his own neck was just another in a series of shadows, like the grave, something that happened before and was not real. The horse's damp hide shone from the moon and Marco's mouth grazed those sweating marzipans and the horse walked backward. Short, hesitant steps, then he jumped sideways, landing a meter to the right. The space between the two places where he'd stood ceased to exist, like a splice of badly censored film. The Americans hollered and La Canaria fell back in the dust, her hair spread out around her, neck open to the stars. I could feel Marco looking at me, feel him smile in a way I'd never seen him smile before. I fell back on the grass by La Canaria. The sky swung up around me and circled in.

Five

After the Mass for Alexis—flowers and no body—I went to the old railway bridge where we'd first seen the piles. He'd kept going there long after I could try to stop him. Walking back from the university along the river, I would see the shadow of his head tuck behind the rails. When he washed his hands in Abuela's kitchen, the rust from the bridge's railing floated in the sink.

On the bridge, with his medallion the police had brought in my hand, I knew if he was anywhere, he was there. I stepped out to the edge where the rails broke off and searched, hoping to find a waterlogged stack of his hand-rolled cigarette butts. The tufts of grass were empty. On the riverbank below the bridge, red poppies waved against the gray water and gray sky. I stood up and went as far as I could, took off my shoes and socks for better balance, and wrapped my bare feet around the wood where the bridge disappeared into air. At the very edge, perched on a broken plank as if he'd written it right as he was diving in, was his tag. *A L X S.* I unwrapped the handkerchief and threw Alexis's wallet in the river. I put the ID in my pocket. Then I took off my medallion. My mother had given it to me for my first communion. I could remember only her hands opening and the medallion inside, nothing else. I threw it in the river, deep in the middle, where it would sink or wash away but not ashore. Looking at the water, at the poppies, I put on Alexis's medallion. San Judas Tadeo, the keeper of helpless prayers.

Grito, La Canaria, Marco, they all knew about the Mass, but only Marco came, and he stayed in the back of the church, tucked away from my abuela's sight. None of them has spoken Alexis's name since.

Someone was shouting, but I heard it through water. The sharp grass was slick under my skin. The scent of goats and rotting grapes. I'd fallen asleep outside Marco's villa, in the grass, but I was wearing clothes, expensive ones. I remembered stumbling through the villa with Marco, laughing, and how he smelled like the horse when he buttoned up my new shirt, linen with tiny abalone buttons. But it was morning, and a woman had hold of my hair and was pulling me through the grass.

"*Puta, puta, puta,*" the woman mumbled. She dragged me across the courtyard to the front of the villa. "My house is full of *putas.*"

I pulled myself out of groggy half-sleep and grabbed her wrist and bit it. My tongue tasted her gold bracelets. She was shorter than me. When she slapped me, I saw Marco in her face for a moment. A face he'd always tried to hide, blooming without shame on hers.

I pushed her to the ground and ran out the open gates of the villa. Marco and Grito were crouched in the doorway of the hut just outside the villa's walls. Marco held a bright red little-kid backpack clutched to his chest. A clump of green oaks hid them from the courtyard.

"Cosme, please," Marco whispered through the wooden

door. "You have to let us in. They're crazy—I swear they're going to kill me this time."

Behind the door of the hut, I could hear soft breathing and the scratch of callused hands on unpolished wood, but no one spoke.

"Please, Cosme. I know you hate me, but you hate them even more."

"Marco!" screamed the woman who had dragged me. Through the green oak branches, I could see her standing with her legs wide and swinging a heavy piece of wood. A man joined her. His bald head glistened with sweat.

"Marco, you *maricón*!" the man screamed.

"*Joder,* Marco," I whispered. "Are those your parents?"

"Unfortunately, yes," Marco said.

"What's the matter with them?" Grito said.

Marco turned away from the door to study the two figures delicately lit by the rising sun. They were dressed in fine country suits, their bodies small and compact, like an atom before it splits.

"I didn't think they'd come back so soon. I'm not really supposed to be here," he whispered. "The last time I saw her, I told her to take her *facha* money and shove it up her ass."

"You said that to your mother?" Grito said.

"You see that thing she's waving around?" Marco whispered to me. "That's what she smashed my head on. Can you believe my mother dragged me all the way down the stairs to the altar before I woke up? San Sebastián's head woke me. A fucking tête-à-tête."

"You get back here, Marco Francisco!" The woman waved the outstretched torso of San Sebastián through the air.

Behind us, the door of the hut swung open. Grito and Marco slammed down face-first onto the packed dirt floor.

"Thank you, Cosme, thank you," Marco whispered.

We crawled in the door, not daring to rise up in case that woman saw us. She was small, but I was scared because Marco was.

"Cosme, they're crazy," he said. "You saved my life."

The room was dark and I couldn't see anyone. The shutters were open only slightly to the purple dawn. I smelled old *bacalao* and drying rice. In the corners were rough bunks, but the lumps in them lay still. I couldn't tell if they were blankets or someone listening.

"Who are these *comemierdas*?" The voice floated out of a corner. Once my eyes adjusted, I could see a young man—the same one who'd been drinking in the yard when we pulled up the night before—leaning against the wooden shutters. He struck a match and lit a cigarette. Grito breathed in deep and fast behind me. My head pounded. I couldn't remember seeing La Canaria after watching Marco on the horse.

"Who?" Marco said. He was standing up, though he was still crouched, his head tucked protectively under his shoulders.

"Them." The young man pointed at me and Grito with the lit cigarette.

Marco looked back at us, confused. "They're my . . . you know—"

"They're not from here."

"No," Marco said.

"I'm your only friend around here, eh, Maria?"

"Yeah, Cosme," Marco said. "For a long way."

Cosme eased the shutter closed with his shoulder and turned on a kerosene lamp.

"My parents are already out working." He nodded at the empty cots on the far side of the wall. "The babies won't say anything unless I tell them to."

Four heads raised out of the cots, dark hair matted against flushed cheeks.

"I knew they weren't sleeping," I whispered to Grito.

"Shut up," Marco said.

"What'd she say?" Cosme said. "She your girl?"

"Yeah, ah, no. Yeah, yeah, she is," Marco said, and he put his arm around me.

"Who is he?" I asked Marco.

"I can hear you," Cosme said.

"All right," I said, and removed Marco's arm from my shoulder.

Cosme was younger than us but his face was burned old by the sun, and his hands were too large for his body. He looked like the boys who would come help my abuelo when he could no longer tie the ropes around the sheep gates or carry the stacks of hay from the stable.

"May I?" I leaned into Cosme and he handed me his cigarette. I held his gaze and blew out the smoke, struggling not to cough. I didn't know what was in the cigarette besides tobacco, but the smoke was a porcupine needle racing to my heart. He smiled slightly when he saw that I wasn't going to flinch. "Are you going to help us out of here?" I asked.

Cosme turned to Marco. "Where's the other girl? The one with the tits?"

Grito looked at me but didn't say anything.

"Maybe she left with the Americans," Cosme said.

"Where'd they go?" Marco said.

"They headed out when Her Majesty came in screaming. Took all the cars."

"Where?"

"They always go to the city when the dons get here. Stay out of Her Majesty's way."

"She's our friend," Marco said.

"I bet she is."

Marco had never used that word before. None of us had. It

was too corny, too soft. It wasn't our own, like he was reading from a card our grandmothers would send, covered in lace and flowers and the clasped hands of Christ praying. *Condolences for a beloved friend.* But Marco using the word made me wonder. We'd all entered something that night in front of the fire, but had we entered the same place or all crossed through our own separate doors that slammed shut behind us? I didn't know whether our words meant the same thing to one another anymore.

"I'm going to Gijón," Cosme said. "I know some people there we can stay with. You'd like them."

"What does that mean?" Marco said.

"They have drugs. They're not a bunch of pigs."

"We're trying to get to Madrid," I said. "Gijón is in the opposite direction."

"Don't want to be late for the hotel check-in, Mosca?" Grito sneered.

"Catch the train to Madrid there, then," Cosme said. "It'll be easier to find a cheap one in a city."

Gijón. I traced the name in my mouth. Alexis hadn't called from there. It was not on the list of cities.

"What do we need you for?" Grito said.

"I have a truck that'll get us to the station," Cosme said. "No one will come out here to pick you up now that they're here. I don't think you can all fit on Marco's horse."

"We'll go to Gijón," Grito said flatly. "Sounds like a good time."

Cosme took a back road toward town, gravel the whole way, sometimes slipping into the brush and almost bouncing down a hill. Even early in the morning, the dust rose through the open windows.

"You've got quite a family, Marco," I said.

"You don't have any idea who he is, do you?" Cosme said to me, one hand on the large wheel of his rusty truck. I was packed between him and Marco in the front seat. His hand grazed my thigh each time he shifted gears.

"They know who I am," Marco said.

We were silent, looking out over the scrubby trees in the purple light. Grito sat in the open back. He fidgeted, tapping his fingers against the broken back window.

"Stop it," Cosme said.

Grito pounded his fists against his thighs. We bumped over a low row of scrub. Finally he spoke. "Are you really that dumb, Mosca? Why don't you tell her, Marco? Since she can't figure it out herself."

Marco kept looking straight ahead. "What do you want, Grito?"

"The house, the money, the fucking peasant at your beck and call—" Cosme swerved the truck to throw Grito on his back, but he wouldn't stop. "You really can't figure it out, Mosca?"

"What the hell are you talking about?" I said.

"He's not talking about anything," Marco said.

"Oh, yes, I am. I'm talking about Marco's famous father. Even us lowlifes have heard of him. Don Lara—the Butcher."

Marco flinched.

"Is that true?" I said.

Cosme grinned. "You stupid fucks."

"I knew it," Grito said. "I knew it the whole time!"

Marco was silent, staring out the window at the dust the truck kicked up.

"Jesus Christ," Grito said slowly. "*You're* the fucking snitch."

Marco turned back to face him for the first time. "Shut the fuck up. I don't talk to the police."

"You're the reason the police were after us—out of that whole crowd, they were only looking for us."

"I didn't tell them anything!"

"You didn't have to. They've probably been following you for years. Making sure the precious Butcher's son doesn't get too roughed up while he plays revolutionary."

Marco's face was white and he was shaking. He couldn't speak. He couldn't deny it.

When we got to town, Cosme pulled his truck underneath a mulberry tree and yanked up the parking brake. "What did you come back for, anyway?" he said.

Marco jumped out of the truck, clutching the red backpack tight under his arm. "I had to get something of mine."

The train slowed once we left León Province and entered Asturias. Whenever we stopped in a town, swarms of striking workers pressed against the windows. In Oviedo, the crowd wouldn't step off the rail, and instead of stopping, the conductor drove through them. They hurled rocks and glass bottles. A man's shirt caught on the car. He was stuck for a moment and we all watched, but the cotton tore and he tumbled away from the rails. The remains of his shirt rippled over the glass, a red flag, as the train picked up speed.

"Should we be on this?" Marco said.

"Believe me," Cosme said, "you don't want to get off here."

Marco had kept the secret from all of us, especially Alexis. Alexis might have forgiven the wealth, the peasants, but not certain family tendencies. An aptitude for torture, a relish. Alexis believed too much in blood to forgive Marco for what his father was known for and what he would therefore consider his true inheritance. The Butcher's son, that he could not

76

forgive. So Marco had lied. The Butcher was famous but the name Lara common enough to not connect Marco to him. In the same way that you'd never confuse two homonyms, never even consider them alike unless they were placed together on a dry, blank page.

It was dark by the time we arrived in Gijón. The train eased into the station, a mess of wires and cement on the edge of the city. The scent of the sea hit us, but no water was visible. The sky hovered low and clouded, air dense with fog. We walked through the narrow streets. Our feet slipped on cobblestones slick with centuries, and picked up clumps of dried rice—the remnants of someone's wedding in the empty trash-strewn streets. A *feria* had just passed. Pink and green streamers hung between the buildings, carrying secrets to those roofs still too sturdy in their foundations to hunch toward one another. Julio Iglesias leaked out of a high apartment window, competing with a recording of Lolita singing a lonesome flamenco on the opposite side of the street. Both sounds floated high above us. Grito kicked a paper devil mask over the cobblestones until it became too waterlogged and melted apart in a puddle.

"I thought you said they lived near the train station," Grito said to Marco.

"That's what *he* said," Marco mumbled back. He kept the backpack tight under his arm. In it was the money he'd taken from his parents' house; he'd bought our tickets with it, and who knew how much more he had. Marco wouldn't speak to Cosme directly, but I could tell he felt under Cosme's power, following him through a strange city in the dark. This shift was new, though they'd known each other all their lives. It reversed something that was as familiar to them as the feel of their own tongue in their mouth. A foreign limb in a too-small cavity: Neither knew what to do with it.

"Are they your family?" I asked Cosme. "The people we're looking for?"

"No. Just friends. Young people. That's why they're hard to find."

He made a quick turn, and I glanced back to make sure Marco and Grito followed.

"How long have you known Marco?" Cosme asked me.

"A few years. We went to school together." I didn't know Cosme and I certainly wasn't going to tell him the truth.

"And he never told you about his home? Or his parents?"

"We don't talk about those things."

"What do you talk about, then?"

Marco and Grito, a ways behind us, stopped, staring down the street to where the city disappeared into the sparkling water. I couldn't tell if they could hear us or not.

"We talk about music, politics."

"Nothing personal, then. What are you looking for?"

I'd been scanning corners and the hidden curves of water pipes, looking for a familiar arc of spray paint, not even knowing that I was.

"Nothing," I said. We kept walking up smaller and smaller streets with no view of the water. The buildings closed in on us. The scent of stale pork and grilled sardines.

"That is what is personal," I said finally. There was no trace of Alexis's tag that I could locate. Why should there be? And what difference would it make? Gijón wasn't on the list, and what did the list mean, anyway?

"Not your family?" Cosme said. "Who do you live with?"

"My abuela." It was the first time since I'd called her at the station in Casasrojas that I'd thought of her. Not about the way she moved after Alexis disappeared but about her in the present, as she must have been at that moment. A life can be built entirely around someone, and then a new life is made without her in it. Her saints, her prayers, and her lace, the jars of old oil stacked neatly by the sink. She opened her black lace fan only when she was angry, in one movement, forcing the flowered cloth to bring her new air. She endured the heat otherwise. I had to forget her; remembering her was remembering what I'd done by leaving. The space I had made was not one for remembering, for staying still, jaw slack with want in the solitude of lifelong grief. It was hurtling ahead, no reason, no sight.

I thought of her smell and her weight on the worn linoleum floors. The farther I moved from Casasrojas, the less I could keep what I wanted hidden from rising up. But I could not picture her. I didn't know if she was angry, fanning herself by the closed shutters or kneeling in prayer in front of the shrine with the old marzipan box filled with a lifetime of funeral cards, her rapidly moving lips almost grazing the rosary beads. In Casasrojas, her reactions formed in front of me into layers of glass, each stained a different color, piling on one another as I climbed the stairs to our apartment, until they were thick enough to be real and I opened the door to her.

But I could not see her then, walking through a new city with a stranger, though I tried. Maybe I had betrayed her so much that I had killed her, this creature who raised her eyebrows and flared her nostrils every time I moved. But I hadn't killed her. She lived. The movement of her palms unknown to me was much worse. I knew what Grito would say if I called her, and I didn't think I could keep it from him. Anyway, what would I tell her? The list of cities swirled in my throat.

"Where are they?" I said. Cosme stopped walking. The street was empty except for two pigeons. A balcony window opened above us, and an old woman turned the crank that brought in her laundry. "They were behind us."

"Maybe they ditched you. They ditched the other girl."

"Maybe you don't know where you're going." I stopped looking down the blind alleys and faced Cosme. His eyes were just visible in the flickering light from a streetlamp a block away. "Maybe you lost them on purpose."

Cosme grinned and stepped closer to me. I had my arms behind my back. I reached until I could feel with my fingertips the damp stone of the building surrounding us. A strip of torn poster plastered on the wall grazed my shoulder.

"And if I did, what would I do now?" he whispered.

I could smell the inside of his mouth and the sweat from the collar of his jacket. "Nothing," I said.

He stepped in closer. "Why's that?"

"You're not who you're acting like you are."

"And how would you know?"

I held his gaze. Whatever Marco had done, whatever his family had done for however many centuries, I wasn't a part of it.

"Because I'm the same way," I said.

Cosme smiled. He stepped away and bit his lips. He'd gotten to taste what he wanted to. "*Mosquita muerta*," he said and passed. "They're unstoppable, you know."

"You don't know anyone here, do you?" I asked.

"In school, I read that in the Arctic, mosquito swarms can kill these giant deer they have there, the caribou. Drive them completely crazy just with tiny bites."

"You were going to drop us here, but they've done it for you." I started walking again, trying to retrace our steps.

"Marco's a *pendejo*," Cosme said. "And that other one doesn't seem any better. Why do you all have such stupid names?"

The streetlamps went out, just like in Casasrojas, and the night flickered into a negative of itself, the sky lit instead of the street. I heard shouting down one of the streets and walked toward it, saw Marco's frame at the end of an alley. Cosme stood behind me and I turned to him. "What did Marco do to you?" I said. I knew Cosme was going to disappear down one of these alleys soon.

"Nothing. He hasn't said a word to me for ten years. His father didn't like the little lord speaking to the peasants." He lit a cigarette and stared up at the rusting gutters. "But they'll lose it all now that el Cabronísimo is dead. Now it's time for the rest of us."

Grito saw us and waved.

"You think I'm one of you?" I said.

"I can see your whole life, Mosca. Your dingy apartment. The fake roses and jars of pickled meat and photos of el Cabro—"

"My family was Republican."

"Was. And what happened to them? People like Marco's family killed them?"

I dug my nails into my palms. "The past doesn't matter," I said.

He knew I was lying. "It's all that matters." He lit a cigarette. "You can always go back to your family. Real people, not royalty, they will always let you back."

He turned into an alley and I couldn't see him anymore. But I knew he was wrong. In the dark, I could see Alexis on the shore of the river, running away from me, running in the sand toward the piles, his legs outgrown his shorts, his messy curls that he wouldn't let Abuela cut bouncing. From the way he held his shoulders and pumped his arms, I could tell he was smiling. When he turned from the weight of the man's hand on his shoulder, his mouth still held a bit of that smile, but it was turning to surprise at this man standing over him. Before even looking at the man, Alexis looked at me. Because I should have shouted a warning that something was coming. It came too fast. I saw it and I didn't do anything.

I rounded the corner without Cosme and didn't bother to give Marco an explanation. Grito shrugged, but Marco ran down a couple of dank alleys and pulled on doors that had been boarded up for years.

"He's gone, *tío*," Grito said, picking a forearm-long strip of green paint off a rotting door.

Marco turned away from both of us and lunged as if to go after Cosme but instead crashed his forehead into the doorway, landing on the rotting wood and just missing Grito's own skull. I thought he was done, but he brought his head back and slammed it against the damp wall. Again and again. Around us, the night lurched into the sea.

Once Marco stopped, we found a vendor who was just closing his cart and bargained for three sardine sandwiches. The fish was cold but the bread still fresh. I didn't know how much money Marco had, but he wasn't acting like he had a lot of it. He might be protecting it from Grito. I would do the same thing. Not that I feared Grito would steal from me but because I didn't want to give him the chance. We walked toward the harbor, not speaking, just chewing, and licking the paper wrappers before crumbling them and throwing them in the water. They bobbed against the docked fishing boats.

"We could stay in one of those," Grito said, pointing to the boats, and I nodded. A night watchman passed by and we sat down on the stone steps by the water, hidden in the shadows and the smell of piss. The outlines of the abandoned steel plants fell in contorted shapes on the water. We waited for the man to walk to the far end of the stone wall.

Our hands greasy from the sandwiches, we ducked below the metal gate and climbed down the slick steps to the dock. Marco pointed silently to the watchman sitting on the other end of the dock, enclosed in cigarette smoke. If we stayed quiet and in the shadow, he wouldn't see us. Then we could duck into a boat and sleep until sunrise.

Grito chose a long boat with a high, solid railing. Even if we couldn't get into the cabin, we could sleep on the deck, curled up by the railing, and no one would see. The lights from the city dove and died in the water. They didn't reach the dock. We were in black air surrounded by light, and nothing could touch us.

The boat barely rocked when we climbed into it. All the boats on the dock were low with large decks. A few other men joined the watchman and huddled around one another, making one form, their cigarette smoke rising and blurring the lights behind them.

"They can't hear us," Grito said.

"They can if you keep talking," Marco said.

The cabin was locked and none of us wanted to risk breaking a window. The deck was damp. We huddled together against a pile of fishing ropes. No one said La Canaria's name, but we were all wondering if we'd left her to a worse or better fate. No one had said her name since we last saw her. The same as after Alexis disappeared. Abuela and I didn't speak about him, but his name hung over us, a flashbulb that would burst suddenly and fill the air with the smoke of his absence, leaving me immobile in the shattered light. Abuela with her rosaries, her knees pitted from kneeling, sucked all the oxygen from the apartment and the tears from my body. There was no room in her grief for mine. No room for a single breath that was my own.

"Do you think she went to Madrid?" Marco said. "That's where we said we were going."

Grito shrugged. "I never know where she's going."

We didn't know how to feel about La Canaria. At least I didn't know how I felt, and I thought Marco didn't, either. I wasn't sure how much Grito could feel. Not just for La Canaria but for anything. In Casasrojas, he never winced at the gypsy children begging or the old men who'd fought in the war and now sat on the park benches, their sleeves hanging empty at the joints. He didn't wince at the smell coming off of them— sulfur and bitter almond—the smell I imagined leaked from the white scars where their arms and legs ended. He'd left me as soon as I wasn't something easy to be around. During the protests, he'd screamed and thrown empty bottles against the cathedral walls, but I hadn't seen him break in any other way for a long time.

I knew that Marco wanted to say that leaving La Canaria, that not searching for her, that not speaking about her, was disloyal, but Grito would have smacked him on the back of the head like a misbehaving acolyte. *Whose side are you on?* Grito would ask. *Want to go back to your mansion and your peasants?*

Loyalty was one of el Cabronísimo's words. Loyalty to the Church, loyalty to the Fatherland. Friendship was, too. Friendship was watching your neighbors; it was turning on them for the chance at a higher number in the ration line. We didn't have words to speak about our lives, about how we moved into and around one another. They had been stolen; they were never ours to begin with. We were animals, wordless and scratching.

Alexis's protection was that he was able to keep some of those words. He guarded them deep within or wrestled them, bloody and almost broken, from the very lips of those he hated most. As a kid, he held my or Abuela's hand everywhere he went. We slept in the same bed most nights, curled together like foxes in a den, safe under thick layers of oak roots and red dirt. Years later, I remembered what he had been. Because the toughness he slipped on, I knew it was an act, a film over each of his movements. I saw the same in La Canaria. Masking something, though with her I never quite grasped what. Which was perhaps why she and Alexis had made so much sense together—even when they fought, it was like watching a drunk punch himself.

Marco's and Grito's breaths landed heavy on my skin, heavier than the damp air coming off the harbor. I could never stand to feel anyone else's breath when I slept except for Alexis's. Marco's and Grito's bodies, anxious not to touch each other, were stiff even in sleep. From where I sat, their shoulders, dashed in fragments of light by the moon, created a separate skyline, like the pictures of American cities I'd seen in magazines, paper puppets against the night, casting their own light, containing their own spheres. I couldn't sleep. Too many names hung above me, each letter a flickering bulb that refused to finally die.

At some point the city lights went out. Or I dreamed they did. I watched the water dance, ushering in new musical movements, streaks of diesel shimmering in taffeta over the surface. In my pocket, I found the bullet La Canaria had given me at the shepherd's shack in the mountains. I couldn't remember how I'd kept it. Maybe Marco had found it in my widow's clothes and had been about to throw it out but I'd grabbed it from his hand, drunk and reaching, and put it in the pockets of the polyester trousers I woke up in, dragged across the dirt by his mother. The bullet fit right in my palm and I ran my fingers over the writing—the name of the gun and where it was made. The same gun my abuelo used for hunting. Alexis went with him several times until he refused to go again. He was twelve. They had been hunting pheasants. The birds hung from their shoulders. Alexis handed my abuelo the gun and his old wool hat.

"He doesn't like killing," my abuelo said. But he didn't mean that Alexis was weak. He meant Alexis understood something we didn't.

La Canaria's bullet warmed in my hand, the only warm and dry thing around me. I pulled at a frayed bit of rope by my feet until I'd loosened a thin strand. When I was young I used to read books aloud to Alexis about these kids whose lives were really terrible but they found this amazing new world where they were kings and queens. The thing about this world was that you could access it through ordinary things—a closet, a park bench, whatever. We always hoped we'd find that right thing that could get us in. Of course, our parents would be there, but we never said that. We were always looking for a way, even after we stopped believing in it. After so much searching, I'd gotten into somewhere, but it wasn't that place. And the things that had been solid before no longer were. No object or act held definition. I floated between the wants realized in sleep and the loss found in waking, unable to distinguish between them.

I wrapped the frayed rope around the bullet and put it over my head. It hung on my sternum beside Alexis's medallion. Gijón was somewhere I had never been, but it was somewhere Alexis had never been, either. Madrid, Madrid was the first city. I felt the name, the shape the syllables had made in his mouth, pulling me. I looked up and met Marco's eyes. I could barely look at him. Marco had lied. But far worse was what I'd already known: he kept Alexis alive in front of me—nothing more cruel or more gracious. I didn't want to want him because of who he'd been close to, what he'd meant to Alexis. I didn't want to be that cruel. But I was. I'd do worse. And I wanted to hurt him for the same reason and because he was stupid enough not to see what I was. I knew what he felt about me and I wanted to punish him for it, for being the one person who could really see I was bloody rocks to break on and chains and gulls at his eyes and he was still following my every move. I would have told him if I could, what I wanted him to bear, but I couldn't meet his gaze long enough.

The water and the lights continued their flirt, a slow torture for no one else to see. If Marco heard the cities I whispered when the moon set, he didn't say.

"I've got money, but it is going to have to last us," Marco said when it was just light enough to see beyond one another's faces to the edge of the boat. "It's not endless."

"No, Marco, it's just your family's land and peasants that are endless," Grito said.

"Do we have to do what you say, Marco?" I said. "Or you'll sic your father on us?"

"It's not very much money; it'll just get us to where we're going."

"Which is where?" I asked.

"I don't know, maybe we could go south, to Cádiz. We could stay there, get jobs, I don't know," Marco said without looking at me.

"Why do you want to go there?" I asked. It was the first time I'd ever heard him mention Cádiz. Grito talked about it sometimes because the rumor was that now that el Cabronísimo was dead, the ban on Carnival would be lifted, or people would just have it anyway. Cádiz was famous for having the best Carnival before the war.

"Carnival isn't for almost another year," Grito said.

"We're going to Madrid, like we said we would," I said.

"No," Marco said. "We should go to Cádiz. We should start there."

"Marco Francisco," Grito said, laughing and using Marco's middle name for the first time. "They even gave you the general's name. Somebody to live up to?"

"Mosca, listen to me—"

"Got more land in Cádiz?" Grito continued. "An uncle you can sell us out to?"

"Shut up, Grito," I said. "Madrid is where we said we'd go. It's where we told La Canaria we'd go. It's where I'm going."

The cities were an itch in the back of my throat. Cádiz was not on the list. Madrid first, then the rest. I couldn't get rid of the thought. I didn't need to talk about it. Why I heard them, why I listened to them, why I wanted so badly to go to them and trace their walls with my fingertips. The want unformed but there, letting me know it wasn't leaving.

"All right," Marco said. "Madrid to start."

"Excellent choice," Grito said. "Maybe you'll become the first Lara to slaughter pigs exclusively."

I touched the bullet around my neck, wondered if that or a thin blade to the throat was better. I had a bullet, but the farther we moved away from Casasrojas, and especially there on the water, the half-light remaking every form, the less I could believe that it was Alexis who had gotten the blade. The less I could see him how I'd imagined him—on his knees, throat pulled back—the more something else twisted in me. It no longer seemed as certain. Other passages felt possible.

In the summer we used to take trips to Abuelo's old farm. That's where our parents' clothes, our mother's childhood toys were kept. I knew Abuela's apartment would freeze until we got back and then be set in motion when she turned the key in the lock. The more I thought about it, the more real that thought felt. I never saw Alexis's body. Without a body, nothing is certain.

MADRID

Six

Her feet before the rest of her, in the Atocha train station, La Canaria's dirty toes curled around the edge of the marble steps, easing into the depression at the center, making home. Then her voice, yelling at the pigeons gathered around her, cupping a handful of bread to keep them close. "*¡Hijos de putas!*" she shouted, just loud enough for it to echo a bit. "Suck it, *¡maricones!*" I knew this act, the crazy one she made when she didn't want anyone near her, when she wanted to feel safe sleeping somewhere strange. "*¡Cabrones! ¡Pendejos! ¡Co-o-o-ño!*"

Looking right at us, yelling at the pigeons, the whole train station, and us. We walked straight toward her, Marco and me first, Grito following, staring at the polished marble floor. She threw a shoe at Marco but missed by a lot. It wasn't hers. "*¡Hijos de putas!*" La Canaria waved the other shoe above her head, moving it with the rhythm of her words.

"Where did you go?" Marco said when we were close enough.

"I tried to run away to America, you *comemierdas*," she said, still waving the shoe above her head. "But they kicked me off the boat!" She was laughing and I couldn't tell how angry she was. I knew that was how she wanted it. "I grabbed this as a goodbye present."

Marco tossed the shoe back to her and she clapped it in her hands before it hit her in the face. She kicked her legs in the air, pretending she was a can-can dancer. She stood up and revealed an expensive-looking suitcase. "The bitch overpacked. Want a bikini, Mosca?"

She tossed it in the air and I caught the bikini—a skimpy gilded thing. With that I let her slip back in, her breath on the back of my neck. The kind of weight you have to turn around for, because what person would stand so close unless she wanted something. And you always turn, not knowing how much you're willing to give or how much you'll be asked to.

"What were you going to do?" I said.

"I got plans, *tía*," she said. "I was heading to Paris—I know someone there. But that can wait." She tossed Marco the suitcase she'd stolen. "It took us so long to get here, let's see this fucking city."

She was wearing a pair of black tights with her sandaled toes peeking through the seams and a green silk shirt that barely covered her ass. Marco wanted to say something but didn't. I knew he didn't want to stay in Madrid but wanted to keep moving, to Cádiz, for whatever reason. "Fine," I said.

Marco walked over to a boy selling newspapers. The demonstrations seemed to have died down for the time being. Instead the headline was the murder of Oscar Luis Romero, a young attorney.

"Well, at least it's better than it was before," Marco said.

"You would think that, Don Lara," La Canaria said. She was walking ahead of us.

"I mean at least the newspapers are covering it," he said. Marco and Grito hurried to catch up, the stolen suitcase banging against Grito's leg.

I'd never been to Madrid, and I'd always thought it would be different from Casasrojas. It was where the demonstrations had started, where all the artists lived, it was supposed to be modern. In Madrid, everything we always talked about had happened, was happening. It was supposed to be much more alive than Casasrojas, a place that couldn't collect dust or suspend you in oil your whole life.

The train station was far more grand than the one in Casasrojas, an expansive metal and glass arcade both delicate and threatening, but the people looked the same. The same men scurrying in their faded black suits and crumpled hats, the same gypsies with dirt worn into the creases in their dark skin, their foreheads bent over the cement, arms outstretched and hands clasped in prayer. The same frantic movements when someone gave them money, tucking a coin into their dresses so their sardine tins always stayed empty. I followed La Canaria, wanting to wash this grime off of me, to see my surroundings for what they really were and not with the tired tinge of what I expected and what I was capable of seeing.

The streets were covered with the smiling photos of all the different candidates, their faces repeated for blocks. Most of the posters were shredded and wilting, but someone could always be paid to plaster more on top of them. Torn pieces crumbled off, adding more trash to the streets. La Canaria kept walking like she knew where she was going, and maybe she did. I never knew when she was boasting or not. She always acted the same way, no matter what spot she was in. The newspapers all had the same photo of the young attorney who'd had his throat slit outside of his apartment in Lavapiés. He'd been trying to prosecute members of the Falange. The centerfolds had a photo of how he'd been found. It looked like he'd tripped falling down the stairs, but blood pooled on the steps below him in a dull gray. All the articles contained the same minutiae about his daily life and the weather the night he was killed, painting a perfect picture and not pointing any fingers.

Marco kept looking at the cafés we passed and I could tell he was hungry. Grito and La Canaria walked ahead of him. I was glad to be somewhere farther south, where it was warmer. In Casasrojas, the sun coaxed each stone warm one by one, and all its efforts were washed away with some rain. It took months to shake the damp and then it was too hot, the city emptied, people piling into cousins' farms in the country, everyone in search of cool water, a window big enough to catch the breeze. But Madrid was full of people. Maybe the weather didn't matter much here. The rules of a job or a crowd's movements probably meant more than the sun. Or maybe it was because there were just so many people that if even half left for the summer, the city would still seem busy to me.

It was around six. All the men were getting off work and stopping in cafés for a *caña* before they went home. The old people had just left the house and were walking through the city. Groups of old men with canes and summer jackets walked arm in arm in front of their wives, who held on to each other's hats when delivery trucks sent up gusts of hot air. The young businessmen tried to skirt the edges of these groups, but sometimes the old people would take up the entire width of the sidewalk. The businessmen kept walking behind the old people, their pace the same, just taking smaller steps, moving like those windup plastic ducks with feet that go really fast but don't go anywhere and that do flips if they're working right. I thought one man ahead of me in a worn green fedora was about to flip right over the old women who had stopped to look at hosiery in a window and were fighting over whether it was indecent to show a mannequin in her dressing gown. They had their arms linked, and though they had stopped, they hadn't huddled together by the window because the one farthest away considered even looking too immodest.

Someone brushed into me and I felt something cold and wet reach right under my ribs and grab my spine. It was a young guy—he looked like Alexis. His head wasn't shaved but he had those same curly lips, the proud way of holding his neck that contrasted strangely with his hunched, defensive shoulders. A few minutes after he passed, I realized I'd stopped looking at the old people and the businessmen. I looked for groups of young people, for young men carrying packages or smoking on balconies. Instead I saw *fachas* in stiff suits, skin wishing to be encased in military uniform, hands drifting to guns that were perhaps still within easy reach. I thought of how the police hadn't questioned my abuela or me when they gave us Alexis's medallion. I'd been relieved, but it seemed strange now, an omission, one that might have to be circled and revisited. We had thought no one was watching us in Casasrojas, but that was because we forgot. Like a child forgetting to breathe, we forgot there were no unsurveyed moments. That was as true in Madrid as in Casasrojas. Nothing was secret.

We passed the huge museums and rows of carts selling used books. On balconies, pudgy women in tailored suits and heavy gold jewelry, wives of the old guard, knitted under parasols. Their feet bulged out of tight leather sandals, arched into high heels even when sitting. Women in pleated pantsuits with matching bright plastic jewelry stood in doorways, smoking and waiting for it to be time to close up shop. We turned down smaller streets that the dipping sun couldn't reach. Last Easter's palm fronds had been woven into the window grates. Children's fingers or the long nails of women about to go out picked at the fronds. The streets were already dark and damp even though it wasn't yet night. It didn't take long for the buildings around us to start crumbling. Empty lots appeared, with kids and old people picking through the rubble like tongues surfacing through missing teeth. La Canaria walked up to a group of young people sitting on the steps of a grimy café, drinking liters of beer.

"Buy us a couple," she said to one of guys. He was skinny and short with dirty pants cut off mid-calf and a dark shirt, the sleeves rolled up like James Dean's. His hair looked like the scruffy hind legs of a circus bear. His face was shaved and his nose turned up like a boy's.

"Why should I?" he said, taking a drink of his beer and looking La Canaria up and down.

"Because we're cute." La Canaria grabbed my arm and wrapped her hands around my waist. Grito and Marco stood back, not speaking. The guy smiled and went inside the store. A group of gypsies had made camp in one of the abandoned buildings across the street and were roasting potatoes in a trash can. A family was asleep in an old Renault 4, the children's faces smudged against the glass hatchback.

"His cousin works here—he gets a bunch of stuff for free," said a tall guy with a Mohawk. A dog sat with his head on the punk's legs, lapping up the cold sweat from the beer bottle.

"Well, I don't do anything for free," La Canaria said. She sat down on the side opposite the dog. The dog pulled his tongue away from the beer bottle and sniffed La Canaria's knees. She ignored him. The guy came out of the café with two beers. He handed one to me and one to La Canaria.

"You *punki*?" La Canaria asked.

They laughed. "Yeah, we are," said the one with the Mohawk.

She introduced us. They said their names but didn't stand up, just waved lazily. There were about five of them, two guys and three girls in leather jackets and miniskirts. Paco brought us the drinks and Borgi, with the Mohawk, had the dog. Marco kept twitching toward them to offer his hand, but they stayed still.

"What, are these your brothers?" Paco said to me, jutting out his beer at Marco and Grito. Marco looked at me quickly and then away. I ignored him.

"No, they're not our brothers," I said.

"*Vale, vale,*" Paco said, stretching out his long fingers to scratch behind the dog's ears. "Where are you from?"

"Casasrojas," I said.

"We came for the protests, but I guess we're late," Grito said, speaking for the first time.

"*Joder,* I thought everyone in Casasrojas was a *facha,*" Borgi said. The girls sitting behind him laughed. When he spoke, his Mohawk flopped around in front of his eyes. He was taller than the others, taller than anyone I had seen before, though he was sitting down. He was as skinny as the rest of us, but his limbs seemed to contain a barely reined current. Paco was stockier; the veins in his forearms pulsed when he gripped his bottle.

"We had huge protests for the Communists," Marco said. "Almost all of the students were involved. A bunch of teachers just passed their students without even looking at the final exams."

"I hope they did that for us," La Canaria said.

"I guess that would have been the only way you could've passed," Grito said. It made him angry when she talked to any other guy except Marco.

"We're not in school anymore," I said. "I don't know why we have to talk about it so much."

"We haven't mentioned it for days," Marco said. "Not since—"

"Then we shouldn't now." I couldn't remember a time when

I hadn't been in school. Everything that I could remember doing had happened while I was getting ready for an exam or after I'd been studying in the print shop beneath the philology library or leaving it. That I'd never do that again was not quite touchable.

"Did you drop out?" Paco asked.

"Yeah," I said.

"Cool. Us, too."

I drank from my beer bottle.

"We're artists," he continued when I didn't speak. "Public artists."

I swallowed my beer and nodded as if I understood. Then I handed the beer to Marco. He was still standing over us, expecting someone to ask him to sit. I don't know why I handed him the beer. It was making me laugh, him leaning, up on his toes. But I wanted to make it clear just what I was accepting from these punks and what I wasn't. La Canaria looked at me and handed her beer to Grito. She grabbed it back when he took two sips in a row. I took mine back too.

"*Coño,*" she said, "public artists, what does *that* mean?"

I peeled off the label of my beer bottle. The beer wasn't quite cold enough for it to come off in one easy strip.

"We make public art," Borgi said. "In the street—wouldn't you say, Zorra?" He reached back to tickle one of the girls' legs. I handed my beer to Marco again and tried to iron out the torn label on my thigh.

"They're just a bunch of hicks," Zorra said, brushing him off. She stretched her long legs out around Borgi and flexed her feet, moving through ballet positions. Then she tightened each of the three ponytails that stuck out in a row on top of her head. "They don't know what we're talking about." The girl next to her nodded and took a slow drag, leaving a ring of bright purple lipstick on her cigarette. Their clothes were nice, the leather jackets new, the zippers shining. They smoked American cigarettes—Winston Slims—blowing the smoke high above them. They were slumming it, but there was no dirt under their nails.

"If you're artists, let me see your art," La Canaria said.

"It's transient," Paco said.

"You mean you haven't done any?" La Canaria said.

"We're having a show tonight," Zorra said. "In the Plaza Mayor."

"That sounds cool," La Canaria said, "but we have to keep moving because we don't have anywhere to stay." She was perfect in these moments. I held my breath, trying to show I didn't care what they said next.

"You can stay with us," Borgi said. "We squat in a big place, an old factory. There's room."

"Well, then," La Canaria said. "Let's go see some art."

Paco got more beer and we followed them a few blocks to an old textile factory. We walked up three flights of stairs through a dingy boardinghouse. The kind without lightbulbs in the hallways, where you know they're not licensed and everyone is constantly terrified of getting evicted. The punks lived on the top floor. The door was off its hinges. Behind it, several dogs whined, pushing their snouts against the frame.

I couldn't tell how many people were living there. It smelled of piss and wet dogs and what gathers on your scalp when it has been weeks since you had a shower. A couple of punks were sleeping on the floor right by the door. Their mutts circled them, panting, but the punks didn't move. It was mostly guys. The girls we'd met glided in and out of the rooms, not touching any surface for long. The drugs they had were too expensive for us.

By the door, the almost-floor-to-ceiling windows were wide open but barely caught the breeze coming off the rooftops. The farther we moved into the building, the hotter and stiller it got. There weren't any doors, just half-standing walls and old blankets hung up between different spots where people were sleeping. Paco's stuff was in the middle, right under a dingy skylight that had been collecting the sun full-force all day. Just sitting there made me sweat.

Paco put on Santana's *Amigos* and set the record to "Europa." Marco groaned and Grito smacked him in the chest. There was no electricity in the warehouse, but they'd rigged a network of extension cords snaking out the windows and over to the next apartment building. Across the room was a hot plate on a milk crate. The cord was that soft woven plastic from right after the war. The wires were visible and frayed.

"It's still so good, *gachó*," Paco said, and passed a joint to Grito. "Listen to *that*." The guitar did sound like smoke, a dangerous smoke that wanted to pull you in and lose you there.

Paco had just a sleeping bag and an old army roll. His spot was sectioned off from the rest of the room with an old blanket. Piles of broken wood—doors, pieces of tabletops, and old signs—were propped against the walls around us, next to buckets of house paint and horsehair brushes.

Paco moved closer to me and laid his hand flat on my stomach. La Canaria had floated into another corner I couldn't see, probably going after Borgi.

"Is it cool, *gachó*?" Paco asked Marco.

"Don't ask him what's cool to do to me," I said, pressing down on his hand.

Paco leaned in and kissed me. I tasted chemicals, bright and burning as the sun on water. Marco was staring straight at me. I took off my shirt. Marco got up and passed through the curtain without saying a word. Out the skylight you could see the splayed forks of pigeon feet moving around on the glass.

Once it was dark there were more people bumping through the building. Grito came and sat by us, but I couldn't see Marco.

"How many people live here?" Grito said.

"I don't know," Paco said. "It's a free space. If someone needs to stay here, they can."

Borgi pushed open the curtain and stuck his head in. "Everyone's getting ready," he said to Paco. "Let's go."

"Hold on. I need my chocolate," Paco said. He unrolled another cigarette and crumbled hash into it. I put my shirt back on. We smoked and then stood up. Borgi had kept his head in the same spot the whole time. His Mohawk was stiffer now and smelled of raw eggs. He nodded his chin to the sound of an accordion player on the street, but his hair didn't move. Then he grabbed a bunch of the pieces of wood around us and handed some to Paco. Grito offered to help, but Paco acted like he didn't hear. He took a bucket of paint, too.

More young people were waiting outside, smoking and pulling on bottles of San Miguel. Zorra stood in the center of the group in a large men's trench coat. Once they saw Paco and Borgi, they all started moving in the same direction, toward the city center. Everyone was getting off work, moving in one current from their offices and storefronts downtown back into the apartments where they lived. We pushed against aging businessmen and young women in pressed polyester skirts and matching jackets. Some of the men cursed us and others looked like they knew—that we were coming up now, that they were the ones to get shoved in the dirt. Marco caught up to us, but instead of reattaching himself to my elbow, he walked next to Grito. He wouldn't look at me.

We walked past a bar playing that stupid disco song, "Fly Robin Fly." It only had six words in it, which these coked-up Germans repeated over and over. Those six words had played a million times on the radio since last year. The place was empty because it was early, but a group of women stood outside the door, dressed in matching metallic pants and halter tops and platform sandals with clear plastic heels, their lips fluorescent pinks and oranges. They were practicing their dance moves and mouthing the words. Grito started walking toward them, shouting the lyrics over the instrumental break and gyrating his hips. They tossed their cigarettes at him.

"Fuck disco!" Grito shouted once we were past them.

"Fuck punk!" they shouted back.

The plaza was full of people going out for tapas and to catch the air, cool now that the sun had gone down. La Canaria absentmindedly traced graffiti letters that spelled out REVOLU-CIÓN SOCIAL on a brick wall, the *a* an anarchy sign and the *r* a trademark. I caught Marco staring at the graffiti. Maybe he was looking for something specific, too.

Tiny pools of water from the afternoon street cleaning reflected the gold and pink lights of the bars and municipal buildings. The streets in the city center were immaculate, scrubbed raw for the soon-to-descend packs of English and Swedish tourists. In each window of the tapas places was a big empty table, but the waiters ushering people inside made them stand at the bar. This so the tourists would think there was an empty table and then get stuck at a bar with the rest of the fools. All the boards outside the restaurants offered the same menu as in Casasrojas—potatoes and red peppers, tortilla, octopus with garlic—but the food the servers scurried past us with was far more elaborate than anything I'd ever seen. The punks didn't seem to notice the restaurants or the lines of tourists and Madrileños alike waiting to get in.

Borgi and Paco walked right to the center of the plaza and put down their pieces of wood and buckets of paint. It was so full, no one noticed them at first. I could hardly see them in the crowd because I hadn't been following them that closely. La Canaria was standing outside one of the restaurants. We were starving. Paco turned over the boards, which had cartoon sketches of political prisoners on them. One had the hammer and sickle in red behind black bars. It was pretty typical stuff. The same that I'd seen on posters and banners at the rallies in Casasrojas. La Canaria took her eyes off the platters of food for a second and glanced at Paco and Borgi. She rolled her eyes.

Zorra stood in the center of the signs and threw off her trench coat. "¡Oyé!" she shouted. "Listen up! Everyone here knows someone who didn't come home. Who one day just didn't show up for work." She was dressed like a flamenco dancer, with a black flared skirt, long black satin gloves, and big gold hoops, red carnations in her hair. In the artificial lights from the plaza, she appeared both young and old at the same time. "We don't even know how many dead there are! How many they marched out into the desert and never brought back!" She moved through the crowd, bringing her long fingers to turned-down chins, carving out a stage as people pulled away from her. "The police give us the medallions, but we never see the bodies—every one of you walking here! But you all saw *his* body—Oscar Luis Romero—throat slit on his front steps because he wanted to know where they are buried and who put them in the dirt. He wanted to know who killed—"

Borgi stepped behind Zorra and shoved her to the ground. I gasped. Paco caught her right before she hit the stones and tossed her in the air. She spread her arms and landed in Borgi's arms, and then they both rolled to the ground. It was some sort of dance. They were fighting, but it was beautiful, too. Zorra kept trying to drag herself out of Borgi's reach, but then he would pin her down again. The people walking in the plaza stopped to watch. Some men tried to get between Borgi and Zorra because they thought it was real. Paco raced in front of them like a startled antelope, his neck arched back and arms out. Zorra got away from Borgi and twirled around and around, leaping into the air, her legs almost completely horizontal when she jumped, turning herself from a wounded doll two guys were throwing into a piece of sailing architecture. Borgi collided with her in the air and they rolled onto the ground. He started stage-punching her, his fist landing in smart slaps onto his splayed palm. Then he drew her up on her knees by her hair and pulled back her head. Though I knew it wasn't real, I believed it. Her neck stretched back like a curve of water. A man rushed toward them and Paco had to hold on to his overcoat. Borgi drew his arm up to Zorra's neck like he was about to slit her throat.

I felt a hand on my shoulder and smelled rust from the bridge in Casasrojas, empty aerosol spray cans, hand-rolled cigarettes. "Watch," someone whispered in my ear. I turned around, but there was no one next to me. When I looked back at the dancers, Zorra was collapsed on the ground, Borgi standing over her. Still holding the man back, Paco motioned frantically at the punks sitting nearby. One stood up and threw a bucket of red paint on Zorra and Borgi.

The punks who'd been watching stood up and cheered. Paco tried to explain to the man what they were doing. The man thought he'd been tricked and kept checking his pockets. Finally he shrugged Paco off and walked away. The punks passed around a hat to the crowd who had gathered to watch. Most people turned away once they saw it and kept heading in the direction they'd been going. Grito was shaking all the punks' hands and hugging them, his ponytail bobbing up and down. A few moving lines of people separated me from them. I walked over, going against the current, searching the crowd around me. I could still smell the bright rust that sticks in your throat, the decaying weeds and algae clumped around the bridge, the harsh burn of drying paint. Still hear that voice in my ear. La Canaria followed me. She hadn't said anything during the performance.

Grito wouldn't stop talking to the punks about the show. I'd never seen him so into something. La Canaria sneaked her hand under his crooked arm and around his waist. He turned to us, beaming. "Could you see from over there?" he asked. "Why didn't you come closer?"

"Yeah, we could see," she said. Grito was waiting for La Canaria to say something more, but she didn't.

"It was just amazing," Grito said to Borgi, who was trying to wash the paint off with turpentine from an old shampoo bottle. The paint clung to his hair, molding it into strips of red clay.

"Thanks, *macho,*" Borgi said. "Glad you enjoyed it."

Paco stood talking to Zorra; their cheeks were flushed. They were in the center of a group of other punks. She stretched her leg out high and straight in front of her and laughed.

"Where's Marco?" Grito asked. "Where's that *pendejo?*"

"I don't know if he saw it," La Canaria said.

"What did you think, *gachí?*" Borgi asked me.

"Look," I said. "It's Marco." He was walking toward us, carrying a brown paper bag. The corners were shiny with grease.

"What's happening?" Marco stared at Borgi's red paint.

Borgi turned away from him and walked over to the others. "Here," Marco said, and handed us each a ham and cheese sandwich, still not looking at me.

"How cute," La Canaria said. "I like rich Marco."

"Shut the fuck up," Marco said quickly. He looked over at the punks.

"You're worried they're gonna hold you hostage for ransom money, *maricón*?" Grito said. His lips were lined in grease from the sandwich. A string of hot cheese hung out of his mouth.

"Why are they covered in paint?" Marco asked.

"They did this art thing," I said. "Some kind of protest."

"Glad I missed it."

Grito swallowed the rest of the sandwich and pulled La Canaria over to the group with him.

"You don't like them," I said to Marco.

"I don't have to. I just don't want them fucking with us."

We followed the punks toward a bar a few blocks away from the plaza. A woman sang on the street corner, one of the old flamenco songs my abuela used to listen to. Zorra danced down the street, circling the singer and spinning away. Her clothes were refined in comparison to the singer's, Zorra's clearly a costume. La Canaria reached out and stole the flower in the singer's hair, but the woman didn't pause. When the rose wouldn't stay behind her ear, she traced it over the graffiti that sprouted haphazardly between buildings, smearing the petals on brick and cement.

I almost passed it. But I noticed La Canaria's hand hesitate for a second and then leap over a patch of wall. There—half hidden by a poster for Princesa madeleines—was Alexis's tag. I pulled up the paper ad to make sure, but I knew the second

I saw the long hook of the *x*. I pressed my hand against the cement until it warmed. La Canaria tore my hand away.

"Don't be stupid," she said. She'd seen the tag same as me.

Grito was up ahead, talking to the punks. I could tell La Canaria was trying to figure out how to feel about them or, more, how to act. Grito seemed really into it and she didn't know if that threatened her or not. Maybe she also didn't know how much she cared.

"It doesn't mean anything," she said. I thought of her and Alexis fighting in the plaza and dancing alone in the parks at dawn. No matter how many times they broke up, they always got back together.

"Down here," Borgi called out, and disappeared below street level. La Canaria followed him and ran her fingers along the crumbling clay and glass mosaics that lined the descent into the bar. Pink-and-purple-tinted shards of mirror glittered back at us, reflecting sweaty corners of our skin. She'd dropped the shredded rose under Alexis's tag.

The bar was underground, full of cramped booths, the stuffing sticking out of the plastic seats. The whole place was lit with only a few red bulbs. It was hard to see what color anything really was. Like we were in one of those cheap horror movies that the censor boards love—the kind that always ends with the main girl dying, not because her vampire boyfriend sucked her dry but because she tried to abort their baby and now she's bleeding to death in an alley. The vampire boyfriend has converted and repented for his sins—the big one being that he'd fucked the dying *puta*.

We squeezed into a booth with the punks. They ordered pitchers of beer with the few coins they'd collected in the hat. Someone shook a salt cellar over the pitcher to settle the foam.

"Watch this," Grito said. He already had a glass of beer half filled with foam. He ran his index finger around his nose and across his forehead and then dipped it in the glass. The foam collapsed slowly under his finger. Everyone laughed. La Canaria laughed really loudly and high-pitched to show how stupid she thought it was. She reached for her own beer.

"I prefer salt to his dirty face," she whispered to me, but loudly enough that Grito could hear.

The punks continued talking. Grito's joke had been a quick interruption; they turned in toward one another.

"It's more dangerous now," Paco said.

"Yeah," Zorra cut in. "After the elections, there's a chance there'll be trials—the *fachas* will actually have to pay for what they did. And if that happens, they want to make sure anyone who could point a finger is already dead."

"But we have to know it's a good source first," Borgi said. "That we can trust them."

"And then what?" Paco said. "None of us even knows how to use one."

"I do," Borgi said. "My father was in the Civil Guard. He was always giving me these fucking lessons. Trying to make me into a man." He flicked his wrist and the punks laughed.

La Canaria, Grito, Marco, and I all listened closely. Grito smiled and nodded along with them; maybe he did know what they were talking about—he'd walked right next to them on the way to the bar. La Canaria had this grin on that she got right before everything started to fall apart in a way she liked.

"What are you discussing?" She leaned into the group, fake-absentmindedly piling her hair on top of her head, doing her best impression of a Soviet spy. What movie we were in kept shifting.

None of the punks answered her. They all stopped talking as if they had forgotten we were there and wouldn't have been talking about this if they'd remembered. But we were right next to them the whole time.

"It's nothing," Borgi said. "Just more art stuff."

"*Cabrón*," Grito said. "No, it isn't."

Marco leaned away from us and looked around the room slowly.

"You can trust us, *tío*," Grito said. "We know which side we're on."

"What about Señor Sandwich over there?" Borgi pointed his glass at Marco. Marco rubbed his eyes and covered his mouth with a half-formed fist, resting his head on it. He met Borgi's gaze but didn't speak.

"He's with us, *tío*," Grito said. "He's been protesting with us all spring."

"This isn't protests we're talking about," Borgi said. "This is serious. This is military defense." La Canaria raised her eyebrows and pursed her lips conspiratorially.

We'd heard the rumors about the old guard in the capital. That they hadn't surrendered their guns. That they weren't as interested as the king in a peaceful transition to democracy. But none of us knew how much to believe. The news in Casasrojas was completely controlled by the old *fachas*. Any event, we read filtered through that lens. When el Cabronísimo was alive, "tension" meant secret arrests. "Skirmish" meant executions, piles of medallions rimmed with dried blood in tiny plazas. But the code was always changing, and we were never quite sure that we'd cracked it accurately in the first place. After his death, there was even less clarity about what the words meant. All we knew was what we had known then, that they may keep information from us but that didn't mean they didn't know how to communicate. That didn't mean they couldn't find you wherever you were, whenever they wanted.

"We have a right to defend our party," Paco said. "We want this country moving forward, not backward."

"Yeah, of course," Grito said. "Us, too. We're in. All of us."

La Canaria looked at me and rolled her eyes. She didn't believe a word the punks said, but as long as it was an act, it was her kind of script.

We stumbled back to the factory and sat as close as we could to the open windows to catch the night air moving slowly over the buildings. Borgi and Paco seemed to be leading things, but they spoke in a sort of shorthand that was hard to decipher. There would be long pauses after one of them spoke. They, too, seemed unclear about what was happening. One of their friends who was a part of the Communist Party had received death threats. They didn't know what to do about it—who to ask for help. The old guard and the new police force were made up of the same people.

"We want to be armed for later, too," Paco said.

"Why?" Grito asked.

Zorra leaned into me. "They just want another war. In a war, they know where they stand."

"We're saying we need to be prepared," Paco said. "The pigs are prepared—"

"Who's 'they'?" I asked Zorra.

"The men, *mujer.* They're fucking terrified we'll start actually expecting all the change they've been talking about."

"That's off track," Paco said. "We need to think about what happens if the pigs try to rig the elections. We need a way to fight back. The people are on our side, we just need a way to fight."

"You're about to drop your balls over anything actually

changing," Zorra said. "Not being a fascist is easy—cleaning the shit stains out of your own underwear is a little harder."

"Not me," Borgi said. "Let the change come, please."

La Canaria nodded along with Paco and Borgi, but of course no one knew her well enough to know how much she was joking. If she was at all. At least no one who knew her was paying attention. Grito hadn't spoken to her all night—pissed at her for flirting with Borgi. The floor of the building was coated with fabric dust from when it had been a mill. Threads and tiny motes of different colors of cotton and wool packed tight between the floorboards. I kept picking at them, pulling out several centimeter-long stretches of compacted cloth, smashed by heat and age into something new, a composite of a thousand forgotten dresses. Marco had bought Zorra's pills and was stretched on the floor, sloping his arms up and over his body.

Sometimes when Alexis was little, he'd get these plans in his head, and my abuela and I would be so happy to go along with them. Once he convinced himself that he was a baby fox and couldn't leave his den until winter was over. My abuela and I spent all Sunday afternoon stretching out blankets and lining up chairs so that he could move from under his bed to the kitchen. We sat under the table to eat, my abuela moving her old knees uncomfortably every few minutes, watching carefully that no scraps fell on the floor. He was giddy to be down there with us, and though he refused to speak—because he was a fox—he kept nuzzling us with his snout and making this sweet growling sound. My abuela had probably never eaten on the floor in her life, or sat on it in decades, but she smiled at his tender growl and even ate a few bites with her hands. She liked things to be very clean, very clear. She was like the facade on the cathedral: thousands of tiny, perfect relief sculptures spread out so far you had to arch your back to see. But each in the exact right place, never moving. Each figure symbolized something directly, a perfect ratio of image to meaning. Alexis could make these relief sculptures shift, make where and when we ate change, make a flower mean something different, make everything mean many things at once. I liked Abuela best this way, all of her attention turned toward keeping Alexis smiling. Even when Alexis got older, she acted like that. Even when she wasn't trying to keep him smiling but just trying to make sure he didn't break through his own seams.

"It's gonna happen tomorrow," Borgi said. The sun was beginning to rise, but the few streetlights on the block were still on. They were the only light in the room. "Tomorrow we'll pick the stuff up." Everyone around him nodded, trying to look focused and determined through their different hazes. The punks kept talking, but I finally fell asleep, their indefinite words passing through my dreams.

I woke up to the sun hot on my face, already sweating, the air in the factory completely still. La Canaria was draped over Grito. Marco had curled up in a corner near the far window. None of the others were awake, though it was late in the day. I didn't want to speak to anyone. I just wanted coffee. I still had a few of La Canaria's coins. I stepped slowly over the stretched-out bodies to get to the door and into the street. The dogs were whining to be let out. I let them go and they disappeared into the alleys ahead of me. It was the first time I had been alone in a long time.

"*Joder,*" I said out loud. There was no one to hear me. The streets were quiet—it was a Sunday, I realized, and all the shops were closed.

It was strange to walk alone and not be flanked by Grito or La Canaria or Marco. I kept thinking one of them would appear and make some comment about how stupid I was, walking through a city I didn't know, looking for a café on a Sunday. I didn't trust my movements without one of them around to contain me. Without La Canaria or Grito or even Marco there to keep me closed in on myself, my arms might just detach and float away.

White canopies stretched across the rooftops to keep the streets shaded. Only the intersections were unprotected from the sun, but there were no cars, so I didn't have to wait at any of them. The air felt cool because it was early, but that was a warning of how hot it was going to get. The cement and stones releasing their last calm breath before absorbing the sun. I passed the red outline of a body splayed awkwardly on the sidewalk. Zorra had said that it was for a student killed when the riot police's tear-gas canister exploded in his face. The outline was painted over every day, but someone sneaked back at night and repainted it. I finally found a tiny Moroccan place that was open. I'd heard about places like this appearing now that the borders were open. Immigrants started up shops again, right where their ancestors had lived centuries before, neon lights flickering under ornate columns with Arabic script.

The shop sold newspapers, pinkie-sized sweet rolls stuffed with pistachio and honey, and coffee with cardamom. It was smaller than my abuela's kitchen, with room for only one person and no place to sit. The coffee was thick with oils, and grit floated near the bottom. The woman behind the counter had on a pale lilac veil. She didn't look up from her magazine, just accepted my coins in her outstretched palm and deposited them underneath the counter. I wanted to stay by her because even though she wouldn't look at me, sometimes she would look out the window through a section that wasn't covered by posters of football players and ice cream ads. She glanced up as if the window looked out over something unimaginable.

I finished my coffee at the counter and tried to read my future in the dregs. It would be nice to know. I wanted to ask her to do this, but she would probably be offended. She already seemed offended. Every part of her body except her face and her hands was covered. It made me feel naked in a way that the shrouded grandmothers never did. My abuela would never speak of the war or before she met my abuelo, but I knew what they did to Republican women when the war ended. There were no photos, just stories passed between women. They stripped them in the squares and made them drink castor oil until shit streamed down their bare thighs, this after the beatings, this after the rapes. A reminder of what those in charge are capable of. Keep your skirt long and your eyes on the ground. There are bad men at night. Keep on the right side; their means of breaking you are very specific.

I spent my last coins on a couple of the pistachio sweets and watched the white paper wrapping glaze with honey in the woman's hands. She looked out the window again and I followed her gaze, almost wishing I hadn't, because I saw someone who looked too familiar to be possible.

I rushed out the door and into the street. I caught a shadow turning down an alleyway. I ran up and down the whole length of it but saw no one. I kept hearing footsteps. I smelled rust and wet weeds. But the street was empty. Around me only cats and stray shadows. I pulled out Alexis's medallion from under my shirt. I kept walking, my heart thudding rapidly.

* * *

At the factory, people had started to stir. No one was fully awake yet. One of the dogs was back on the steps, but he didn't want to come in. It was cooler on the shaded stone, and I figured the other dogs had found a better place than the factory to spend the day. La Canaria had her arm stretched over her eyes, and the paler underside of it caught the light. The windows lit the room in elongated rectangles. The only people who had moved were the ones unlucky enough to be caught in that orange space. The dust from the old cloth clogged in the light. Fine powder we shouldn't breathe.

It took half the day for everyone to wake up. I didn't know why I couldn't just go back to sleep. I didn't like sitting and waiting in a hot place for anyone. It opened up too many rooms, a hundred books spread out in front of me, and I had to learn them all but each letter was melting, dripping colors. The cities in my throat.

Paco got up to piss and then smoke on the landing. I came out into the light and asked for a cigarette. He didn't seem surprised that I was there. I wanted to ask him what they were planning, let that lead to the real question I had, but I didn't know how to shape the words so that I didn't sound ignorant. I also didn't want to give him too much attention.

No one mentioned the plans all day. Grito was itching, too, I could tell from the way he kept looking at Paco and Borgi, opening his mouth, and then shutting it without speaking. Borgi passed a joint. Something was supposed to happen that day. They'd said so the night before. The orange rectangles of light got smaller and smaller until they disappeared and the sun was overhead, lighting the place through the dirty glass of the skylight. It got so hot that just sitting made us sweat. Paco got up again and disappeared behind his curtain. I could hear him moving in there, the wet sound of a brush dipping in and out of paint.

La Canaria spread out the clothes from the Americans' suit-case and we swapped with the punk girls for what we wanted, a striped T-shirt and a pair of black jeans for me, two jean jackets, a woven backpack from Guatemala. La Canaria kept most of the Americans' stuff because it was nice but got some money for the suitcase. As the day passed, it seemed both more and less likely that anything would happen. Each time I would stop thinking and remember I was waiting, I would be relieved that it hadn't happened yet and therefore probably wouldn't. Then I would also be scared, because it just meant that if it was going to happen it would probably happen soon and I hadn't figured out what to do about it yet. Besides my abuelo's old hunting rifles, I'd been close to a handgun only once before. I'd been studying in the bar under the philology library and had come up to my abuela's apartment for siesta. The door was unlocked. All the lights were out, but it was still early in the afternoon. I sat down at the kitchen table; the television buzzed from just being turned off. On the table where Abuela kept her magazines was a gun.

"*Joder*, you scared the shit out of me," Alexis said. He'd just walked into the room and hadn't known I was there.

"What is that?" I said. Of course I knew what it was, but I didn't know what it was doing there.

He picked up the gun and pointed it at the television. He pulled the trigger. I flinched. It was empty. "I'm just keeping it for someone," he said, looking at me and smiling. "Don't worry, it's not loaded."

He sat down next to me, which he hadn't done in a while. As a kid, he was never on the same eating schedule as me and Abuela, squirming at dinner, gorging on biscuits and candies before bed. Years later, his stomach always hurt, and it kept him up at night. He was thin unless he was in a drinking period. Then the extra weight coiled heavily around his neck. I'd notice it suddenly, as if I hadn't seen him in months. But he'd wake up and start running in the mornings, do push-ups in front of Abuela's telenovelas, and he'd be thin again. Neither ever lasted.

"Turn on the television," he said, teasing me. "I want to watch the game." He knew I hated when he bossed me around.

"You never watch anything," I said. "You don't even know who's playing."

"Just turn it on." He was playing with the gun, scooting it around the Formica table, moving it between the neat piles of magazines and porcelain figures and the baby Jesus like he was trying to get it out of a maze.

"Why are you keeping a gun for someone?" I asked.

"A friend asked me to." He was trying to maneuver the gun through two porcelain angels. His black hair was buzzed short, a style Abuela didn't like. She said it made him look like one of the prisoners from the war. Alexis said at least that way it was more honest.

"Why would you do that?" I said. "I wouldn't do that." I didn't look at Alexis when I said this, just pointed at the gun. But I tried to keep my voice even, tried to use as few words as possible.

He never asked me for anything, not since almost a year before, when he'd broken his arm jumping over the fence by the train tracks. The bone had cut through strips of skin. The doctors shot him with morphine before he left the hospital, but he wanted me to go get him brandy and I wouldn't. I was studying and didn't want to leave the house. I was worried, too, that the two drugs together would be dangerous. He laughed at me, said he could handle it, had handled worse, but I wouldn't leave. I was trying to protect him, but he stopped laughing and got so angry that I wouldn't do this one thing. How amazed I'd been at the weight of his hand on my cheek. I couldn't stop the tears that came to my eyes, couldn't keep them from thickening my tongue. Not pain but surprise that the casing around my body had been broken and how easily. I remembered that moment then, and I knew he did, too.

"I have the same reason to care," I said when he stayed quiet. "About what you're doing. Who you're fighting."

"What do you know about what I'm doing?"

"Nothing," I said. It was true, really.

"Good."

When he was young, our abuela would cut his hair short in the back, letting the top grow long and curly like a Botticelli cherub's. In the days after she cut his hair, I used to love running my hand along the back of his head. Even though his hair was just as short in the back now, I never would have dreamed of reaching my hand to his head.

"But you're right," he said. "And if I asked, you'd help me." He smiled like it was a joke.

I nodded. I hoped I would.

He stopped playing with the gun, thrummed his fingers on his knees. "Do you think you'll stay here, Mosca?" The television buzzed in and out. He got up to try to fix the antenna.

"What do you mean?"

"In this *comemierda* country? Or will you leave?"

"I don't know," I said. "I guess it depends on how well I do on my exams."

Alexis laughed. He'd dropped out of university and teased me for studying all the time. When he was really young and we first came to live with Abuela, he was always in my room. He'd even get dressed there, sprint naked through the apartment to grab something he forgot, and run back to my room even if I wasn't there. Or the door would be locked and he'd be inside under the bed, playing with his toy soldiers. Even though he had a room of his own, he slept in either my or Abuela's bed, sometimes leaving mine in the middle of the night to move to hers. I never knew what made him switch, what woke him and made him sure he wasn't safe where he was. It drove me crazy, but it stopped right when it should have. I don't know if Abuela told him or he heard it at school in that silent language just being learned. All of a sudden he couldn't even look at me in a swimsuit.

"I wouldn't stay here," he said.

"I guess I'd want to go to France," I said. "To Paris."

"Paris, yeah," he said. "Me, too. We can meet up at that Sacré-Coeur—where you intellectuals love to go."

"When?" I said, playing along.

He shrugged. "When we haven't seen each other in a while." He smiled that curly smile that made even me blush. No matter what he was saying, he could get anyone to smile when he wanted to. He sat down again and started pushing the gun around.

"Paris," he said. "That's where I'd go. That's where I'll see you."

The gun squeaked against the tabletop.

"I don't like it," I said. "What if you get caught?"

"They can't touch me, they have nothing on me."

"They don't *need* anything."

"He's about to fall, Mosca. We're winning. We're taking him down."

I didn't want to say that even if he was right, and I knew he wasn't, a cornered animal is the most dangerous kind.

"I wish you wouldn't."

He brought the gun to his temple. I froze. He pulled the trigger.

"It's empty," he said again, smiling. But he meant it as a warning.

It was dark and we'd been inside all day by the time Grito opened his mouth and finally decided to speak.

"Isn't it going to happen today?" he said. He didn't look at anyone when he said it. Borgi and Paco were both nearby but didn't turn toward him. "You know, with the transfer."

Borgi got up and went to the room with the hot plate in it. He came back with a bottle of wine. Grito didn't like it when people ignored him. He was getting angry. "Well?" he asked again.

"Oh yeah, *macho*," Borgi said. He took a swig of wine and passed it to me, then lay down on the floor. "Probably not today, soon though. Pass it on, Mosca."

Grito nodded and went to get more wine. La Canaria crawled toward me on all fours, away from Zorra and another girl gossiping about the latest Kaka de Luxe show they'd seen and what had happened backstage, flicking their syringes and holding down the other's veins. Zorra took a close-up photo of the other girl shooting up.

"Now you can tell they're good anarchists," La Canaria said loudly, slurring her words and jerking her head back toward the girls. "They fuck everything that moves. Good little anarchists." She bounced her head to the words and tickled Borgi's chest with her ponytail.

Grito came back into the room. "What are you doing?" he said.

She ignored him. "Only fascists don't put out," she said.

Borgi snorted with laughter, but kept his arms stretched out on the floor. Grito pushed La Canaria but that only made her lean closer into Borgi. "*María la O . . . ¡todo se acabó!*"

Once everyone forgot that we hadn't done anything all day, the punks started to talk about their plan again, to collect arms, it seemed, but they spoke in vague terms and never added new information or details. Perhaps Paco and Borgi didn't trust us yet. Perhaps they themselves were wading in the dark. Grito got really excited and La Canaria acted like she cared.

"Tomorrow, tomorrow," Borgi kept saying.

Everything that was going to happen was always going to happen tomorrow.

I sat in a dark corner, trying to stay cool. Marco walked over to me and sat down. I didn't move, waiting. He leaned in and kissed my shoulder, like a question.

I pushed him away. "You don't get to touch me," I said.

He stayed sitting, looking out at the rest of the room. "But some asshole you never met, that's fine?"

"I don't give a shit about him," I said.

"Do you give a shit about me?"

"I don't owe you anything, Marco."

He stood up, surprised. "That's not what I think," he said.

"Then what do you think? Huh?"

"I think—" He paused, tilted his head back to the ceiling. He was more than a little drunk. "I think—I hated him as soon as I found out who he was. I wanted to kill him."

"How could you not tell us?"

"I didn't want you to hate me. I didn't want Alexis—"

"Shut up," I said. We didn't talk about this and he knew it. We didn't talk about who knew what and the consequences of that knowledge. We didn't speak his name. Not to each other.

He stepped back, arms out. "Please, Mosca. I'm sorry."

I pushed against the wall to stand up and walked away from him, into the dark.

Before el Cabronísimo died, before the police handed my abuela Alexis's medallion, I was at an illegal party in a warehouse on the edge of Casasrojas. We were all stuffed in the basement, haggling for beer and thrashing around to these guys doing a horrible job covering Led Zeppelin. Their own songs were even worse, but it mattered only that they were loud. The place was so full of people that even if you weren't too far gone, you could pretend you didn't know what was happening. Nothing really was happening.

I'd come out with Grito but didn't know where he was. He always left me in a crowd, reaching out to strands of people he didn't know, more interested in a face that wouldn't last the night. I didn't care—when I was near someone who knew me, it was harder to pretend I wasn't anywhere, harder to just feel the slick skin of the crowd pressed against mine and close my eyes and scream and have that scream disappear into unknown bodies. The only lights were on the band, and that helped, too. Someone handed me a hash cigarette and I sucked it in and passed it on. It was stupid—these places were always getting shut down, but there were too many of us there that night. We couldn't be stopped.

Someone pushed into me and I pushed back just as hard. A face leaped into mine: it was Alexis. He stuck out his tongue. He was making fun of the band and me and everyone there, but he was doing it, too. I laughed and kept dancing, really just moving my arms and legs fast and yelling. I didn't want to hang out with him, and he didn't want to stay by me, but we were each glad the other was there.

Some *tió* shoved me again and I was about to push back, but he grabbed my chin with one hand and threw me back into the crowd. Marco shuddered up behind him. He hadn't seen the guy hit me, he was angry at him about something else.

"Get the fuck out of here," Marco shouted. The guy was way taller than Marco, with milky *facha* skin that came from never having to do much. It looked even paler in the light from the stage. His hair was short and parted neatly on one side. He even wore a polyester shirt, brown with a big pointy collar.

The *facha* stepped up to Marco, smiling. "Listen, I don't want to fight you—we're on the same side."

"The fuck we are." Marco raised his arm to punch him, but just then one of Alexis's friends appeared out of the crowd and put his hand on Marco's shoulder. He whispered into Marco's ear, and Marco's face collapsed as if someone had cut his puppet strings. The *facha* turned away from both of them and moved through the crowd. He didn't belong there. He knew it and didn't care. Pigs never do. They think they own everything around them, and they might.

Across the crowd, leaning close to the speakers, Alexis and La Canaria were dancing next to each other. It took me a moment to realize why they looked strange; they were the only people in the crowd really dancing. Their bodies pressed against each other like old-fashioned flamenco dancers, hips slung low and legs wired to the backs of the other's kneecaps. They'd found a slow beat beneath the noise, so close to the speakers that a whole separate terrain rolled out before them and they were alone beneath a starry sky, lit by a desert bonfire. Seeing them, I hoped they'd get back together. Making sure La Canaria didn't spin out kept Alexis in this orbit. I'd take that even with the beer bottles they'd fling at each other across the plaza, the people they'd fuck to make sure the other was watching. But somewhere in the middle of a keyless dirge, La Canaria pulled away from Alexis, stuck her finger in his face. He curled over her in mock supplication—only I knew how real it was—making baby faces, cooing at her until she shoved him and melted back into the bodies flailing to the ruin of sound. It took her only another song to find someone else.

I found Grito and told him I was leaving. He said he'd meet me when he finished his beer. I stood outside waiting, smoking a cigarette. The street was silent and dark. In the distance cars sped over the highway. The silver guardrail across the street was the last visible thing before the ground dropped off into darkness. It was a good spot. The sound of the music throbbed faintly, like that heart buried under a mattress. No one could hear the party going on under the stone, and in this part of town, no one would care if they did. I stayed in the shadow of the warehouse. I couldn't see much, and I hoped no one could see me.

The door to the basement opened slowly, but it wasn't Grito, it was Marco. He didn't see me. The *facha* from inside followed him out and put an arm around Marco's shoulders, pretending to be friendly, but the gesture was closer to a head-lock.

"Why are you pretending you don't know me?" the *facha* said. "You've known my family for years. You think you're too good for me?"

"Get the fuck off me, *maricón*," Marco said. He reached behind the *facha* but was too slow. The guy grabbed his gun from the back of his fancy wool-blend pants and hit Marco across the face with it. Marco fell back and slid over the cobblestones. The *facha* kicked him in the gut.

"You don't remember me?" the *facha* said. He knew how to hold the gun, though his pose had a self-conscious quality. Maybe he'd only practiced playing the gangster in front of the mirror. Not that it mattered to me. I tried not to breathe. I didn't want anything to move, scared that someone would open the door and make the *facha* jump, scared that he would see me only a few meters away.

Marco leaned forward and started to rise. The *facha* was crisp and clean—he looked so different from us. But he was our age, from Casasrojas, just a completely different version of it, a different version of what he wanted it to be. The *facha* kicked Marco again. Suddenly, Alexis stepped out of the darkness on the other side of the door. He punched the *facha*'s hand holding the gun, and his fingers splayed apart.

I didn't see it happening even as it happened, I had to remember it to see it for the first time. Alexis bent his knees and bucked himself sideways against the *facha*, who skidded in the air and landed at my feet. The gun was over by Marco, still on his knees, watching Alexis, fixed not by pain but awe. Alexis picked up the *facha* by his greased-back hair and dragged him over to the guardrail. He smashed his face against a post and smashed it again. Blood and spit arched away from him, shone in the light from a streetlamp half a block away. Alexis made to slam him again into the metal. Instead he let him drop to the cobblestones. He picked up the gun and shoved it into the *facha*'s face.

"One more for our arsenal, little piggy," Alexis said. He walked over to Marco and gave him a hand, pulling him to his feet.

"I don't know what he was talking about," Marco said. "He was crazy or something—thought I was someone else."

"Don't worry about it, *che*," Alexis said. "I trust you."

Marco grinned as if someone hadn't just smeared his face on the cobblestones. I knew Alexis had seen me—he must have been waiting outside for the pig to come out. He'd just stood there while I stood there. I understood it. He could be by me without having to say anything, without having that silence mean whatever he was afraid it might.

"You keep it," Alexis said, handing the gun to Marco. "It's your hit."

They walked away, shoulders tipped back toward the flickering streetlamps. I waited for Grito, the only sounds the buried music and the thin rasps of the *facha* on the ground.

Zorra cornered me in the hallway. Asked for a light and then grabbed my wrist.

"You have beautiful bones," she said, and held my arm above my head so it cast a shadow over her face. "Like a dancer's. Why did you leave Casasrojas, anyway?"

It was dark and I could see only the harshest outlines of her features. She smelled of geranium oil and gasoline. "To join the protests here," I said. "What do you care?"

She placed my hand on her hip like we were dancing. "I'm saying if you're trying to find a place to lay low, maybe this isn't the spot."

"What do you mean?" I said. I didn't move toward her or away.

"There's been this guy—a *facha* trying to pretend he's not— hanging around outside. He's looking for some students from Casasrojas."

The instant she spoke, I could see this man, gave him the same face as the man by the river, layered over the shifting features of the police who had brought Alexis's medallion.

"He says they attacked a policeman. Maybe it's not you, but I don't think specifics matter that much to them."

"What did you say to him?" I said.

"Nothing," she said. "I didn't say anything. But why stick around and push it? We have our own shit."

"I think you're exempt from anything that happens here," I said. I removed her hand from my waist. "Don't worry, we won't stay long."

I knew I should tell Grito or La Canaria what Zorra had said, but I didn't want to leave yet. I was waiting. Not for Paco and Borgi's plan but for an unsettling to occur in me. The punks seemed like Alexis's crowd, the kind of crowd we wanted to be, but I wanted to be sure. Maybe they had some information, something that would answer a bit of what had been left so raw it had to be ignored.

I hadn't spoken Alexis's name since he'd disappeared. I'd say *my brother*, or with my abuela, simply *him*, because there was no question where all our words and thoughts were focused. His name put too fine a point on things, an arrow at the mangled bits of me. I wanted to make sure I had a reason to say it.

I found Borgi leaning up against a window, drifting deep into a cloud of his own mixture, and I thought then was the moment to ask, when he couldn't tell the difference between me and his dreams.

"I think you may know someone we know," I whispered.

"We know a lot of people."

"He came down here a lot," I said.

"Doing what?"

I hesitated—again I wished for the right words but remembered they were the enemy, too. "What you're doing."

"What we're doing."

I tried to describe Alexis to Borgi. Not too tall, thin, black trench coat. I tried to use words that didn't sound tender, that didn't compare him to birds or animals lost in the dark. "He had dark eyebrows, a shaved head, a mole beneath his right eye." It had been a detail he hated. He thought it was womanly, which was why the girls loved it.

"Lexi?" Borgi said.

"Alexis," I said without meaning to. The letters sank down to the floor. They were heavy and I wanted to hide them, but they swirled around my feet, tenebrous and dense.

"Yeah, Lexi. I liked him. I haven't seen him in a while. He was going to Paris the last time I saw him."

"When? When did you see him?"

"Not that long ago. Why? He jilt you?"

"He said Paris? How long ago?"

Borgi sat straight up, alert to something beyond the factory walls, but if it was there, it was hovering three stories in the air. He turned to me, eyes wide and focused, though not on anyone in the room. "Not long at all," he said, and leaned back against the window.

"And it was Paris? You're sure?"

"Yeah, he was going there. He was in trouble, so he was going to Paris."

"How long?" I said, my voice weak. "How long ago?"

But I couldn't get him to say anything coherent after that.

From across the factory, I could just hear Zorra talking about the music scene in London and New York. Those were too distant for me to imagine. They were past the edge of space. The other cities in the back of my throat—Granada, San Sebastián,

Barcelona—faded and dissipated. They didn't matter anymore. They were replaced by one, swelling to burst. Paris, where Alexis had told me he'd go. Paris, where he'd told Borgi—*not too long ago*—he was heading. He might be there, and if he was, I might find him. Paris, Paris, eclipsing all other maps.

Seven

"I said, don't touch my girl." Grito shoved Borgi. It was afternoon the next day. Grito was much smaller than Borgi, but he was drunk and high and, like a Chihuahua, didn't seem to notice his size.

"I didn't touch your girl." Borgi stood up straight, smiling, his shoulders relaxed.

"Why are you so hung up on ownership?" Paco said from the corner. "Even Señor Sandwich over here has let go of that." Marco rolled closer to the window, pretending he hadn't heard. "Monogamy is for fascists."

"Yeah, share and share alike, sexy," Borgi said, and tousled Grito's hair.

"That works great for you all," Zorra said, walking into the room with a bottle of wine and her camera. "What about us?"

"It works great for you, too, if you relax a little," Paco said.

"*Cabrón*, shut up." Grito moved toward Paco.

"Let's get out of here." La Canaria pulled me up off the floor. "This is boring."

We left the factory and walked west toward the outskirts, passing a market selling fruit, olives, and sandals.

"Don't even bother," the vendor said when he saw La Canaria finger a pair of espadrilles with blue ribbon.

"It's not really my style," she sneered at him. Our feet were filthy, the delicate suede sandals stolen from Marco's mom disintegrating after too many nights in the rain and mud.

We walked past bags of garbage lining the street. An old boardinghouse was getting cleared out. Women picked through the bags, avoiding the worst-smelling ones.

"He's not even interested," La Canaria said.

"Who?"

"Borgi."

"Not everyone likes you," I said.

"No, I mean he's not interested in girls."

I stopped walking.

"You are such a prude, Mosca. I wish the guys would all just fuck each other. Leave us alone." I realized she was sober—the first I'd seen her in a while. "We don't want it as much as they do."

I nodded, though sometimes I felt like I wanted it enough to kill. What I'd done with Paco or on the mountain wasn't it. Sometimes I felt like I'd chop off my hand if I could kiss someone the way I wanted to. But that was when I felt anything at all.

It started raining, so we stopped outside an old building with a sign on the door that said MUSEUM. FREE TUESDAYS.

"It's Tuesday, right?" La Canaria said.

"I think so."

"Let's go in, then."

It wasn't that big, just a single story of an old house. We thought we'd see some art, but the whole place was only toys—antiques from a hundred years ago or collected by anthropologists in Latin America. The old man behind the desk smiled when we walked in, and I gave La Canaria a look that I would kill her if she made fun of the place. She gave me a look like she didn't understand why I was looking at her. Instead she flirted with the old man, which was probably the nicest thing I'd ever seen her do. While she talked to him, I wandered around. The place was empty of other people, the rain streaking the windows. There were hardly even signs by the toys; a few had a stock paper card that said the year they were made or where they were from. There were pre-Columbian figures, miniature tin cars from Germany with chickens and rabbits in them, and weird life-size porcelain dolls with hair that looked real. Some of the toys had been made by hand, each probably the only one a kid had. In the center of one of the rooms was a tower, and hanging from it were marionettes of all the characters in Carnival. They were old and had the same costumes that I'd seen in books from before the war. The harlequins and witches were dressed in faded oranges and greens. In the center hung a skeleton, the death figure, its bony grin stretched wide. They moved slowly, lit from above by a small window near the top of the tower.

La Canaria made a strange sound. She'd stopped talking to the man and was on the other side of the room from me. I walked to where she was bent over, looking at something in a case on the wall.

"Look," she said, pointing, her finger bent against the glass.

"At what?" The case looked the same as the others. Packed full of different dolls, hand games, tiny planes.

"It looks just like mine," she said.

I bent down to her level and followed her finger to a tiny doll between two British bears. It had brown skin, a white headdress, tiny hoop earrings, and an old-fashioned dress of bright patterns. The placard said it was from Cuba, mid-century.

"It's just like her, like my dolly," she whispered. Our breath fogged the glass. I didn't know what to say. "But she couldn't really be here."

"No," I said.

"My sisters all had ones like it, too," she said.

"Your sisters?" I said. She'd never spoken about her life before Casasrojas.

"Their dolls all matched them, except mine. I was the only one with light skin. They buried them with their dolls." La Canaria pulled away from the glass. She traced the doll's outline with her thumb. "You know I really miss him, don't you?" I knew she was talking about Alexis. "I'd still do anything I could to get him back." She wiped our breath off the display case with her hand. "And I'd hurt anyone who hurt him."

She turned from me and walked out of the museum. The old man stepped out from behind his desk. I twirled my finger around my temple to say that she was crazy, but I didn't mean it.

I remembered one morning in Casasrojas, I was walking back from the bakery and saw La Canaria sprawled out on a park bench. I didn't really believe it was her until I got right up to the bench. It was one of the first warm days of spring and right before Alexis disappeared. The sun had reddened her face so that it looked swollen, about to burst like a pimple with too much pressure on it. She woke up when I stood over her, blocking the light.

"Have you been here all night?" I said.

"No, just a couple of hours. I was with Alexis—"

"You're back together?"

"For about two seconds we were, but he was being so stupid, I ditched him and went to El Llano." She sat up and crossed her legs underneath her. El Llano was what we called a corner on the edge of a run-down park frequented by drug dealers. I'd never been there alone. It was a meat market—you went there only if you wanted to fuck somebody and didn't care who.

She ripped off the heel of my bread and stuck it in her mouth, chewing slowly, shaping the crumb into a ball with her tongue. Then she turned around on the bench and puked up the bite of bread and a lot of red wine. Some of the vomit hit my sleeve. She didn't apologize. That's what women in Casasrojas did. They apologized and they bent their heads and prayed and then they smacked the next small body they could catch and pin down long enough. La Canaria just smacked, no bending, no praying, then licked our upturned faces with her scratchy tongue. I waited beside her until she stopped puking and then she got up and left. She acted the same as always, but she looked back at me before she left the park.

"How is he?" she said.

"Alexis?"

"Yeah. He seemed worried."

"He's fine," I said. "You know him."

But she just shook her head. Her face was impossible to read.

I caught up with her on the street outside the museum. "Your sisters?" I said. "What happened?"

"I don't want to talk about it." She stopped in front of a candy stand and pointed to a purple Chupa Chups. "Buy me one, will you?"

We headed back toward the factory and passed the same woman we'd heard the first night, singing "Chant du Levant." She looked older in the daylight. Her body was as small as a child's, skin yellow and puckered, with dark circles underneath her eyes.

"Why do you let us call you La Canaria?"

"Because I don't care. Why would I care whether a fake name fits?" Her mouth was bright purple from the candy. "Do you think Grito will stay with them?" she said. He hadn't been clinging to her in Madrid, not ignoring her, exactly, just acting like Casasrojas didn't exist or that we were the visitors, not him.

"I don't know," I said.

When we got back to the factory, everyone was outside. Smoke billowed out of the top-floor windows. Grito, Borgi, Paco, and Zorra stood in a close circle, whispering. The boardinghouse tenants were dragging everything they could down the narrow staircases and throwing clothes out their windows. Handkerchiefs and slips caught in the air, mixing with scraps of burning paper drifting slowly down.

"Hey, you *pendejos*," Paco shouted at us. He broke away from the group and ran at me but stopped too close and backed up. I could feel the pulse of him running at me, trying to still and unable to. "There's someone looking for you."

"Who?" I said. "What do you mean?"

"Some old guy, clean-cut, smiling all over, he looks like an undercover policeman."

"I don't know anyone here," I said.

"Borgi said you were asking about Lexi," Paco said. "Whose side are you on?"

I moved away from both him and La Canaria.

"Do you see what's happening?" Grito said when we came over to him. It was the first time he'd spoken to me directly in days. "The fire—it's sabotage." He was looking in every direction at once, his face red and eyes strained.

"What do you mean, it's sabotage?" La Canaria said to him.

"The old guard, the *fachas*—they started this! It's arson!"

Grito said, practically screaming. Two men were trying to push a bureau through the front door onto the street. An old woman shouted behind them to hurry.

"Hey, you *maricones,* help us with this!" one of the men holding the bureau shouted.

Grito waved his hand to ignore them. "There's no way that's coming through the door," he said. "Everyone's gonna burn up if you don't move it."

"I don't know," La Canaria said. "That place looked like it wanted to start on fire."

"It's you that started it!" one of the men yelled from behind the bureau.

"It's you that ratted us out to your *facha* friends!" Grito shouted.

"Ask your girlfriend who the *facha* is!" Paco shouted.

"She's not my girlfriend!"

Marco had been standing apart from us, his red backpack slung over his shoulder, talking to a group of tenants and passersby. He walked quickly over to the doorway. He tried to pull at the bureau, but one of the drawers was caught in the doorway. He pinched his fingers in it.

"*¡Joder!*" he shouted, and pulled his hand away from the door, shaking it in pain. "It's not moving. You'll have to push it back if you want to get out."

The windows on the first floor were barred with iron lattices. The people inside either had to get out the front door or jump out the second-floor windows. Grito looked warily up at the windows. The show suddenly wasn't as much fun as it had been a moment before.

"Help us push it back, then, *cabrón!*" another man behind the bureau shouted.

Marco pushed at the dark wood, his hands balled up in the

center of his chest to keep them from getting pinched. He looked like a rag doll someone had pulled the arms off of and thrown against a wall. The bureau creaked and sighed but didn't move.

"How did you even get it in there?" Marco shouted, now pressing with his hands and nudging the legs with his feet.

"It was my great-grandmother's," an old woman behind them shouted. "She had it assembled in her boudoir."

Marco couldn't help laughing. He hadn't asked anyone else to help him, and no one was offering. I knew the thing wasn't going to move no matter how many of us helped. "Hand her out to me," he shouted. "Then climb over."

The old woman's black orthopedic shoes appeared first, the sun glinting off her leg braces.

"This is shameful!" she shouted. The men lifted her higher and pushed her over the bureau. "Ugly, lazy, absolutely shameful!" she paused to yell, perched on top of the bureau, crouched between its ornate posts and the low entryway ceiling. Marco jostled the bureau and she cried out, crossing herself repeatedly. "It's me and the bureau or neither me nor the bureau!"

The men behind her tilted the bureau up. The old woman began to slide off. "Shameful!" she shouted, falling. Marco was looking down the street at a fast-approaching fire truck. He reached out to try to catch the old woman but missed, and she slapped his arm for seeing her slip and garter belt. The men climbed over after her.

"What a hero!" Grito shouted behind him.

Marco turned away from him. The punks stared at the fire truck down the street. It had to stop at the corner because the road was too narrow for it to pass through. Firemen were jumping out of the truck and trying to hook up their hose to the water main. They were mostly volunteers in this part of the city, but the police would follow them.

Borgi held a big canvas army bag and kept looking at it, then at the firemen. I walked up to them. The bag was full of guns, the long ones the old guard used to carry when they stood on every street corner, slung nonchalantly across their backs like an extra limb. I felt fingers wrap across my arm, but I didn't really understand that it was my arm or that a living limb could bend. Marco pulled me close to him.

"Paco said a policeman was looking for us—" I started.

"I know. I saw him. We have to get out of here now," Marco whispered.

"Did he see you?" I whispered. "The policeman?"

"No, I was on the roof."

I nodded twice, my chin jutting against his sternum, feeling something gurgling within me and the light outside fading. Soon I would be a body, running or not.

"They have another place where we can stay," Grito said.

"Come on, follow us," Borgi hissed. He was just as nervous about the crowd from the boardinghouse eyeing us all, listening to the old woman shouting and waving her arms.

"We're not going anywhere with you," Marco said.

"What do you mean, *tío*?" Grito asked. "You chickening out?"

"We're leaving," Marco said. He hadn't let go of my arm. I didn't know where La Canaria was.

"I'm not going anywhere," Grito said. "Doesn't this mean anything to you?" He pushed himself close to Marco. I was pressed between them both, Marco's fingers tight around my arm. I couldn't remember how to move, that I could shake him off or try to, that I had in the past. I didn't feel arms were made for that.

"We have to get out of here," Marco said. "The police are looking for you. They're looking for Mosca."

"And whose fault is that?"

Marco was silent.

Grito leaned in close to him. "What are *you* afraid of? No one's going to arrest the Butcher's son."

"These people are *idiotas*," Marco hissed. "They're not going to do anything. The only thing that will happen is that they will get themselves killed."

"That's what I thought," Grito said, stepping back and holding his arms out wide.

"Where's La Canaria?" Marco asked.

I couldn't speak, and my eyes hadn't left Borgi's bag.

"What do I care?" Grito said. Marco started walking away, pulling me with him. Grito stood still, staring at us. "You're nothing but a pig at heart."

I could feel Marco tense, but he didn't turn around. In front of me, La Canaria stepped out of a shadow made by laundry hanging out to dry. She started moving in the direction Marco was heading, not looking back at the firemen or the burning building or Grito. Marco pulled me around. I couldn't see Grito anymore. But I knew the second he slipped from my view that he was going to follow us. It was easier to. He probably looked back—saw the neighbors shouting, the punks twitching with the weight of their new weapons, Paco pointing at us. Grito would drop the punks and whatever they were going to do and come with us. Because it was easiest. But he'd drop us, too, if that became easier.

Eight

Outside the train station Marco squeaked his finger across the greasy glass that covered the map. Along the border were the strips of wasteland that had held thousands of war refugees. The map like a gravestone, some clean way to show the dead.

"I think we should go to Paris," I said. I looked down when I said it. I hadn't meant to let the sounds out.

"Why?" Grito said.

"I want to see the museums."

La Canaria rolled her eyes.

To say why I wanted to go would make it sound like what it was: desperate. All the other cities had disappeared—there was only one left. Borgi's word wasn't much, but it was more than I'd had before, and it was all I had. I couldn't look at Marco because I was scared that as soon as I did, he would know why I wanted to go to Paris. But maybe he wanted to go there, too. We would go for the same reasons and help each other; we didn't need to say why.

"I think we should head south to Cádiz," Marco said. "We can hide out there."

"You and Cádiz," Grito said.

"No way," La Canaria said. "They found us in Madrid. I want out of this *facha* country."

"We're not voting," Marco said.

Grito moved his finger across the map, undoing our steps, pulling our clothes from the bonfire, tracing rings around Casasrojas.

"I'm going to Paris," I said. Marco hadn't seen Alexis's tag and he hadn't talked to Borgi. "I'm going whether you come or not."

Marco's face was still, his gaze fixed beyond us. He nodded, deciding something, though it took me a long time to figure out just what it was. "I'm staying with Mosca."

"I don't need your protection," I said. He said nothing to that, but his eyes were the firmest I'd ever seen them. There was no pleasure in his words, only certainty.

"I know a place in Paris we could stay," La Canaria said before Marco could answer me. "In France, once you're in a spot that no one else is in, they can't kick you out." I didn't care about the details of what she was saying, so long as it would get us where I wanted to go. And I was glad to have the attention pointed away from me. "This guy has a huge apartment, lots of rooms all shuttered off that he doesn't even use."

"So you *don't* have a place for us to stay," Marco said.

"No, I do," she said.

"But we'd have to sneak in," Grito said. His hand spread across the map, blotting out the whole country.

"Well, *I* wouldn't, and I could probably get Mosca in, too—"

"Into what?" Marco said.

"Once we'd been there a couple of days, I'd sneak you in. He's a total brat. Always traveling—actually, his place in the country would be the best, but we'd have no way to make money."

"How long have you been thinking about this, *chica?*" Grito asked, leaning close to her, playing a nervous rhythm on her shoulder, easing himself back into the space around her body as if he'd never left. But I could see how many escape routes he kept open.

"I knew for a long time that I'd fail my exams, and there's no way I'm going back to that sugarcane pit. No one's gonna find me in France."

"How did you meet this guy?" I asked.

"On the island. He was vacationing with his parents. We met on the beach."

Marco and Grito shared this stupid look. They were trying to guess what that meant, like it was a secret to figure out. I wasn't too curious about what La Canaria had done that she felt she could stay at this guy's house. What I wanted to know was what he'd done that she felt good bringing in squatters. That's what would matter to us. But that wasn't why I was going, and I didn't plan on spending time at the house or with this guy. I couldn't say what I wanted, just that it was moving me forward. The reason was climbing up my tongue, getting ready to form.

La Canaria and I stood by the road with our thumbs out.

"Why can't we take a train, Marco?" La Canaria had asked.

"The money has to last us," he'd said. We didn't mention the policeman in Madrid again, but I knew that was partly why he'd insisted we hitchhike. He wanted to move fast and stay out of places where we might be seen.

If a car that seemed safe stopped, Marco and Grito would climb out of the green oaks that lined the highways, trying to look like they hadn't been hiding. If the car sped away, fine, we'd wait for the next one. If not, we'd climb in, heading north and east, through Castile, La Mancha, and Aragon. We slept half-nights, or during the day in the back of worn-down vans. We listened to the drivers' old radios playing French love songs and shitty disco and news of the ETA kidnappings. The price of oil and the number of unemployed rising.

In Catalonia, the Castilian signs had been spray-painted over with their old Catalan names. We got stuck in a traffic jam from a protest. We asked the driver what it was about, but he refused to answer. He stuck his head out the window and listened to a young guy in a jean jacket who was shouting about separating from the rest of the country and creating an autonomous nation. The driver nodded earnestly, and spoke to the young man in Catalan, gesturing back at us with a jerk of his head. After that he wouldn't speak in Castilian. The young people outside the car windows looked like us—ragged clothes and grubby faces peeking through black and red bandanas—but they spoke a language we could barely understand. The radio played new songs by protest singers, bare, rough guitars being plucked under lyrics spoken rather than sung, all in Catalan or Basque. These languages had been banned for decades and sounded much older than our own.

It took a couple of days to get to the border of France. Then another day over the Pyrenees Mountains that had been the first border. Closer to a week in all. We crossed at dawn on a small road, sitting in the back of a truck filled with metal canisters of milk. I'd never left the country before. I'd thought about it so many times when I was a kid—I'd imagined the sky expanding, my lungs lifting with it, my whole body growing so large and light. But I felt just as small and crouched as before, a rodent scurrying from one tunnel to the next.

On the northern side, the mountains were filled with Dutch tourists, their pale skin burned pink, with small bags fastened in front of their crotches and cameras covering their faces. The mountains did look like paintings. On them stood clean sheep and white dogs as big as bears. The wind spread their fur, making them look even larger.

"I wish I had a camera," Marco said.

Blond cows were visible at the edge of a crag, bending their heavy heads, collared in red embroidered leather and bells, down into the grass. Light and shadow played to make the animals and mountains flat, as if they could be touched from where we stood. The man with the milk canisters dropped us off in a town that was a ski resort in the winter and had mostly closed for the season. Locals led small groups of tourists around the town, into the tiny church, up to a spring whose water was supposed to keep marriages together. Grito laughed.

We hitched through southern France, not the ocean resorts but inland, the terrain not much different from the scrubby hills surrounding Casasrojas, more desert than countryside. Then the soil turned from hard-packed red sand to black dirt. Instead of green oak shrubs, spread out and stunted in search of nonexistent water, lindens, chestnuts, and pines loomed tall over the road. A driver let us off in a small town circled by mountains. On the flat roofs, black-and-white sheepdogs paced and kids threw stones up at them to catch in their mouths. We walked to the train station and Marco pointed at where we'd ended up, the Cevennes, a different set of mountains, in central France. We'd never heard of them, and there were few roads going into them, no cities. On the map they rose green and unmarked out of the red hills.

"Paris is a straight shot to the north," Marco said.

"Who gives a fuck about Paris?" Grito said. "Let's just get out of this hick town."

Marco flagged down a van, and the driver said he'd get us going in the right direction. He wasn't much older than we were, but he dressed like an old man, and his face had deep lines cut into it by the sun. In overly formal Castilian, he told us that people had moved here to drop out of society and get back to nature. La Canaria rolled her eyes, but Grito leaned forward.

"It's so much work," the man said. The highway was wide but flanked by mountains and held few cars. "The farms have been vacant for decades. It's wild here. In the winter, you're trapped up on these roads. Snowstorms can come even in the summer and block you in. Then when the snow melts, it washes out the roads. But you can grow what you want, eat it, barter the rest, try to eliminate the cash flow. The farmers need helpers, if you're looking for work."

"What the fuck?" Marco said, ignoring the driver. He was digging in his red backpack frantically. "Where the fuck is it? Where's the rest of it?"

Grito lowered in the front seat and muffled a snicker.

"Give it back," Marco said. He threw down his bag and grabbed Grito's shirt. "Give it back!"

"I can't, *tío*," Grito laughed. "It went up in flames!"

"What the fuck are you two talking about?" La Canaria said.

"Let go of me," Grito said. "It really was an accident. I just took some money and put it where I was sleeping, for safekeeping!" He laughed again.

"You stole from me?" Marco said.

"I just thought you needed to share a little more. Each according to his abilities, each according—"

"You stole from me! That money was supposed to last us!" Marco slammed his fist into Grito's seat.

"Watch out!" the driver said. "I'll leave you right here."

Grito turned around to face Marco. "Guess you're just like us now," he said.

Marco dropped his hands and his jaw wilted.

"We'll work," Grito said to the driver. "If there's work, we can do it."

The driver nodded and in a few minutes took a turn off the highway. We drove between jagged cliffs that would settle suddenly into small plateaus covered in crab apple and chestnut trees. The lindens were just budding out, pushing frail neon-green blossoms into the light.

"That was fucking stupid, Grito," La Canaria said.

"It's Marco's fault we're in this shit anyway," Grito said.

I looked to Marco, who avoided my eyes. I couldn't insist on going to Paris right away without letting on why, and without money there wasn't much I could insist on. We climbed higher into the mountains, turning on increasingly narrow roads. Finally Marco spoke. "We'll make some money and then we can go to Paris."

"What kind of work?" La Canaria said. "I'm not doing anything unless I get paid."

"I don't need four workers," the driver said warily, looking back at Marco in the rearview mirror. "Just two."

"We'll stay together," Marco said.

"You're like orphans in the war," the driver said. "My grandmother would tell me about them. Packs roaming the hills and spilling off trains, looking for work but never getting any because they wouldn't be split up. The big packs were the scrawniest because no one could take them all in at once."

Outside the window, timid new ferns uncurled and began to swell, breaking on the mountain rocks. The pine needles and fallen leaves hid the depths of each valley, as if to say falling here would not be so far.

"I know a family who needs help," the man said. "Their workers left them for a better deal on the other side of the valley." He took his hand off the steering wheel. Where his finger pointed looked close enough to touch, but to walk there must take several days, to descend and to climb again. "They have a large plot, they could use you all."

"Could they pay us?" La Canaria asked.

"I think so. They're good people. Young, with three children."

I could see them in my head, the way kids on the edges of cities looked. Like shrubs I didn't know the name of, kids all seemed the same to me. Sweetened milk caked around their mouths, dirt in rings around their necks. As if their mothers held them there when they dipped them in dirty water for protection, leaving the most important parts exposed, white top of the throat, white eyelids.

When we got up to the farm, the kids did look like that—matted hair, a blur of taut bellies not completely covered by worn shirts. They galloped over the crumbling stone walls and down mossy stairs. The farm was built on a few slivers of level ground, each building sharing a wall. It had been a large family hamlet once. There was only one structure intact. But the kids were smiling at us and tugging at our jeans. They weren't like animals everyone kicks. There were two boys and a toddler girl. The older boy had the thin, pinched cheeks of not having settled into a recent growth spurt. I looked at the younger boy, blond hair and open, eager brown eyes, and was smacked by the memory of Alexis crying over the death of a spider after Abuela ironed the spring linen. It tormented him for weeks. He wove the spider's life for it, described in agony its agony, as if he didn't know what else there was to hurt for, as if he needed more.

Marco knelt by the boys and pointed to something in his hand, and they laughed. I walked up to the mother.

She was only a few years older than we were, and her oldest kid was around five. She was like the girls I'd see in the plaza in

Casasrojas, long hair down their backs, tight bell bottoms on, laughing. They'd turn and their stomachs were huge, proof they had only a few weeks left. There were doctors in Madrid who would do it, and women in every town willing to shove a piece of bamboo up your cervix for all the pesetas you had, willing to lie when they said it wouldn't kill you. A wealthy girl could fly to London, but for most of us, it was a life sentence one way or another.

The mother, Berta, was pregnant, and she had this surprised look, like she really was one of those girls in the plaza who couldn't believe the huge weight suddenly attached to her. She had blond hair that massed uncombed down her back and a faded blue kerchief folded in a triangle on top of her head. She blinked repeatedly. When she smiled, first at her boys, then at me, there were thin lines forming around her mouth, just the faintest pencil strokes quickly erased, only slightly visible. We tried to find a common language.

They were German. She could speak some Castilian but had English, good English. I felt La Canaria drift up close to my body, affixing herself firmly to me. I wondered again how much I would tell her, what I would leave out and why. Berta's husband, Franz, walked up to us and La Canaria watched him. He walked behind us, held his hand out to Marco and Grito. He was older than Berta was, not by much. He looked younger somehow, seemed to weigh much less, his hair long and downy. They weren't made to be outside and certainly not high up on this mountain, so close to the sun. Even beneath the sunburn, they had a gleam to their skin that only the wealthy have, a sort of elasticity in the way their fingers and lips moved. The kids didn't have it.

Brushing aside a wall of vines with bright yellow flowers and a swishing fly door, Berta invited us into the house. She left the door open and the kids and Franz followed, pressing against one another into the dark of the kitchen. A cat ran in after them with half a salamander in its mouth.

The kitchen was filled with smoke. The once-white plaster walls were blackened in layers of soot, darkest near the open chimney. Rows of shelves snaked the small space, dividing it so we couldn't all stand together. We had to separate and drift in between the different cupboards. They were filled with jars and secured by twine to the ceiling. The wood wobbled if touched, the movement jittering into glass.

Berta made a rich quick bread with eggs, brown flour, and cinnamon. She carefully tore open the bottom of the bag of flour and shook into the dough the final dusting caught in the folds of paper. We ate the bread with stew that had a few potatoes and carrots but was mostly water. The boys ran laps around the table, sitting still only to steal food from each other, one eating the carrots the other set aside to save until the end. The eldest boy ate only the insides of his bread, draping the crust to frame his face. He swore when Berta reached to pull it off his face, and then his father, who hadn't looked at them all dinner, yelled sharply in German. Berta spoke to us slowly, balancing her daughter on her leg beside her swollen stomach. I could tell she was smart, but it was clouded. She had to sift through so much just to shape her mouth in a way we could understand. She said that when they came to the mountain, the room we were in was the only one intact.

"It still is," Franz said, trying to make a joke.

"It's very slow work here," Berta said. "Everything keeps falling apart. And the soil is very thin."

"We're not really farmers," Franz said. "Isn't that obvious! But you can make a place fertile if you have enough water, which we do. There are springs everywhere, clear good water just coming out of the rock. Yes, that's one thing we have enough of, water—and babies." He grabbed the eldest boy racing past and pulled him close to his body, kissed him on top of his dirty blond head.

"We put up a great deal of food for the winter," Berta said proudly, gesturing back at the shelves stacked with glass jars. "But the spring has been slow in coming." Most of the jars were empty.

"We thought the winter would be the hardest," Franz said. "But it's now—when you can almost taste the food, even though it hasn't grown yet."

Grito looked up at me. He had finished his bowl of stew and was slowly chewing his bread, an old trick to make it last. This was the way the old people used to talk. Spring hunger would surprise you if you didn't know how to plan for it. They said that during the worst years after the war, spring was when the most people died.

"We need money for seeds—" Berta said to no one.

"No, we can't just eat grass like the sheep," Franz said.

"But we're very glad you're here," Berta said, smiling earnestly. "Tomorrow Franz will sell the lambs in town and bring back seeds and we can all get to work."

We nodded, except for La Canaria, who had stayed silent and still the whole meal, moving just to eat. Marco was the only one who didn't look worried. He spoke comfortably with Franz and Berta until Franz got up to check on the sheepdogs.

"We don't have the nicest place for you to sleep, but it will be your place. We won't go in it," Berta said.

Outside, the ground and steps were wet from the gathering dew. Cool air settled around us. All that was visible were pines and bare green hills rolling into dark. A pink and orange sky with clouds as big as the mountains rising behind them, their movements slow and dramatic as armadas. We picked our way through the broken rocks, unclear which piles were mountain and which were ruins of the farm that used to be there. Behind the kitchen and sharing one of its walls was a huge open room with the roof mostly intact.

"This is where they used to dry the chestnuts to make flour," Berta said. Off to one side, the old wooden floor fell away to several meters of darkness, what was below it invisible in the twilight. From underneath a tarp, Berta handed us several sleeping bags that smelled musty but seemed dry. "I'll wake you up in the morning for coffee." She looked down at my and La Canaria's feet. "And I'll find you some boots. You can't work in those."

La Canaria and Marco unrolled their sleeping bags. Grito followed Berta out. When he didn't speak, she handed him the flashlight and disappeared behind a crumbling wall covered in green moss. I realized we hadn't discussed getting paid.

We needed the flashlight, especially inside, where the light from the ringed moon didn't reach. The air and the stones, everything we touched, was wet. I could understand that water came out of rocks here, the whole world dripping. Sheep bleated and Grito kept opening his mouth and closing it. I was so tired it seemed that he was the one making the sound. I was about to tell him this when he spoke.

"*Noche que la noche nochera,*" Grito whispered. It was a line from a Lorca poem we used to read aloud. The night that night made night. In that moment it made sense like it never had before, looking out over the pines blackening into a black sky. An entity defined by its own existence, made into itself by what it already was. I wanted to reach out and touch him. Just to say that I remembered that line, even if I didn't want the whole memory anymore. But I didn't know how much of it I did want. I tried to remember the rest of the poem—necklaces of almonds, a city of doors and sowing flames—but the next line didn't come.

Grito turned to go back inside, taking the flashlight. I didn't move toward him. In the poem, gypsies make suns with their small fires, but here there were no scattered lights, the pines enclosing. We were on the edge of the space we'd made, and we were cutting even the twine that bound us. That was how Grito wanted it. But the night didn't need more night to make it what it already was. And in the end, it was still only night, unchanged and alone. That wasn't enough for me anymore.

Nine

Franz was out working by the time we came into the kitchen. The boys were off somewhere, too, the silence of the chestnut trees interrupted often enough by their shouts that Berta didn't worry.

She gave us a weak, gritty coffee that completely filled our teacups, and sweet biscuits.

"Americano," Marco said.

"Watered down," La Canaria whispered to me. "At least they don't eat like those Brits. I can't take breakfast this early. I think I'd puke it up."

Berta carried her cup and we followed her out into the garden. She led us to a hill already drenched in sunlight. The land had been carved into terraces, some very narrow. She tied her daughter to her waist like a goat. "I can't have her falling off," Berta said. The terraces must have been made long ago. The corners were rounded into tired knuckles, and the edges had crumbled into piles on the lower terraces. Tall grass covered remnants of structures, cornerstones hidden under years of matted debris.

"This is our project for the spring," Berta said. "This area was a hamlet. It had been empty for twenty years when we got here. This used to be the vegetable garden."

"You want to make this into a garden?" La Canaria said.

"Yes, see there, that will be the tomatoes." Berta pointed to a thick clump of brambles taking up half a terrace. "For market. We'll try to sell some."

Berta had Grito and Marco start breaking up the sod with long, thin shovels. La Canaria and I followed her up the hill. The buildings were stacked on narrow sections of somewhat level ground, their corners carved back into the mountain. Every step we took was slanted. Berta moved quickly up the hill, as if she had hooves instead of boots, even with the girl tied to her. Some of the buildings were completely buried by earth and grasses. I'd think I was stepping up a really steep part of the hill, and when I looked back, I could see the shape of a wall, corners dulled beneath the sod.

Behind the chestnut mill where we'd slept was a somewhat intact structure. It was once several stories, but the roof and the second-story walls had crumbled years ago. It was now just a stone box emerging out of the grass. Berta picked up a ladder from the ground and swung it against the wall. She untied the girl and handed her to me, then climbed up the ladder.

"You can help me bring the dogs down," she said to La Canaria, who looked at me and tightened her lips. Two sheepdogs stuck their heads out over the edge of the building, whining in high-pitched notes. They circled the structure's flat roof, scenting the air and wanting down.

La Canaria didn't move to climb up the ladder. She wouldn't even look at the dogs. "I'm not going near them," she said. I put the girl at her feet and went up after Berta.

From the top of the structure I could see Marco and Grito working away at the sod. The grass was thick and its roots dug deep into the soil. They had to peel off almost thirty centimeters to get to clear dirt. Marco bent down and curled up strips of sod that Grito had loosened. They had barely spoken since the car ride. At the edge of the terrace was only blank blue sky.

On the roof, the two dogs ran up to me yapping. My abuelo had the same kind of dogs in the country—black and white with short hair, long, lean bodies. I ignored them until one jumped up on me. I struck him firmly but not too hard on the snout.

"Good," Berta said. "You know how to treat them. They're not pets."

We brought the dogs down off the structure. They stayed still in our arms and then leaped away from us when we set them down, circling the building and moving outward. La Canaria stood looking at the girl with her eyebrow raised and mouth set, daring her to move.

"Marie," Berta said to the girl. "Do you promise to stay close and then I won't have to put you on the lead?"

Marie nodded slowly, not taking her eyes off La Canaria.

"She fell off one of the terraces last month and twisted her ankle," Berta said. "I'm terrified to let her out of my sight, but I can't work with her so close to me. She's too big to carry and too small to let play with her brothers."

We followed the dogs up the hill to a fence with a wooden gate. The fence sloped down the mountain in one direction but stopped abruptly on the other. The pines emerged again at the top of the ridge, but for a while there was an empty stretch of grass and stones.

"You could tie her to the fence," La Canaria said. "If we're not going far."

"Yes, all right." Berta took the rope from around her waist and tied it to the fence post and to Marie. She could move a meter in any direction. The girl stepped as far as the rope would let her and then stood staring at us. Berta kissed her cheek and stood. "Today we have to separate out the lambs so Franz can take them to town. We have to make a temporary pen, and then we'll have it when they need to be sheared."

Berta shook a bucket of grain and called out for the sheep. The dogs bolted away from us and disappeared over the other side of the hill. We could hear them barking to each other and then sheeps' bells and their dull bickering. A ewe with a red collar and a large brass bell jutted her head over the hill, followed by the rest of the herd. When they came close to us, Berta started to count them. "There's one lamb missing," she said, frustrated. "We'll have to go find him."

The ewes circled us, fighting to stuff their long heads into the bucket of grain. Their warm bodies pressed up against my legs and I could smell their sharp wool. None of their tails had been clipped. Mud and dung clung to their backsides like stew dripping out of a pot. Berta kept tossing the feed away from her to give us space, but the ewes knew where it came from and kept tight around us. La Canaria pushed through them and started down the hill. Berta watched her walk away without speaking. Marie was straining toward one of the lambs on the edge of the herd but not getting any closer to it. Below us, I could see La Canaria speaking to Marco and pointing back with her shoulder at us. Marco put down his shovel and came toward us.

Berta made the dogs stay with the herd while we searched for the lamb. "If we can't find the lamb soon, I'll come get them," she said. "Marie, be good, we'll be back."

Marco saw the lamb first. We had come up over the first hill on the side where the forest reappeared. The lamb was down the hill near a gully. Patches of dirty snow still clung beneath overhanging rocks and in the roots of large trees. I didn't know how he told the difference between the lamb and the dingy clumps of snow stuck with dried leaves and briars.

The lamb's leg was caught in an old bear trap. The metal probably would have gone right through its leg, but it had hit high on the haunches and dug down to the bone. The trap was covered by the broken branches of a thorned shrub. Though the trap itself was old, it looked well maintained, oiled recently and without rust.

"What's this doing here?" Marco asked. "Isn't this your land?"

"I don't know," Berta said. She bent down to put her face close to the lamb's and cooed at it. The lamb's mouth was open slightly, its pink tongue swollen in its mouth. Breath came rapidly but without any strength. The air could not get past the tongue and instead circled the crowded mouth frantically.

Marco pushed the branches away from the lamb to see its leg better. The wool around the wound was matted with dried blood. The lamb didn't even flinch when Marco touched its leg. It just kept its mouth open, pink tongue sticking slightly out. It must have been trying to bleat.

"Where's its mother?" Marco asked.

"She's a bad one," Berta said, her face turned away from us and looking down the hill. "She's probably back with the herd, stealing feed."

Marco felt carefully with his fingers around the trap until he found the release. The spring snapped, but the metal clung, buried in the lamb's leg.

"It's stuck in the bone," Marco said. "Do you want me to even try?"

"I'd like to—my flock is too small as it is," Berta said. "He was going to be our ram."

Marco pressed his hands down on the lamb's back. Its breathing seemed to slow, and it lowered its head toward the ground. Berta stood up and looked again down into the gully.

If the trap had been set there, we'd never have found the lamb. Even low on the hill, you could see only parts of the ditch. You didn't know how much you couldn't see.

"One of the neighbors went to visit her sister," Berta said. "This was a long time ago, when there were more people here. The snow was deep and she got caught in a storm. She was only going over one hill, but she never got there. They had to wait until spring for the snow to melt so they could search for her body."

I was looking at the gully, imagining what it hid. Wondering what else hadn't been found there, what had to wait too long to be looked for. The dark wet leaves and pine needles that made up the ground seemed to move, to come closer and edge away. To swirl as if someone were stirring them. Marco struggled with the trap. He had not stopped to look up while Berta spoke.

"I'll get the iodine," Berta said. "I think I have to put it on the wound as soon as you get it out." She ran up the hill, holding her belly.

The trap's metal teeth flashed in the sunlight. The air was too bright for this. Where we stood, there were no shadows to cover the lamb's thin tissue, still pumping blood to ruined flesh. Marco pried slowly at the trap, trying to wedge it out of the lamb's leg. The lamb jerked upward suddenly, remembering it was alive, and caught Marco off guard.

"Help hold him," Marco said to me. I shook my head, the rest of my body not moving. He bent back toward the lamb, his face a dropped curtain, closed in on itself and pushing the set around in the dark.

The lamb struggled under Marco's hands.

"I need you to hold its leg, Mosca," Marco hissed. The lamb thrashed again. "Hold it here."

He wanted me to hold the lamb right by its wound so he could get the metal teeth out of its bone. He wanted me to press down right where its insides met the air and curdled.

"I'll go get Grito," I said.

Marco grabbed my hands and pulled me onto my knees. He put my hand where he had pointed. The wound was wet, but the only smell was blood.

Looking at Marco's hands, the lamb's blood welling around them, I couldn't stop the memory, the one I least wanted, I was back in the kitchen in Casasrojas, the cathedral bells calling home the storks, Abuela out with her last friend still alive, to walk beside the pigeons and piles of sunflower seed shells in the Plaza de Colón. Alexis looked up at the cheap clock with gold-plated plastic chimes that hung above her altar. We had about an hour before she got back. She could hardly hear anymore, but Alexis said he had something important to ask me and he wanted to be completely sure she didn't hear any of it. He said she needed to know nothing.

Alexis turned away from me and Marco, fixing us both some espresso. I'd never seen him make anything in the kitchen be-fore. No matter how late he came in, Abuela would get up and cook him whatever he wanted. But he didn't fumble with the parts of the moka pot, and he even knew where she kept the wooden brush to clean out the old grinds.

"Thanks," Marco said when Alexis placed a small white cup in front of him. The cup jittered in Marco's hands. Alexis kept adding sugar to his espresso. I hadn't known he took so much—perhaps that was new. Alexis started another pot for me and I stayed quiet, waiting for the hiss of the coffee sweating out.

The photo was on the table without my seeing how it got there. Alexis turned away, fiddling with the espresso. I knew why he hadn't explained what he was doing with the militants until that moment. If I'd known what it was about, I would have tried to help, but he didn't want to ask until he needed me.

I looked at the photo on the table. A cheap snapshot, black and white, blown up. The grain was too large. Our parents had disappeared when Alexis was four—he'd seen only a few pictures since. He needed me to make sure it was really them.

Alexis handed me my espresso without looking at the photo. It was clear he hadn't spent much time studying it, if he had looked at all. He was waiting for me to tell him it was real. I nodded once, and only then did he face the photo. His fingers moved to pick it up. I must have made a sound to stop him. I needed to look, too.

Our parents were turned toward the camera, their necks taut, looking over their unnaturally squared shoulders. Their hands were bound and they were on their knees. My father's face was partially hidden by my mother's, his thick mustache disappearing into her black hair.

"It was taken before they were executed," Alexis said.

Marco ran his fist over his mouth again and again, bringing blood to his chin, marking it as with smeared lipstick.

Whoever had taken the picture must have surprised them, because they had turned quickly, the movement caught in the shape of their eyes. They must have thought it wasn't a camera behind them. They must have thought that was the moment they would die and not the one after. They were looking straight into the camera, unflinching.

Alexis picked up the photo, rotating it slowly in his hands. "The people I'm working with—they say they can find who did it."

The photo was the proof of what we'd suspected. That our

parents had resisted. That they were killed for it. That they weren't coming back.

"Do they know why?" I said. "Why they were—"

"No, but we could find out. The militants trust me. I've done enough for them."

"Where did they get the photo?" I asked.

"There's a lot of them showing up. When the old *fachas* die off. Or someone kills them."

I imagined a room of these photos. Thousands of faces, shoulders all pinched into the same position. Their heads turned, facing the bullet that would kill them. First I thought of a room with all the different dead. Then I thought of one filled only with the same picture, endlessly repeated, a strand of my mother's hair caught in my father's partially open mouth.

"I'm glad you told me," I said.

"You don't have to be here, Marco," Alexis said. "It's not your family. It's not your fight."

"It is my fight," Marco said. I knew why he was there. The pig outside the warehouse hadn't really been Marco's hit. The gun they got from him was because of Alexis. Marco needed to be there because of Alexis, Alexis only, who hadn't even asked him, and Marco was so proud of that. He'd volunteered before he could be asked. I didn't mention La Canaria. The last time I'd seen her, she was strung between two guys crossing the plaza past midnight. Alexis had seen her, too. We would all pretend she didn't exist until they got back together again.

"Are you sure, Mosca?"

I nodded.

Alexis sighed—out of relief or fear, I couldn't tell.

"I didn't want to ask you," he said. "But it'll be safe, I promise."

"We're meeting at the library," Marco said hesitantly. "And since you're always there—"

"No one will suspect you," Alexis interrupted. "You're always studying, that's why it'll work." He was smiling, almost, excited about the plan, excited to play the part he'd practiced. They had talked about it together. Which meant Marco had seen the photo of my parents before I had. Alexis had shown him first.

I nodded again. "I'll help."

Alexis and Marco would meet the militants in the philology library to exchange information. I would be the lookout, signal them if anyone came too close. I wouldn't know anything else. Alexis needed us, and we would do whatever he needed. We would help him find the men once we had their names and addresses. My task would end at a certain early point. I wouldn't see them, I would be asked to walk away. We made the plan and promised.

Marco left before our abuela came back. Alexis slipped the photo into its envelope and rolled it carefully. I watched it disappear into his jacket. He rubbed his thumb and index finger over his clavicle.

It had been almost a game. The phone calls from new cities his bragging rights: playing spy, playing soldier. But whether he knew it or not, in that moment Alexis's body told me what the game had become. I looked at him and knew what he would do when he found the men he was looking for. He thought he was invincible, his sternum pressed proudly against his white T-shirt. But I knew how each muscle would coil and spring, their future actions already wrought into them. If he found those old men, he would make them scream, and I would hear their screams, louder than I imagined but gentler, too, radiating off of his skin every time he moved. He wouldn't be able to deny those sounds. I wanted to turn away from the violence already written into his body, but the inevitability followed me like a spell.

Marco pressed down on my hands on the lamb until I wasn't trying to pull away. He lined up his fingers beside the metal teeth where he could grip the trap without cutting himself. Berta called for us on top of the hill.

"Now," he said.

I pressed down into the wool and muscle, bringing blood to the surface, the lamb struggling beneath me. Marco pulled on the trap. With the sound of a rubber boot squelching up through mud, the metal came out.

"Bring him here," Berta called. The dogs were behind her and raced up to us, sniffing the trap and barking at Marco.

Marco picked up the lamb and ran up the hill with it. My hands were covered in greasy blood and lanolin. Berta squirted the wound with iodine. The wool around it turned the yellow of a sunflower just about to die.

Because I didn't go. I promised Alexis I would help him and I didn't. I didn't show up at the library that day. The night before, I had followed Alexis in my dreams, just awake enough to panic, followed him to where he would take the men when he found them, saw him standing over two wrinkled *fachas*, his back to me, his face nothing I would see again.

An English exam was rescheduled at the last minute—it was just the excuse I needed. I took the exam, did well. Really, I was too afraid. I thought of Mamá standing in Abuela's kitchen, handing us sweet crackers and saying she'd be back soon. The policemen knocking at our door. The piles by the river.

And I thought, If I don't go, the plan stops. Alexis's muscles won't have to coil and kill. There will be no more men on their knees. No one will be held accountable, and our parents' names will rest where they had for years, buried deep in the silt of memory, asleep, asking for nothing. I was wrong.

Marco didn't mention the lamb at dinner. Berta placed it on the hearth, as close as she could to the fire without singeing its wool, and wrapped it in a blanket. It hadn't moved since Marco pulled it out of the trap.

We had taken too long to gather and separate all the lambs. Franz would take them to the town the next day. The sound of the grieving ewes echoed over the hills, down into the stone chimney, coating our meager dinner. La Canaria and Grito were silent, trying to speak to each other without words but neither knowing how. If they found a way out of this, they had better tell me. I was worried they would only do so if they needed me. I picked at the blood under my nails.

"Why did you care so much about it?" I asked Marco when Berta stepped outside. There was even less food that night than the one before.

"It doesn't matter," Marco said. "It's going to die anyway."

Ten

The snow came the next evening while we were peeling wrinkled potatoes and dumping the black bits into a dirty bin. We'd spent the day getting the plot ready for the seeds that Franz was supposed to bring back from town. Berta was worried because he hadn't returned, and all evening long she kept looking up as if to make him appear.

The lamb rasped in the corner by the hearth. It was beginning to smell. Its meat ruined. The window in the kitchen was small and held only a view of a stone courtyard with a finger's width of sky. We didn't notice it cloud, and we didn't see the snow start. Out the window over the stone stable, only darkness was noticeable, twilight forgotten and now night. There were no lights to glint off the snow. We didn't even know we were working in the dark until we could hardly see. The night piled layers of cloth slowly over our mouths, so thin we didn't notice until we couldn't breathe. Berta lit a kerosene lamp and put it in the window, and then we saw the snow. Falling, it caught the light the way water does. I gasped in surprise and Berta did, too. Only she knew what it meant.

She placed her face to the window and cupped her hands around her eyes, held her breath to not fog the glass. She wiped the glass from the heat of her skin and leaned in again. Then she left the kitchen and opened the door. The wind shook the jars and the shelves. Marco had to help Berta close the door. We all looked up at her, waiting for her to speak, but she didn't. She just sank to the floor like a glob of spit down a wall. She was whispering quietly and quickly; I couldn't understand her. Marco leaned down next to her and she turned her face away, mumbling, her hands covering her mouth.

"Is Franz still out there?" Grito asked, and Marco nodded.

I went to the window. The snow was falling fast.

We stayed in the kitchen all night. Dawn was just a slight shift: the air outside the window turned from a wall of easing black to a wall of cascading grays. The snow kept falling, pressing against the warped glass of the kitchen window. It had a texture and mass that I couldn't keep my eyes off of. Each flake possessed a huge strength, to support its own weight and not collapse the way my lungs felt they would. The glass jars on the shelves jittered constantly, moved by the wind coming through all corners of the room, calling attention to their emptiness. Berta kept a small fire going, but the woodpile was shrinking. The smoky wet logs did nothing against the wind. There was hardly anything to eat. We huddled close to one another, the air stale with our recycled breath yet cold, too. The lamb died and Berta opened the door enough to put it outside because it smelled so bad.

"Where did that trap come from?" Grito asked Berta. He'd finally gotten out of Marco what had happened to the lamb.

Berta didn't answer him but stroked her daughter's hair, which was matted and dark with grease. A thin line of black grime circled the girl's neck. The gray light was an in-between place, one I didn't want to be in, one where I didn't belong. The fire didn't do much except make the shadows at the window look alive.

"Is the trap yours or what?" Grito said.

"It's not mine," Berta said, looking out the window. "No one comes up here to hunt, either. At least not that I know of. And they wouldn't put a trap where my sheep are."

"Whose is it, then?" Marco asked. "It was hidden. It was supposed to catch something, but it couldn't have been there long."

Berta kept looking out the window. She was no longer expecting Franz to appear but something else, something she was afraid of seeing. She wouldn't answer about the trap. They stopped asking, and the words she could have said circled the house silently until they batted up against the window harder than the wind.

"Franz's uncle wants to take the boys to live with him," Berta said, still turned toward the window. "He thinks we can't raise them all by ourselves here."

"But that's the point, isn't it?" Grito said. I was surprised he'd even been listening to her. She wasn't waiting for an answer. "This is something you do by yourselves. Getting help would ruin it."

Berta didn't seem to hear him. The boys were too skinny, proof of how far their plan of independence had failed.

Marie waddled slowly over to where Grito and La Canaria were sitting by the fire. She touched La Canaria on the knee and said something. She had the look that children get when they've decided to love, no matter what it is. It can happen so quickly, a squash with a curly stem, a rabbit in an alley, someone passing in the park they will never see again. The girl looked at La Canaria and spoke, her hand still on La Canaria's knee, her tinny voice rising in a question. I couldn't tell if it was baby talk or a language I didn't understand. The words seemed formless, too soft and particular to contain meaning.

La Canaria got up quickly and Marie stumbled back. She

didn't hit anything. I looked up, but Berta hadn't seen. La Canaria knelt next to the boys, who were sprawled out on the dusty floor playing game after game of tic-tac-toe on an old newspaper. The youngest one was debating where to put his next *x*. La Canaria bent over him and whispered in his ear. It was hard not to look at the boys. All day they'd been edging closer to me. The little one threaded his bottom lip behind his teeth, concentrating on what La Canaria was trying to show him. It wasn't enough that he looked just like Alexis, who was blond before his hair turned black; he had to move like him, too. I tried not to remember the boy's name. Listening to La Canaria, the little one held his hand over each square until she nodded and then he made his mark. The older one cried out. "It's cheating!" he said in English. La Canaria just shrugged and whispered again to the little one. He drew a new game and on the second round placed his *x* in the same spot. They kept playing, the little one always winning. The older boy didn't get it; he kept thinking he would win the next round.

"He's right," Grito insisted. "I used to hate it when people would play like that."

"It's a dumb game," La Canaria said. "If it's that easy to beat."

Grito was pissed off, but it was too close in the kitchen to yell at La Canaria. None of us wanted to go out to the barn where we'd slept. The floor was probably covered in snow.

"You can't just tell him how to win," Grito said. "It doesn't make sense as a game now."

"Why do you care?" La Canaria said.

"Don't they have any books they can read?" Grito asked Berta. She'd been staring out the window, really at her own reflection. The window was completely snowed in.

"Excuse me?"

"Books, you know," Grito continued, trying to sound nicer. His hands wouldn't stop moving, picking at the bits of scalp clumping at the nape of his neck beneath his hair. "Books or games, so they have something to do."

"They're fine," she said. "Look, she taught them a game."

I could tell Grito was angry, but I was the only one besides La Canaria who knew that. His nails worked a patch of skin behind his ear over and over. He picked up Marie, who was leaning too close to the fire, and sat down holding her. "Do you like living here?" he said.

"I don't think she understands you," La Canaria said. Berta had already turned back to the window.

"Do you like living here?"

Marie pulled at Grito's ponytail and then rubbed her hand across his nose, leaving it speckled with ash from the hearth.

"She doesn't know how to talk," La Canaria said.

Grito stood up, holding Marie awkwardly, and she squirmed, too loose in his grasp to trust him. Berta turned toward them, and Grito placed Marie on the ground by her brothers. "I'll show you something," Grito said to the children.

The boys bent their heads over the newspaper, bored of the game and drawing pictures of houses and animals that might have been sheep or dogs. But they were too bulky to be distinguishable and instead seemed threatening, their mouths big, and not easily named. Grito laid a new piece of newspaper over the old one. The boys both cried out. La Canaria stood over them and pointed down at Grito. Right then she was the magician's assistant, wearing only feathers.

Grito drew a new tic-tac-toe game but added extra lines and lines that intersected the new ones. The grid became more complicated, branching out at different angles. It took him several minutes, but then he gave the boys their pencils and stepped back. He nodded when the little one put down his *x*. He nodded when the older one drew more lines to intercept his brother's *x*. "That'll keep them quiet for a while."

"They were quiet," Marco said. I didn't know he'd even been paying attention.

"They were until she pissed them off."

"I'm bored. And I'm hungry." La Canaria said the last words louder, looking over at Berta, Berta at the window, Berta not turning. La Canaria brought her face a centimeter from Marie's nose. "What have we got to eat, little girl?"

Berta could probably understand La Canaria's Castilian. She was speaking slowly, as if to an animal.

"Find me something to eat," La Canaria said. Marie giggled and stuck out her tongue. La Canaria bit at it. Suddenly, the little boy looked up, looked right at me. There was no way he could look the way he did, exactly like Alexis, almond eyes and curled lips almost too pretty for a boy, so much that I couldn't look away this time.

"Do you think Franz left before the storm started?" Marco said in English. His words brought the walls in closer. A bleeding in the air, layers of sense tearing. I listened to the one city still inside me, Paris, Paris, blocking out all other sound. The boy kept looking at me. Beneath his hand, the game Grito had made stretched the whole length of the newspaper and continued unabated onto the stone floor. The brothers were no longer playing with or against each other, just extending the game, placing their marks farther and farther away.

By afternoon the snow had stopped, but Franz hadn't returned. Berta made us coffee, weak and mostly chicory. She handed us the cups. "You have to leave," she said slowly in Castilian.

None of us had spoken in several hours. The boys were upstairs sleeping and the girl sat silent where the lamb had been.

La Canaria stood up quickly. "We're not going anywhere."

Berta didn't move and didn't look at La Canaria. Berta was really small. Her body formed around tiny bones, not an extra ounce of fat except for her belly, a tumor jutting out of her. She bent down to pick up Marie and spoke to me in English. "I don't like to do this, but I can't keep feeding you. I'm sorry. You can make your way to a road that's been cleared and get to town. I can't go anywhere with the children."

"We're not going out there," La Canaria said, stepping closer to Berta.

La Canaria probably wouldn't hit a girl holding a baby, a pregnant girl, but we were all shaky with hunger and cold. La Canaria wouldn't really have to do anything. Berta was alone and was acting strong, but there were four of us. "I'm not going out in that snow. You haven't even paid us."

"I don't have any money to pay you with. We obviously don't have any money."

"You *puta*. The guy that brought us here said—"

Marco stepped between them and turned to Berta. "We'll leave. We'll get to town and come back to help you."

This wasn't what Berta had said, but it was a way that Marco could accept what we were being told to do. I didn't think he was ready for the alternative. He didn't look at Grito but kept talking. "This is a freak storm, right? The snow will melt soon and we'll be able to get back here. We'll find Franz and we'll come back."

Grito nodded and La Canaria stepped away from Marco. Berta gave us extra sweaters and plastic bags for our boots.

"Follow the river," Berta said. "It will lead you to the highway."

Eleven

The snow kept betraying us. In some spots it held, supporting our weight, and we were able to take several steps on top of it. Then it would collapse. The sound of our boots on the ice grated against our teeth and clung to the insides of our ears. We'd never been in deep snow, never been this cold or wet for this long. We kept walking, trying to follow the river but not get too close. It had frozen in some spots, a thin skin over shaded eddies, and black water rushed underneath.

"We have to keep this mountain on our left," Marco said, pointing at a peak I guessed was to the west of us. We nodded, but we'd lose sight of the peak when we climbed down into gullies, and its position would shift by the time we got back out. There were dips and tiny streams. It was hard to know if we were following the right river anymore. The snow swallowed. Even my breath entering the air became white and indistinguishable from the ground around us. If I closed my eyes, all I knew was the sound of my heartbeat, fast but buried deep. I wondered if it was really my own or the sound of the snow expanding and bringing everything it touched inside. Or if it was someone behind us. I thought this and not that it was the sound of Marco's or Grito's heavy, wet breaths. At first I felt the sound inside me. But we kept walking, and more and more I felt the sound around me. It was larger than I was, and following.

The edges of the forest disappeared into darkness. I could see only in black and white. Snow clung to our clothes, seeping through the wool and layers of thin cotton. My legs were thin sticks, toys a child would hit together to make noise and see which would break first. We shouldn't be out in this weather and we knew it. La Canaria and Marco slowed down, leaning into each other and stumbling.

Grito was farther ahead, moving toward a deep dip in the snow. It was getting dark. Grito fell through the ice and into the river.

You say what you don't want to only when there is nothing left to say. When that thing is all you are, all you've become. No words, breath disappearing, legs brittle movement, collecting patches of wet lichen that fall off too quickly. When Grito fell into the ice, I saw Alexis at the edge of the frozen river. Not someone who looked like him or a memory of him. Him actually there. He was standing in the deep snow, wearing his long dirty raincoat. He looked at Grito, Grito falling, Grito taking in huge gulps of watery air. He looked at me. La Canaria screamed in my ear and Alexis was gone. There was only Grito in the water, trying to dig his nails into crumbling ice.

In Berta's son's face I had seen Alexis, in Marco sometimes before dark, in the pigeons that came fast around stone corners in Casasrojas, chased by something they certainly could not name. In what chased them, I saw my brother. I saw him at the riverside when we were kids, turning, that man's hand on his shoulder, smiling, then his smile changing, thinking it was me, turning and knowing it wasn't. But I saw that, saw that smile turning, so I didn't have to see other things. Picked at a scab to ignore the termites making a home in my spine, crawling into my organs, forming lace of my bones, dyed red and dripping.

The night after I was supposed to help Alexis, I came home late from the library. My abuela had left me a plate of ham and chorizo and the last of that day's bread. I'd been trying to avoid Alexis and expected the house to be quiet, dark, Abuela sleeping and Alexis out for the night. But the kitchen lights were on.

Alexis and Marco were sitting at the table. They had been talking, I could tell from the suspended flecks of unclosed verbs in the air. They were silent when I walked in. Not silent because I was there but because of the burnt words passing between them. Marco got up to leave without looking at me, and Alexis held his pocketknife in his hand. I sat down at the counter and stared at the drops of blood where Marco's hand had been.

I don't know why I sat down. I needed to explain why I hadn't met Alexis like I'd said I would. To tell him that it wasn't just cowardice, that in my own way, I'd been trying to protect him. But I couldn't speak with our abuela in the other room. Alexis was churning within himself, like he was too big for his skin. It made him still as he was never still. Completely silent, the knife stuck in the table, stuck there at some point between Marco leaving and me staring at the drops of blood.

"Where the fuck were you?" he said.

I knew I should get up. I knew I shouldn't stay in this room, where my breath itself was a challenge. But I had to try to speak. Instead, Alexis stood up and left the knife in the table.

Later that night he came to my door, like he did when he was a kid.

I was in bed listening to the dump trucks, the clang of metal echoing down long channels of stone. I kept my room bare, almost empty, except for a plywood desk covered in books and my narrow bed. Years before, Abuela had tried to throw away everything that had belonged to our parents. I saved what I could. My mother's old journals and christening gown, my father's university papers, notes and torn kerchiefs, I placed in cardboard boxes and wrapped them tightly with twine. I shoved the boxes under my bed, against the far wall and beyond my reach. I never looked there again, but I knew what was there, sleeping over a whole ocean I didn't want to touch but couldn't let go of. At night our street was an underwater cave: me floating above what was left of our parents, the lamplights bouncing off formations made of exhaust and burnt coal, a drunk calling down the alley just to see how far the sound would carry.

"*Coño*, Mosca," Alexis hissed. "Where were you?"

He stood just inside the door, and the sound of his voice skimmed over the cracked linoleum floor. Alexis never knocked when he came into my room and would swear and slam the door if he found me undressing, like I should have warned him. I knew he couldn't see my face that night in the dark. The lamplights lit a yellow stripe that hit the wall above my head, punctured by red stars from the dump truck. To me, he was just an outline, a figure I knew should be there, and I filled in the rest.

"I'm sorry," I said.

"You said you'd help. We were going to get the info on those *pendejos*."

"Look, I said I'm sorry. But I didn't want you to go. It's too dangerous. Marco said he would tell you, and you wouldn't go without me—"

"*Joder*, Marco—"

"I know it's what you wanted, but it won't bring them back. Finding who did it. The whole thing will only get you into more trouble."

I could hear him ease the door shut behind him. He stopped before the latch clicked. The cheap metal rested on the frame with an almost silent intake of sound. The black space that I had filled in to make him moved over to my desk.

"Something bad happened, Mosca."

Alexis was crouched over, leaning against the desk, cupping in his hand a cigarette he'd just put out or hadn't yet lit. I didn't move, didn't even sit up, as if staying still would stop what I feared would come next.

"What do you mean?" I said.

"Everything was fine, we met my contacts, exchanged info, but then the police showed up. They knew we'd be there. They spotted me and I ran."

"You—you still went?"

"I need you to do something for me."

"What do you mean? What do you mean they saw you?"

He moved, and the streetlamp lit up half his face. Except for the cigarette, he looked the way he had when he was a kid and was scared and wanted to climb in bed next to me. And it would be fine if he did, if I just said he could.

"I have something important. All the information I've been collecting—a lot of work went into it. The *fachas* don't know I have it. But if they find me with it—"

"Well, get rid of it!"

"I can't. It's too important. Please take it, just for a few days. They don't know about it, and they don't know anything about you."

"Get rid of it—get rid of it right now," I said.

"Look, Mosquita, I'm leaving soon, and I'm taking it with me. But I need you to hide it first."

He'd set a box on the desk. Just bigger than a small bag of flour, one dented cardboard corner catching the light. I didn't want to see it. He was desperate or he wouldn't have asked.

I sat up, though I didn't get out of bed, wanting to keep as much distance between me and this thing as possible. "What about Marco? Can't you ask him? Did they see him, too?"

"No, they didn't see him!" His voice suddenly cracked in anger. "Look—just fuck Marco. You stay away from him."

"La Canaria?" I said. Her name made him flinch, I could see that even in the dark. "She'd do it for you—and even if you're split now, you'll get together next week."

"She doesn't know anything about this," he said.

"She doesn't have to. Just give it to her—don't tell her what it is."

"She doesn't know anything about this, and it stays that way."

He wanted to protect her. Maybe it was his desire to protect her over me that made me refuse.

"No," I said. "Just throw it in the river. And get out of here. You need to leave. You'll be safe if you leave."

"It's small, just keep it for a few days. You have to."

"No," I said again. "I won't. Leave me alone."

"Please, Carla."

He said my name, my real name, which no one had called me for years. But I thought of our abuela praying for our parents. I didn't want to be another laminated card on her shrine.

"You said you would help," he said.

I turned my face to the wall. I heard him pick up the package. There was a long pause and the sound of him moving across the room. The door opened and closed.

Grito was in the water, and I must have run to him, reached for him, and fallen in myself, though I don't remember. All I remember is seeing Alexis, clearly, deep in the snow. Then La Canaria screaming and the water, the water like nothing water could be. Change could come without warning, a storm arrive to kill us, and tomorrow it wouldn't even be there. The snow must have been melting, making the water stronger, making it more, it must have been more, to be so much. Warmth on my arm and ice scraping across my face. Marco grabbing my arm and whispering, "I've got you, I've got you, just you." He'd been saying this for so long, that there were two of us to save and he got only one.

Grito wasn't where he'd been in the water—there was only water and ice breaking around us. We ran down the bank of the river. If Grito was in the water, we couldn't see him, we kept running, the branches and the snow stopping us, feet sinking, the shoes that had never fit getting caught, dropping off. We were mimes, so hilarious, the snow muffling us, too scared to speak, trying to move fast and falling. Grito moving beneath the water or caught somewhere, stuck when we rushed on. Perfect globes of air floating through the black water, going up and no way to push them back in, they would not go back in though his mouth was open, though he was trying to bring them back. Dark, darker than any night under his sheets because there were always streetlights, under the ice the snow covering the ice only water and not clear, filled with everything the water wanted to be filled with except light.

When we found him, his body curled around a branch brought there in the same way, his thin arm bobbing in a break in the ice, we didn't know how long he'd been there. How long we'd been pantomiming through the snow. How close or far we'd been from saving him.

Marco grabbed his arm, and with La Canaria's help, we dragged him out of the water. Grito lay there in the snow, his face swollen and his sweater torn and clinging to his skin, leaving parts exposed and purpling. Sheep bleated above us; we wondered how far we were from the farm, from anyone. The sheep could be lost, too, they could be stuck, faced with their own inescapable mass of weakness, blood that can spill and soft marrow. Grito's skin shifted at our touch, a mood ring's waves of pigment responding to heat. There was perhaps a pulse inside him, breath that knew we were there. If we can get him warm, if we can get him dry. Marco grabbed his wrists, and me his feet, but we couldn't move forward that way, the snow was too deep. We took turns dragging him. We didn't know where we were going, and he was too heavy. Getting darker, the trees rushing up to meet us, appearing silent and solid against the anti-night of snow.

Two weeks after I refused to help Alexis, the police brought his medallion to our door.

I wish I could say that was the last time I saw him: when I stared at the blank void of his body and refused. But Abuela made us lunch the next day and he laughed, placing his hands too hard on her shoulders without knowing it. Only I noticed her quick wince and knew that even if she were someone who complained about physical pain, she would never do anything that would stop him from laughing. He even joked with me, imitating the ridiculous way I walked when carrying my heavy backpack, doing a perfect impression of my English accent. When he didn't leave town, I lied to myself that he'd figured a way out of what he was in. I thought he'd destroyed the box and that was enough. That it hadn't been that important. He'd blown it up because of the dark, because of whatever he was on, because his mind had turned toward that thought and refused to turn away.

But when the police came with his medallion, I knew. I knew he hadn't been angry because he'd already known what would happen. He had slipped that night from their black leather gloves and cement interrogation rooms, he'd run home through the dark streets, but they would come, they would find him. He knew what he had chosen.

The problem with a body is that it's entirely inescapable. It is entirely before you and you can't cover it and it weighs so much.

We never found Grito's body. I lied about that, too.

I later dreamed we did, dreamed there was even life left in it. I could see myself carrying him as we searched in the snow, but he slipped beneath the water and we stumbled after him, following the river as much as we could, not daring to get too close. He must have hit his head because we saw him go under and he didn't come up again. Trees brought down by past floods or forgotten by loggers lay across our path. They reached back into the forest, their branches spiraling upward beyond our sight. For hours we screamed Grito's name, until it was the only sound echoing back at us, arching across the mountains, and then we stopped speaking, still going forward. The road appeared silently beneath our feet and we almost crossed it without knowing. But La Canaria grabbed my arm and held it, waiting until I heard the sound, too. A small white van, narrow and high, drove slowly toward us, flashing its lights. My vision was only light and darkness, no stars, no sign of the river, on then off, on then off, for I didn't know how long. Marco was about to disappear back into the gulch, to keep going after something we'd lost, we didn't know where. I grabbed his wrist and his arm felt wobbly, unhinged.

"Marco," I said, feeling sound pass through my mouth after

so much silence, noticing the shape of his name on my tongue for the first time. He turned around and looked down at his arm where I was holding him.

I wanted to push him back into the gully, watch him skitter into darkness, fall into the water with Grito and everything else I'd lost. Marco who had stood by Alexis and yet couldn't stop everything that happened next. Marco who knew I didn't go and what I was. I thought I would crush his wrist. It takes as much pressure to bite through a human finger as it does a carrot.

Marco pulled his hand away from me. He knew what I wanted. "I can't feel it," he said. "Where you were touching me." In the headlights I could see his hand was white with splotches of yellow, blood retreating from the fingers and allowing the flesh to freeze. "You're soaking wet, Mosca."

The van door opened and we got in.

We drove, back and forth on the same roads or different ones, we didn't know, jumping out of the car to stare and scream into the dark until the driver said no more, either we would go where he was going or we would be left in the snow. La Canaria shut the door tight against the cold. We couldn't bar what else entered. We left nothing behind, and what followed us was all that remained of the thin and pitiful world I'd made.

PART II

THE BLOOD AND
THE ALPHABET

I thought they would come up from the cobblestones, the basements of high-rises, out of the sand at the edge of the city gates. But the dead come from the walls, warmed all day by the filtered light of this drowned city. If they were really dead, they'd rise from their graves, but they aren't really dead. They never were. Delicate Phoenician wives and Moro children who look more like us than we'll ever admit. They feed the dirty cats and kick pigeons. They bring coffee to your blind aunt and she thinks it's you. They are unmistakable from everyone else.

Sometimes I see others like me. Walking through their private layers or stoking themselves up to head to a train station or plaza, any sort of crowd. I see them waiting in a group inside an empty hotel. Their faces are sky with clouds moving across. I ask them what they're doing, but no one can tell me. I don't know if they're lost, too, or if it's only me. It's a different city for each of us. Some are in pain and some are frightened and some are followed.

Not everything here is abandoned or broken, some places are so full of life it sucks you in. It takes a certain amount of holding on to not disappear into them—the crowds at the open-air market or circling a courthouse. It must be what it's like to gnaw your leg out of a trap. The need to do it, knowing you don't have the strength. Some stay all day in the crowded spaces, where life is too strong to keep to its own side. They walk around, trying to touch a living person's hair, trying to get the guts.

I walk into a room or down an alley and see all the things I've done. The city's walls are so thin. You can slip right into a new room without even noticing. Eating with Mosca in our abuela's apartment. Drinking with Marco outside the cathedral. Dancing under the streetlights with La Canaria. Many layers, many times it's happened. The room has this ability to hold all you're capable of—your whole life—between those thin walls. I open the door to Mosca's room. I tell some assholes I'll do a job for them. Even things that happened only once have layers. I can see everything I've ever done reflected in those few words. Boiled down into a thirty-second paste. I can taste it. I spit it out, and it floats in a white cloud through the water around me. Some days I just want to stay still, to keep that taste off my tongue. It slips in anyway. I open a door. I'm carrying something I don't want to. I'm bringing it to Mosca.

Mosca is looking for me. It's not me she sees. Don't you know that? I try writing, hoping my words will get through. I search for phones with her on the other end. I try to get the phone just before the first ring. It happened once in Casasrojas, when I was trying to call Abuela to say I'd be out late, and Mosca picked up the phone before it rang. I could hear her pausing, looking up a number in her notebook and biting on her lip, which she did when she was deciding something. She didn't know I was on the other end of the line. It was nice to listen to her that way, when there was nothing we had to be saying to each other. I hung up so she could make her call. I try to catch that moment now. I walk through the city picking up phones, searching for an opening to where Mosca is. I need to reach her soon.

The city is a sunken harbor. One lifetime built on top of another. Built on unburied bones. Layers of white stone, femurs as mortar. The city is an extension not strong enough for its own weight. The final crust on the edge of a peninsula, stuck out at the edge of the ocean like a dare—the kind that you know you won't live through but that you go for anyway because you're young and you don't give a shit and there's no backing down. But the city is old. It keeps daring itself not to bury its dead. It grows on them. And it keeps growing, stretching into the water. It exists in every city. It's almost the same city but with the thinnest film layered over, just enough to gray all surfaces, just enough to allow me to speak.

When we finally got to Paris—after weeks of slow thawing that never really completed, days when we turned around to bum a ride in the opposite direction and tried to find our way back up that mountain and to the river where we'd lost him, days when we didn't eat and our clothes were soaked from walking in melting snow and sleeping on wet ground, waking and walking again because we were shaking too hard to sleep, days I can barely remember because I was not completely alive during them—La Canaria opened her brass cricket box that I'd plucked from the coals in the mountains outside Casasrojas. It was empty of money, but folded at the bottom was a piece of paper with an address carefully written on it. The address of the apartment we were going to squat in and the meager culmination of our plans. Paris, Paris, the word had bullied me even through the freeze. La Canaria held the scrap in front of my face. The crowds of tourists jostled around us. The paper was creased and the ink blurred. I read it again and again, as if I could find something more in the few words but also because they took so long to harden into legible shapes. Finally she let the paper drop. It fell on my boots and we stared at it. Marco slowly bent to pick it up. At one time he would have caught it before it fell.

It wasn't hard to find the apartment. A huge gray stone building just off one of the wide boulevards. A wealthy neighborhood, close to all the museums and in the very center of the city. The front had a marble staircase and a doorman and balconies with bright red geraniums. We sneaked around to a side alley with small windows and narrow doors used only to carry out dirty laundry. We climbed a back fire escape to the top floor. Through the window we could see a large bathroom and hall, but we kept climbing to the very top, a garret right beneath the roof. The window there was smaller, and the casings hadn't been replaced in decades. It was too dirty to see through and held shut by a rusty latch. I used a knife La Canaria had taken from a roadside café to force it open. Inside was only a bare room, a water closet—the door didn't quite close—and a cracked enamel basin that cold cloudy water spurted into. On the floor was a mattress and an old phone, its dial tone intermittent. It must have been a servants' quarters once. A low door in a corner opened to steep stairs going down. Marco tried the door at the bottom of the stairs, but it was barred from the other side and wouldn't budge.

We didn't care what led beyond that door. We'd spent all we had left getting there. Climbing the metal fire escape, I felt like the bottom of a ceramic bowl—Paris, Paris, the voice scraped inside me. No other cities mattered. And yes, we were finally in Paris, but I was hollowed out, and any effort racked me with a grating peal. No one would see us come in and out through the fire escape. The room was all we needed.

Once inside, La Canaria wiped the grime off the window with a scrap of newspaper crumpled up in the corner. Over the buildings you could see the Tuileries garden: rectangles of blurred green sectioned off neatly by gray pathways and speckled with dots of people. It was the height of the summer tourist season and hot in the room. She laughed a cold bark. The only sound I'd heard out of her all day. It was early evening, but we fell asleep as soon as she closed the window. We all slept on the mattress, as far away from one another as we could.

In the morning I walked north, to Montmartre. It was where Alexis had said he would go that afternoon in Casasrojas when he held an empty handgun to his temple. Paris the target and the Sacré-Coeur Basilica the bull's-eye, where he said he'd be waiting for me so long ago. I'd retraced that memory so often that it had worn out completely. It was more a gap than anything else. But Alexis speaking, his voice, remained, and I could feel the letters in my blood. I slipped out of the room while La Canaria and Marco were sleeping. We still hadn't spoken a word.

I went slowly, taking side streets and stopping in alleys. It was midday by the time I met the steep hills and the dark-even-in-daylight cafés packed with students. I'd told myself when I was leaving the room that morning that if Marco or La Canaria woke up, I'd say to them I was going to get food. But I couldn't eat. I'd walked and walked, curving slowly around narrow corners and into dank alleys. We had hardly eaten while we hitchhiked to Paris. Every time I opened my mouth, I saw Grito's mouth opening and river water rushing in. Food made me worse than nauseated and played a trick on my throat more horrible than a gag.

Down a narrow street I saw a patch of color—red poppies and yellow mullein—and followed the color to a section of train tracks lined on either side with makeshift gardens. Behind the flowers and drying vegetable growth, the cement walls were covered in graffiti. Mostly murals, a fake Aztec sun and women planting sunflowers that bloomed in the shape of hearts, cheesy hippie stuff they probably took for granted here but which still felt slightly dangerous to me.

I walked the narrow series of tunnels and passageways that lined that section of the tracks, picking my way through overgrown melons, broken glass, and the sodden pads of cardboard someone had been sleeping on, my fingers trailing the cement walls. No voice seeped through, nothing but echoes I knew were my own straining. You can make sounds in your head if you want to and know only after they've passed that you've turned a truck backing up into an old lullaby, a feral cat yowling into a voice calling your name. The one word I was looking for was nowhere among the graffiti and murals. My fingers collected only soot.

I walked back into the streets in the condensed light of late afternoon and, on the buildings and outside of museums, read the history of the arrondissement: It had declared itself its own country a century ago, a barricaded, bloody little island of attempted democracy. I touched a brass plaque on the corner of a stone building that detailed how thirty laundresses had held the army back.

It took me all day to get the guts to walk up the basilica steps. It was such a white, unblemished building, rising like a blister over the steep hills. When Alexis had mentioned it in Casasrojas, I hadn't understood why he would go there, but thinking of those laundresses, I figured he must have wanted something like that. A battle in the streets that was remembered, mythologized, set to music. Not that he cared much about whether he himself was remembered, but I think he wanted his fight to be something you could talk about, not just a hollow, grown in on itself and silent.

The steps leading to the domed cathedral were covered with painters and tourists and couples making out and little kids in matching summer shorts racing one another up and down, but the stones were scrubbed clean of every mark and every face unrecognizable. Everywhere I looked was so empty of what I was searching for that the basilica steps might have been vacant, rid of all people and pigeons, rid even of the cathedral. The entire city was like a smooth blank page too heavy to turn.

"Well, we're here," La Canaria said when I climbed back into the room. It was late, maybe midnight. Even with the bare bulb hanging from the ceiling turned on, a foggy dark ring hung around my vision. "Now what?"

"Excuse me?" Marco said. He was lying on the mattress looking up at the ceiling, moving his hand in and out of the light. It was a position similar to one he'd struck those days in Madrid—like he was waiting to move on but didn't care either way. The act felt different in that room.

"Now what?" La Canaria repeated, not bothering to look at Marco. "We're in Paris, which was the big plan, so now what?"

Marco started laughing. I flinched at the sound and so did La Canaria. It echoed off the tight walls of the room, no hallways or furniture to soak it up. He rolled over, the sound ricocheting out of him and onto the floor. When he was out of breath, he still rocked back and forth silently, an awful smile plastered on his face. Finally he wiped tears from his eyes—his nose had started running—and looked up at me. "Yeah, Mosca. Now what?"

I knew he regretted his words immediately, but he had started speaking and simply couldn't be stopped.

"Are you going to call her?" Marco whispered.

"What are you talking about?" I said, not looking at him. "Who?"

"Who?" he suddenly shouted. "Who? Grito's fucking abuela,

that's who! Who is going to tell her we let him die in a fucking river?"

"Shut up, you *pendejo,* I'm not calling her."

"This was your plan, Mosca! You got us here!"

"It wasn't my plan!" I backed away from him until I was pressed against the wall, the window shooting hot night air against my neck.

"Then whose was it?" La Canaria sneered.

"You want to go back to Casasrojas, La Canaria?" I said. Marco's words had loosed the words within me. I, too, couldn't stop them. "The police are looking for you. You don't know anyone. Your little deal—whatever it was—has dried up. You really want to go back?"

La Canaria flicked me off. "You have no fucking idea."

"Marco, you should go home. Slither home to your *facha* father and slip right back in. You probably have a good job waiting for you if you grovel enough—"

"Shut up," Marco said.

"It wasn't my plan and it's not my fucking fault! It's your fault, you *facha*!"

"Don't call me that!"

"That's what you are! You're the reason the police knew who we were! You're the snitch!"

"Don't call me that! I didn't tell anyone anything!"

"You didn't need to," La Canaria said slowly and quietly. "Just being what you are is enough."

Marco turned away from us, crouched against the wall and waiting for another blow, but I was silent.

I drew in air like I'd been held underwater, and the air hurt, too. I'd said what Grito had said, his exact words, and though I couldn't speak his name, it was like I'd heaved his body, waterlogged and decayed, between us.

La Canaria relaxed her clenched fists and held her hands up and out, empty palms tilted toward the ceiling.

I climbed back out the window and down the fire escape. We didn't have anything else to say.

On the final rung, I froze, one foot stretched out into empty air. La Canaria was right. Paris was where any semblance of a plan ended. Since the bonfire, we'd been aimless, but it had been possible to pretend we were having fun, that messing up was an end in itself and even if it wasn't, who cares, we wanted it. But that particular masquerade ended when Grito fell through the ice.

The cities were just a lie I'd told myself—that I could find Alexis, that I could undo what I'd done. But when I saw him on the edge of the river, I knew I couldn't. It didn't matter what memories I swirled up from the mud. Skipping my final exams couldn't erase the exam I'd taken when I should have been helping him. The space I'd created on the mountain after the bonfire had no power. It was just a wasted brown field. It could undo nothing. I thought I'd seen him in Madrid, thought that with Borgi's words perhaps I could find him in Paris, but when he stood on the snowy riverbank, I knew he was gone.

The road had ended in darkness, not just a break in pavement but the path split clean as the end of a dock. We could have gone back to Casasrojas or Madrid, left the continent, gotten jobs, done something, yet hanging from the broken stretch of dock was a rope dropping down into pitch. I grabbed hold of the rope and, eyes closed, began my descent.

"Mosca!" Marco called out when I got to the bottom of the fire escape.

The window with his face reaching out of it was like a swinging golden pendant against the night sky. I didn't answer him. I turned away from the ladder and started walking into the dark. We had nowhere to return to and nowhere to go.

PARIS
January 1978

Months dropped out from under us, the rest of summer and fall. I opened my eyes and it was winter and nothing had changed except we were skinnier and the room was cold. We didn't talk about what we feared or what we would do next. Instead we tried to anticipate the need for speech, rotating who went out to get food, who rolled the cigarettes that made us need less of it. We did nothing except keep off the steepest edge of hunger, the kind that would let us stall completely, let us slip into stillness. We were parts on a body, moving without speech but unconnected, too, loosed from any sense of common organ. That common organ was known, though we didn't name it. It had curdled, preformed, in our throats. We didn't think about Grito. We were gray with not thinking about him. Lonely anemone all attached to the same rock, tendrils shooting off in different directions, colorless beneath water beneath clouds.

After a few months, La Canaria found a job that paid nothing and lost it, found another job that paid nothing and lost it. Her last job, she complained to the boss that one of the stockers kept grabbing her in the back room and the boss asked to see her papers. She didn't want to work after that. Her ankles were swollen, and what food we had she could barely keep down.

Marco and La Canaria seemed foggy to me. Sometimes

there'd be a carton of cold fries or half a grilled ham sandwich sitting on the mattress for me when I got back inside, but sometimes there wouldn't be anything and I wouldn't eat all day.

Marco's money was running out. La Canaria said he should ask for more, but she also told me she couldn't imagine anything really being his, certainly not anything as powerful and as real as the money a family like his must have. I felt the same. Nothing seemed to belong to Marco. His grip was tentative, easily unmoored. He couldn't even kill himself right. He couldn't even own that. Except for the night when he was on his horse—but the horse wasn't something that could really be his.

The city was empty of Alexis. No tags, no one knew him. I could feel that emptiness clinging to my insides more than I could feel my hunger or the cold. I spoke his name again and again—to the too-clean punks, to the vacant-eyed men who slept on the streets. Who would trust me? I followed half-formed thoughts and hunches, but I said his name too many times. It became a lie, hollowed out and rattling inside me.

We had moved so quickly. Marco, La Canaria, Grito, and I. Through cities and over borders. A blur impossible to slow in present tense and clarify. We had moved without reason and we had left behind no memories. No one could say we had been there because we had not been. We were not anywhere. No one could know who first edged our books to the fire. We had smudged even that. But Grito's death had stopped us. A wall stretching up to the sky.

We were lodged where he was, wherever it was we'd left him, under a black log, cold water rushing over our heads.

Grito drifted down to join Alexis. There were two names, two different rivers merging, but we hadn't seen either body.

We didn't speak either name. We were frozen in fear, in loss, in longing. How unformed it felt. An impermanent mark, but we could not shake it. Time slipped by like sleep. We dreamed of never waking.

Then something grabbed me by the throat and shook.

January, the streets empty, the tourists returned home, the old people inside away from the cold and the young people left on the first train for their jobs in the city center. The parks had been green when we arrived in the summer, stretching wider and longer than the streets, leading to the palaces turned government buildings, palaces turned museums, palaces that were war relics and allowed to remain palaces. The plane trees had been cut, their summer growth carted away, only stubby knuckles left. A sky heavy enough to collapse.

I thought I'd walked every street, but in the early evening I turned down a street I'd never been on. The sidewalks were empty and it was beginning to get dark. The advertisements coating the brick walls were faded. Children holding up bread with Nutella, their faces turned gray and smiles streaked with green dye from the detergent ad above. At the end of the street I could see railway wires and tracks, but the nearest stop a long way in either direction. A dark matted thing batted up against a corner of the chain-link fence—whether trash or an animal, I couldn't tell.

Maybe it was the walking and hunger and wearing down, a chafing away of the grit and sand of myself until I was a smooth stone as thin and light as a sheath of skin, that made me able to see what I saw. I couldn't really see the streets around me. I couldn't find what I was looking for, I'd never find that, so I saw nothing at all. But being so next to nothing for so long, walking without thoughts or the strength to keep walking, maybe that was how I was able to slip, without noticing it, into somewhere else entirely.

The last shop before the train tracks was set away from the rest. Inside, the store was dark, the merchandise generic, past its expiration date, and cheap.

I grabbed a loaf of stale bread wrapped in paper. Alexis's medallion and La Canaria's bullet were cold when I pulled them out from under my sweater, even though they'd been right by my skin for months.

"Is that how you're going to pay for this?" Alexis said, leaning up against the filmy counter. His hair was short and he was too skinny, but he was smiling. That smile I rarely got to see, that made my abuela walk soft to make it last.

"This is real gold, *macho*," I said. "And this bullet's a war relic. Republican memorabilia." I was trying not to laugh. When he teased me, I could never keep from laughing, even if he was making fun of me.

"Listen, Mosquita, you know I don't care about that Republican memorabilia shit." His smile changed. "Isn't that my medallion?"

"No, it's mine now." I stopped laughing.

"Where are you?" I said. "Tell me where you are."

The store was empty. I'd crawled in through the broken boards on the windows. A car's passing lights lit up the dusty air. No one had been in there for months. I found a dented sardine tin under one of the empty shelves and crawled out the way I had come.

I didn't know what I had just seen; Alexis, yes, as solid as I'd seen him on the river when Grito fell in, as alive as in my dreams. But I didn't know what it meant. I'd seen him once and thought it proof he was beyond finding. Seeing him again, a different space opened, a different possibility. I couldn't name it, but I lurked around the space, waiting for an opening.

I climbed the fire escape, shaking and scared that what I'd seen was smeared all over me. More, I felt that I had been skinned, and when I climbed through the window Marco and La Canaria would see not a skinny girl in dirty clothes but a flayed thing, rotted and not worth picking at. But Marco barely looked up at me, and La Canaria was asleep on the mattress.

Marco crouched on the floor, counting his money to come up with the amount we had to live on the next day. The number kept getting smaller. I sat down next to La Canaria on the mattress. Heat uncoiled slowly off her body and I wanted to relax into it. We slept next to each other, but we slept as if separated by mile-high bundling boards, tense and not touching. Moving close to her might help me warm up, but if I did, I'd only get cold again, and that return wasn't worth it. Better to stay numb than to know the details of your frostbite.

Marco stared at the money. His fingers were dirty. Washing meant splashing cold water from the sink onto body parts already recoiling from exposure. He seemed to be diminishing as the money did, whittling down to not much at all.

But I could see him clearly for the first time in months. Sweat-stained clothes, rings of grime around his neck. He spread his coins out on the wood floor like a magician setting up a trick with cards. I wanted to reach out and touch him—and the feeling was so strong and surprising I winced.

"Mosca?" he said, as if he could hear that want, something

he'd been tense listening for. It had been so long since someone had said my name out loud. It was just one word, but he was looking at me, when he said it, hoping for a response.

I turned away as if I hadn't heard him. If there were a bridge between us, neither of us was in shape to cross.

La Canaria pushed herself up on the mattress. She seemed different, too. Maybe after what I had seen, maybe something else had changed.

"Why don't you just get more?" she said.

"What?" Marco said.

"Get more. Money."

"I can't," he said.

"Why not?"

He stacked the coins into a pile and pushed them over to the phone. "Because there isn't any more. My parents have been broke for years. What I took from the house—what he—in Madrid—that was all that was left."

I got up early the next morning and said I would try to find us something to eat. I always said that, and no one believed me. Out on the streets my eyes strayed toward graffiti-coated walls or the faces of homeless kids clumped at the edge of markets, looking for familiar slouching shoulders. If I'd seen him the night before, perhaps I could see him again. La Canaria followed me all day. I didn't pay much attention to her. She was good at finding spare change, knowing who to ask for a light and get a whole pack. She had changed, thickening in some spots, thinning in others, silent and flashing her teeth when least expected. Out walking, she could become almost transparent, blending with cement and prismed pigeons.

At dusk, I looked through the windows into a café, full of

mirrored light and students in fitted dark clothes, the women with fine leather handbags at their heels. They bent over marbled tables, heads close together. Cigarette smoke, mimicking their words, circled tight and then dissipated. The students listened to the same music we used to, but they had more of it. Record shops advertised all the new albums with uncensored covers. Even the punks seemed cleaner, outfitted in brand-new black jeans and crisp Ramones T-shirts. The girls dressed like Jane Birkin, miniskirts and gauzy see-through tops even in winter. Their hair fell long and shining, not from grease but health, over their faces. They smiled coyly down into their steaming mugs of Moroccan mint tea, flashing turquoise rings from Tibet and Arizona.

La Canaria held out the few coins she'd collected, but the café was too nice and our clothes too dirty. I turned back to the crowd skittering from work to home, each person grabbing a baguette or chocolate or a bunch of radishes. I walked toward the street, trying to shake La Canaria, and for a moment the crowd opened.

The people walking didn't notice the opening, but they moved around it just the same. The space was hardly big enough to detect, but I saw it and stopped. In the space were shadows with a heft unlike any shadows I'd seen before. I recognized the smell—rust from the bridge in Casasrojas, aerosol paint, mud at the bottom of a river, and an added scent I couldn't quite place. The shadows got thicker until I stepped inside them.

I looked back at the crowd, and it was gorged with people. Not just the ones I'd seen from the sidewalk. Scrawny children in homespun rags, hobbling men in old-fashioned suits. They were faded slightly, these new figures, and they walked around and into buildings that no longer existed. There were layers of them, growing on top of one another, squished together and weightless. More, the more I looked, centuries of life moving over the stones. I opened my mouth to speak, hoping that one, just one of them, would turn to me and hear, but no sounds came out.

La Canaria grabbed my arm and pulled me back against the café window. "What are you doing?" she said.

"What?" I felt dazed, like I'd been pulled from a deep sleep.

"You were talking to yourself."

I was still stunned, but I didn't bother trying to fight her. "What did I say?"

"Nothing I could hear." She looked back at the spot where I'd been, but the opening was gone. An old couple walked through where the shadows had swirled, their scarves tucked neatly into fur coats and shoulders bent against the wind.

"Come on, you fucking *loca*," she said. "Let's get back. I'm cold."

We climbed the fire escape, familiar with its creaking rungs, which ones were slippery, which rusted weak. The room smelled like an unwashed mouth, and the air was emptied of anything but hunger. But Marco didn't ask us for food. He barely saw us enter. He was pacing the room, banging his head against the wall and then spinning around like a doll. On the walls, at the level of his head, were small ovals of grease where his forehead had landed on the grimy plaster. He slapped a rolled-up newspaper against his thigh.

I helped La Canaria through the window. Her sweater caught in a piece of broken wood on the pane. I tugged at it and it ripped. We both lost our balance for a second, and when I turned around, Marco was centimeters from my face, holding up the newspaper and grinning anxiously. "You must have seen this?" he said.

La Canaria jumped down from the window and focused on her sweater, but she backed up almost imperceptibly from him.

"You did, didn't you?" he said, moving closer to us.

"See what, Marco?" I said. I couldn't decide whether to stick by La Canaria or try to get out the window.

"The news, the news—"

"Marco!" La Canaria snapped her head up. "Just shut up and sit the fuck down."

It was the old La Canaria speaking for a moment, fully in her body and voice, commanding, not questioning. Marco crumpled onto the floor. He opened the newspaper on the floor and folded it so that only one article was visible. He pressed and pressed the paper with his palms, smoothing the pages and blurring the ink. I turned to La Canaria, but she was her faded half-self again, looking out the window, no trace of the voice that had calmed Marco.

I knelt beside him and stared at the article. I read aloud: "'The performance art group that was arrested in Madrid for weapons possession, arson, and conspiracy has been sentenced to a military tribunal. Citizens hopeful for a democratic resolution to the case—'"

"See?" Marco said.

"We don't know it's them," I said.

"Arrested in Madrid—right after we were there," Marco said. "We have to get out of here. It's not safe for us in the city—too many people can see us."

"No one knows we're here," La Canaria said.

"They will soon. Those punks—they could tell them about us. Borgi knew where we were going," Marco said. He smoothed down the paper. The tips of his fingers were black with ink.

"Even if that's true, what's it to you?" she said. "You're not going to get in trouble over anything."

"They might be looking for you and Mosca," he said.

"And I'm still wondering why you care so much." Her voice was harsh. "Don't let your guilt make you paranoid." La Canaria closed the window and bolted it shut. She ran her fingers around the wooden frame, weak in some spots from mold, and then pressed her face against the dirty glass. I didn't know if she meant guilt over his family or Grito or something else. Marco stood staring at La Canaria, his mouth open and his breath like sharp bird heartbeats. I wanted to touch Marco, to calm him, but I couldn't. It was better to stay as far as possible from each other.

"No one can find us here," I said.

Marco folded the newspaper and then fiddled with the rotary phone he'd dragged into a corner.

Alone, we had believed we were safe. All summer and fall we thought it was only together, speaking to one another, that we created a door that allowed entry to all we couldn't name. If we stayed apart, the opening would dissipate. Instead it had stretched, forcing us against the damp walls, threatening to fill our lungs with ice water. I recognized that space. The same contours as the widening in the crowd, but this space didn't want to listen, it wanted something from us. We couldn't travel far enough away.

La Canaria opened the window, gasping for air. Exhaust and the scent of fried potatoes entered. It wasn't like she needed something clean. She wanted only to slow what would happen. We both knew the opening would expand to every corner of everywhere we went, until finally, our backs against the last wall, it would go down our throats.

I couldn't sleep. Marco and La Canaria buzzed with life

they'd lacked for months. I needed silence. I needed to understand what I had seen in the opening in the crowd.

I climbed out the window and down the fire escape. Turning the corner out of the alley, I could hear La Canaria landing on the damp pavement behind me.

It was late, but the bars were still open and bodies pressed against each other in the shadows and in doorways, extending goodbyes. I found my way back to the spot on rue Marguerite where the crowd had parted and I'd seen those almost solid shadows. No one was on the street. The streetlight reflections felt encased in pearl, contained in the puddles on the sidewalks, the brass doorknobs and plated windowpanes. Always a drop of water for light to bounce off, or a gilded corner, a white-domed roof. But all the light made the street feel colder and less alive, like shopwindow mannequins illuminated past closing.

I stood right where I had stood and waited, opened my mouth and tried to speak. But nothing came out. Damp air swirled in my mouth, but there were no special words; there was no torque in my tongue that would hinge the opening I sought. The street held shadows but not with the ones I'd seen when the crowd parted.

I kept walking, trying to shake La Canaria, but she followed me without shame. I ducked into one of the Métro stairways leading underground though I didn't have enough money to ride the subway. But there, on the wet stairs leading underground, circling just within reach, were the shadows I'd seen in the crowd. I stepped down, afraid to get too close. The air coming from the shadows was different from the air of the subway—dank and damp, yes, but the shadow air smelled like rust instead of urine, like salt and the sea. The shadows swirled over the steps, and I knew they were an entryway to a much deeper passage. I saw what I had seen before, hundreds, thousands, of filmy shapes, ghosts walking up and down the subway steps, pushing, slipping on broken stairs that had been mended decades ago, hurrying to homes long burned or bombed.

I opened my mouth and my lips moved as they never had, speaking to Marco or La Canaria or the name lost beneath the ice. A weight passed over them with each syllable, an ancient language I was only just learning, the words themselves painful to shape. The shadows were earth-black, deepest water–dark, cold and briny. I wanted to speak to them. I wanted them to listen. I had a message for them to carry.

Back in the room, I curled up on my corner of the mattress. La Canaria eased through the window I'd left open for her, but she didn't speak to me. I closed my eyes. I didn't sleep; instead I traced my steps that day. With my eyes closed, I saw it as a different city. Covered with a shadowy film, coated with layers of the shadows I'd seen. That city was still deep below me. I had a long way to descend, but the shadows showed me that I'd found the entryway. I was going down.

I opened my eyes to see La Canaria leaning out the window. She breathed in distance rather than air and pulled a small mirror from her pocket. I knew what she was doing—trying to re-create the language I had spoken in the subway stairwell. There was a length of syllables—a single word, though she didn't know it yet—that I had repeated. The streetlight lit the mirror, giving a distorted glimpse of her mouth and tangled hair, nothing more. La Canaria tried to move her mouth as I had done. Again and again she twisted it toward the shape, hesitating at first, then adding sound, until slowly, slowly, Alexis's name began to form on her tongue.

Grito had loosened something in me. It had taken time for this object, once affixed, now straying, to surface, but it had. And then it was all I could touch and see. It was movement, a drive that might break me. It didn't care. When Grito fell beneath the ice, I'd seen the disappearance instead of just waiting on a void that didn't fill. He opened up a crack into that world for me to pass through. I had slipped somewhere I had not been invited, and yet it was the place I was seeking. The shadows had woken me, but I was not in the same place anymore. And I felt not joy or gladness but a surety from it, a response so foreign that it took a while to notice the taste in my mouth.

Because Grito had been wrong. No one is a shard of sound bouncing off rocks. You can't chop off limbs and expect to remain whole. Grito gone and we were only soft tissue tearing. It was Alexis I saw on the riverbank, if only just a part of him, an echo, a shadow or shade, and what I saw in the subway tunnels was the same. Hobo markings on friendly houses, they would lead me to him. I was more in my world than theirs, but I had crossed into a blurred perimeter. I knew Alexis wasn't in Paris or Madrid or any of the cities I'd polished in my throat. He was somewhere else. And if finding him meant tracking the shadows into their depths, into the city I saw when I closed my eyes, let La Canaria follow me. I never knew anyone who wanted to stay alive more than she did. Let her be my tether back.

Alexis? I said to those shadows. Where is he?

How do I bring him back?

The streetlights were on and it had just rained—cold and pestering drops on my face and shoulders. The fire escape ladder was slick under my hands, almost too numb to grip the rungs. I still had only the work boots Berta had given us. They were sturdy, but the soles had thinned from my months of walking, and my feet slipped unpredictably inside them. I moved methodically up the ladder, slowly releasing one hand at a time and then closing it on the next rung, knowing no one would come looking if I fell and that an injury was not something my body could support.

I eased open the window, but the room was empty.

I'd never noticed how small it was. More of a closet than a room, and we had been living there for months. The room stank of rancid grease from fried potatoes and our sweat. It felt as small as it did because it was empty, as empty as it had been when we first climbed in through the window. Marco's red backpack, La Canaria's jean jacket, the sleeping bag from the farm, they were all gone. The dwindling stack of coins and bills was gone, too.

I could hardly register it. I'd been lopped off. True that we hadn't interacted much in those months, but Marco and La Canaria were the only people I'd spoken to since Berta sent us into the snow. The only living people. I kicked the phone and watched the two pieces of the headset split apart. One skittered across the room to land in the opposite corner. The phone was made of hard old-fashioned plastic. It didn't shatter when my foot hit it, just came apart. I picked up the errant piece and stuck it back on the headset. I held the dial tone up to my ear. It clicked on and off, like someone on the same line was trying to make a call. The plastic nestled comfortably back in its cradle. I did a quick sweep of the room, but there was no trace besides our smell that we had been there. I left the window open so that, too, would fade.

I climbed back down the ladder. The rain had started again, but it had a sweeter fall, more like mist rising off the pavement. I didn't know where I was going next. There was nowhere else I could go, no one else I knew. I didn't want to go back to the room. It wasn't pride but a feeling that it was haunted by their leaving.

Below me, there was the sound of sneakers on the pavement. A cat or a rat moved out from under a cardboard box that had blown into the alley after the last storm. I stayed where I was on the ladder, a few rungs from the bottom. The figure moved closer to me, but I didn't go up or down. It was too dark to see the ladder or anyone on it until you were right next to it. That had made the alley a perfect entryway. With the rain, it was too dark to see anything. The footsteps got closer. I closed my eyes. I should have moved up the ladder, jumped down, done something. A hand closed around my ankle like it was reaching for the first rung. I kicked it off and screamed.

"Mosca?" Marco called into the dark.

I jumped off the ladder and landed on the wet pavement, slipping a little. "You *comemierda*," I said.

"What are you doing here?" he said.

I walked out of the alley and onto the sidewalk. I wanted to see his face to make sure he was real. His voice was raspy from a cough he'd had for a few weeks. The streetlight lit his face, so much skinnier than before. Rain had soaked his hair as if he'd been out walking for a long time.

"I didn't get the memo," I said. "You know, the one that said you were gonna ditch me?"

"Ditch you—what are you talking about?"

"Did you forget your hair comb, maybe some cologne?" I wanted to be sarcastic, but it took too much energy. I turned and started to walk away.

"Mosca, wait, what are you talking about?"

"You left me—" I said.

"We talked about this today." He grabbed my arm and spun me around. "La Canaria heard one of the maids say that the owner is coming back. We had to get out of the room before he got there. We decided this morning where to go—"

I turned away from him, hoping my confusion and the blush that came with it were masked by the darkness. His words pulled something up, but it was unclear whether that was an actual memory or what the words themselves had shaped.

"We decided—Mosca, you don't remember?"

"Of course I remember."

I did once he said it. La Canaria had shoved herself through the window, talking excitedly before she was fully in the room. She'd heard a maid on the balcony below us complain that her boss liked his house just so and she would have to clean every room.

"She'll be coming up here," La Canaria had said. "She hasn't seen us yet, but she will."

"*Joder*." Marco had started pacing again. "What are we gonna do?"

"We'll just go to that country home he's got—he's not going there in the winter."

"Won't it be freezing?" Marco said.

La Canaria shrugged.

I had been there, I had heard them, but it took Marco's words under the streetlight for me to remember it had happened.

"It's just—"

"I know," he said. "It's hard—to keep things straight. It—all of it—wears on you."

He put his arm around me and we were standing close together in the dark, in the warm bowl of the streetlight, the rain coming down or misting up.

"When you were gone in the morning, I looked for you and then went with La Canaria to the mill. I thought maybe you'd gone ahead. Then I came back—I couldn't find you."

He was dripping with rain and his clothes smelled musty, but when I leaned into him, it was as if he had a familiar place buried inside, somewhere healthy and clean, a patch of grass or dry pine needles. He raised his hand to brush my hair from my face—it had hardly grown since summer, just gotten more tangled and split at the ends. So gently, tentative as a fawn, he moved my hair and set his hand, wet but warm, on my cheek. His thumb grazed my frozen earlobe, coaxing it back to life.

I leaned my forehead against Marco's and breathed in his exhales, sour as my own but familiar. My arm circled beneath his jacket without my asking it to.

"Why even bother coming back?" I said.

"I told him I'd protect you," he said.

The streetlight blackened everything out of its reach. Yet right at the edge of the orange light, I saw a swift-moving shadow. Instead of holding still and beckoning, it hurtled toward me, taking form. I turned away from Marco, his arm falling from my shoulders like I'd shrugged it off, turned to face the approaching shadow, but it disappeared the second I stared at it full-on.

"I don't need your protection," I said, and moved away from him, searching for the shadow. "Why are you still chasing someone who doesn't care about you? What do you owe him?"

"Just let me take care of you, stop walking, let me—"

"Next time you want to leave," I said, "have the guts to actually do it."

Marco was offering me his hand, off the rope and onto solid ground, or onto something, at least, large enough for us both to stand on. But I wasn't going to take it.

* * *

The mill was on the outskirts of Paris, an hour on the local train, in a small, fading village. It was freezing when we got inside, the building not meant to be occupied in winter. Marco fiddled with some switches on the wall, but instead of lights turning on, there was a low groan and the creak of iron on wood from behind a stone wall.

"That must be the old waterworks," Marco said. "I don't think it's connected to anything now."

"Leave it on," La Canaria said. She stood in front of an ancient fireplace, thin smoke moving around her. The fireplace was big enough to step into, with thick iron bars across it for hanging pots. The whole building hummed from the grinding turbine.

Marco handed me an old blanket. The dampness hung tightly to us. Above us, a staircase climbed toward the vaulted ceiling and led to hallways and rooms. It probably would have made more sense to stay in one of those rooms, but most of the doors were locked and I couldn't stand the idea of being in an enclosed space after those months in Paris.

"How long do you think we can stay here?" I asked Marco.

"I guess until that guy shows up. Which could be anytime."

I slept all night and most of the next day curled by the fire on a pile of blankets and sofa cushions. It was already dark by the time I woke, evening come early so deep in winter.

Marco handed me a cigarette he'd rolled, and I lit it on the low coals.

"What are you going to do?" I asked him. He stared at my cigarette, which was canoeing toward my lips. He licked his finger and killed the ember.

I both wished and dreaded someone would ask me what I wanted. Would ask me anything, because then the air bubbles might escape from my throat and into the water, my words unable to be shoved back down.

"I don't want to stay here," Marco said, looking up at the ceiling of dark interlaced wood. La Canaria had crossed to the kitchen and stood staring at the black window.

"And then what?" I asked.

He opened his mouth, and I thought I'd done to him what I feared would be done to me. That words and air would come out of his mouth and water would rush in to fill the vacuum and there would be no way for me to reverse the process, to exchange air for water. I thought that he was finally going to speak.

"There's someone at the door," La Canaria said.

"Just ignore them," I said. I was trying to act the way I thought she would. To slink on that bravado and act like anyone who was watching was too mesmerized to move. But she was tamped down and had been for months, giving me no mirror. She went to the door and opened it. Marco took my arm and pulled me into the shadows, where the light from the fire didn't touch us. I wanted to stand up to hear what La Canaria was saying and who she was speaking to, but I was so worn that even the slightest resistance was more than I could fight against. A breath could have blown me down.

"Who is she talking to?" I whispered.

"I don't know—a neighbor? The police?"

"Shut up," I said. "It was stupid to listen to her."

"I didn't hear you say that when we decided to stay at his apartment."

"Then why don't you go back?"

"How can I?" he said. He moved his hand to mine and

opened my clenched fist. Traced his fingers across my palm and then between my knuckles. "Return with your shield or on it."

It should have been easy to say something back to Marco, to react to his fingers hovering over mine as if my skin were too hot to touch. We hadn't lost a shield, we'd abandoned a limb, a self, a friend—that's what Grito was—we couldn't name, to water too cold to speak of, instead we waded through it all night long. I couldn't move my tongue and I couldn't move my arm. I doubted Marco's hand, I doubted any words I might shape, I doubted everything but the slow beat of my pulse and the shadows I saw when I closed my eyes. My words to them, my chase. I saw the room as an undeveloped film of itself—different versions of different shots. Exposed paper about to disappear into a tub of chemicals. Only the red light of the darkroom visible until the images took shape from blankness. Then there were so many choices, a crop here, a different exposure, all a matter of light and perspective, of aperture. These choices in that red room changed who entered the door. First it was whoever owned the mill. He slipped his arm around La Canaria. It took him a moment to notice us, but when he did, he changed and it wasn't he who walked through the door but Marco's mother, holding folders full of papers and screaming. Then Grito came in. Each of these entrances etched on top of the other. They weren't even different shots to choose from but the same strip of film, exposed again and again. Grito's old white shirt was wet. He came in dragging the branches and weeds of the river behind him like those old-fashioned ghosts who carry their sins in labeled chains around their necks. And then it was Alexis rolling a cigarette, lifting his face to the rafters.

La Canaria stepped back inside and closed the door behind her.

"Who was that?" Marco said.

"Just a neighbor," La Canaria said.

"Are they suspicious?"

"Yeah, I think so."

"I don't know how much longer we can stay here," Marco said.

La Canaria laughed, a sharp, broken sound. Her skin hung off the bones in her face. She was yellowed as old ivory worn down by someone's hands.

Marco went outside to see who she'd been talking to. I rubbed my hand and wrist. There was a cold feeling in my palm where his hand had kept me warm. Return with what you came for or why return at all.

I woke again to an early twilight. No one was in the big room at the mill, but I heard something above me. The sound clear but the location uncertain. I climbed the stairs and walked to the end of the narrow hallway at the top of the stairs. The mill was hundreds of years old. The wood stained in a way no varnish could replicate. La Canaria materialized from around a corner, carrying an armful of flattened cardboard and plastic bags of rags and wire. Since we'd gotten to the mill, she hadn't stayed put. She'd wandered around the mill or outside of it, come back with cardboard, cloth, bits of wire, and plastic crates. The geography of the place revealed itself to her. Its halls mirrored the twists of her veins, and she didn't get lost or spooked like Marco and I did.

"What are you doing with all that trash?" I asked.

"Marco coughs too much at night. I'm looking for a place where I don't have to listen to him." She looked flushed and tired.

"But what is all that stuff?"

She moved past me without answering. Perhaps I could not be heard. I no longer knew when I was speaking. If the words actually came out, in what language. She had been close enough to touch me, but instead of warmth, I got only a fetid scent coming off the layers of sweaters she wore. The same scent that lurked behind me when I walked.

"I said, what are you doing with that *mierda*?"

She stopped in the hallway and moved her hands up into her shirtsleeves. She wriggled slowly until both arms were against her torso, sleeves hanging limp.

"Who are you looking for?" she said.

I pushed past her. She couldn't catch her balance and stumbled.

"When you're walking around? Who do you think you're going to find?"

The hallway stretched behind and in front of me. I turned around and she'd disappeared. I hurried down the stairs. Marco was out. The fire a weak, suspended string of smoke. I started to make it again, shivering and not looking behind me. When I was a kid, sometimes I would get scared and scare Alexis just by being scared. Then the only way we could fall asleep was to check every room in the apartment, under the beds, press back the clothing in the closets, check behind the shower curtain, until we were certain no one but our abuela was there. We had to move strategically through the apartment so no one could double back and get into a place we had already looked, a place we thought was now empty. It made it worse, though, thinking of all the places someone could be and all the ways the body could bend and shrink. There was no way I could search the whole mill to make sure no one was there.

I went outside to collect more wood. I crossed the small iron bridge over the dam that directed the river underneath the mill. There were no lights on the street and the outside world was a black curtain, no stars or moon. I don't know how long I stayed out there, long enough to start shivering. I was so pliable—anything was enough to make me forget what I was doing. Through the windows I could see Marco walk into the kitchen and La Canaria follow him, as perfectly lit as a play. He'd been outside and was holding a paper—he must have come in though the back door. I could hear them talking through the leaden glass.

"I think you're afraid of her," La Canaria said.

"That's ridiculous," Marco said. "Why would I be afraid of her?"

"You're afraid she'll find out what you did."

Marco put the paper down on the ancient farm table covered with our trash and cigarette butts. He stared at the glass. I was inches from him, but he couldn't see me. He lit gold by the kerosene lamp, I covered in night. He moved his hands over his face as if smearing his skin. I could tell his hands were cold from how white they were—he'd had to walk a while to steal the newspaper. The pressure from his hands turned his face red. I wanted to stay like that, just for a minute. To read what his face held when he thought he was turned to a black wall, as if I were entering his sleep and walking there with him. But he stepped away from the window.

"What do you know about it?" he said.

I opened the door and they both looked up at me.

"They're killing the whistleblowers." Marco gestured toward the newspaper on the table. "Anyone with information."

"This is your news?" La Canaria said. "They've been doing that for decades. It's the party line."

"This is different," Marco said. I couldn't tell if he was worked up about the news or what Canaria had said. "Remember what they said in Madrid? Before, you accuse an officer of killing a militant, an artist, so what? He'll never face trial. After the elections, they don't know what will happen. They might have to pay for their crimes. They're making sure they'll never have to."

"But what does any of this have to do with you?" La Canaria said. She dug our pouch of tobacco out from under the newspaper and began rolling a cigarette with a page of an old book we'd found upstairs.

"It has nothing to do with us," I said quickly.

"Then stop talking about it. I'm sick of hearing about shit that's happening a million miles away. Unless you did something that you can fix, shut up." She finished rolling the cigarette and walked out the door. Cold air entered and shifted the moldy curtains across from the fireplace. They wavered as if they held a melodrama villain who'd just been found out.

"How much does she know?" Marco said once La Canaria was gone. I cupped my face to the glass and I could see her on the small stone bridge, leaning over the dam. "About what Alexis was doing?"

I stopped moving, my fingers pressed against the windowpane, my breath clouding the small range of vision I'd created. I held my breath and tried to see through the fog. I couldn't remember the last time Marco had said Alexis's name. He stumbled over the sounds, as if both wary to speak them in front of me and unaccustomed to their shape.

"I mean—I think," he started again, voice strained, "I mean—they were broken up when he disappeared. He told me he didn't want her to know about any of it. I don't think she knows what happened—"

"Don't," I said. Marco had crossed a chasm with only a few letters, but I stood unreachable across many more.

"Mosca, we have to figure this out. If there's anything that could link us to the militants Alexis knew."

"We're not even in the same country anymore," I said. "No one cares." I moved my hands away from the glass, slowly straightening up, my movements as controlled as if I were drunk and trying to hide it.

"It's happened before. Remember that writer they poisoned? He was in Chile."

"Yeah, but he was a big deal. He had big secrets," I said. "Names and photos, lots of them."

Marco turned away from me. "The package Alexis had was important, Mosca."

I wanted to ask what he knew, why he was afraid, even here. But I couldn't. I couldn't talk about that night and the part I'd played in its aftermath.

"We need to be careful," Marco said. "We need to figure out what we're doing next. We can't just wait here for something to happen."

I couldn't listen to him anymore. La Canaria came back inside. I moved past her, through the door, and the night fell on me. I could just make out someone leaning against the wall of the mill, shoulders hunched against the cold and smoking a cigarette. Though the night was dark, the shadows seemed to start at that cigarette, as if it were their entry port. Through the windows, Marco and La Canaria bent over the farm table, not speaking, just staring, each into their own empty space.

I walked toward the shadows, but when I crossed to the bridge, there was no one. On the stones was the end of a hand-rolled cigarette, fragile and still damp from landing by the water, still glowing faintly.

Back inside the mill, I wrapped the end in a scrap of newspaper from my pocket and placed it in La Canaria's cricket box. She'd left it in the middle of the tiny room in Paris after all her money from her last job was spent. The box fit in my palm. There was a compactness to it that I liked. So practically made for something so silly. The cigarette end proof of what, I wasn't sure.

"Where did you go today?" Marco came up behind me.

I turned and La Canaria was there, too, as if he wanted a witness.

I didn't answer him. I didn't want La Canaria to hear. Maybe if it were just him, I would have said it or said something else in a way that he would know what I meant. Maybe he already knew. He knew he couldn't follow me on my walks—I would have fought him. And I think he knew that I was very tenderly affixed to him. He had to look at me askance if he wanted to keep me in sight. His grip was so loose as to be almost nonexistent.

La Canaria looked up. She was interested. It was strange to see that expression on her face. She suddenly had awareness of us that she hadn't in so long. She usually looked less like she was listening to us speak and more like she was watching fireflies in a dark room.

"I just walk around," I said, and tried to get past them. They hadn't moved, but they'd created a wall with their questions.

"What are you looking for?" Marco asked. It was the first time he'd confronted me about what I did all day.

"Who," La Canaria said, as if to correct him.

"There's no one I could be looking for," I said.

I'd said the words aloud in Madrid and almost believed them. But when I said them again and knew they were lies, they frightened me all the same. I didn't know how much power words had in the place I'd entered, but speaking them proved that they could be possible—that there could be no one I could find.

Just then there was a knock on the door, and I felt that prickle of damp breath at my neck that I would feel standing in Abuela's apartment and waiting for Alexis to come back. When I would open the door to nothing, the emptiness was as sharp as a hangover landing. This time I didn't turn.

La Canaria walked slowly to the door. Marco stepped toward me once she passed, about to speak, but he held the words in his mouth. La Canaria opened the door.

"Good evening, darling."

My body had lied again. Though he was French, the man spoke almost perfect Castilian. His accent was old-fashioned, as if he'd learned from the first lisping king and was here to show us how it was done. He stepped inside and saw me and Marco for the first time. "Oh my, will you introduce me to your friends?"

La Canaria was silent but grinning. Looking at her, I was looking at someone I'd never met. Her smile dripping like caramelized sugar off flan. Her whole face saturated.

"This is Jean-Paul," she said. "Can you believe he came while we were here? How lucky!"

"A pleasure," Jean-Paul said to me, and kissed my cheek. He held out his hand to Marco.

"It's Jean-Paul!" La Canaria said, trying to jog our memories about this amazing event that was going to happen today because it was a fucking holiday and why couldn't we remember. "He's here!"

"Jean-Paul," Marco said, and took the hand that had been hanging there a second. "That's just great. Really great to finally meet you."

"I've got some things in my car," Jean-Paul said. "Groceries.

Though I didn't know we'd have guests, you naughty thing."
He reached out and tugged on La Canaria's nose. "This is quite
a surprise!"

La Canaria giggled. A sound I'd never heard out of her, not
in all her characters and parts.

"Mind helping me?" he asked Marco.

"Of course." Marco followed him out the door, glancing at
me for a second—terrified because he didn't know what he was
supposed to say, what role to play.

Inside the mill, our wimpy fire issued a thin veil of smoke and
green scent. The lights from the low candles threw our reflections back at us. I knew I had only a few moments to speak and
understand before the reflection warped and Jean-Paul appeared
before us again. But the only word I could form was the one I
knew I couldn't speak. Grito's name bubbled up, large enough
to choke on. La Canaria's face in the glass turned from a grinning pastry to an old chalkboard passed over many times with
the same dusty eraser. The board doesn't get clean; the chalk
smears into a uniform layer until rain comes and every hint of
what was written is gone. She met my eyes in the reflection and
opened the door.

I understood then that the certain words we had never been
able to say would now never be said. Whether we should have
kept looking for him—whether he could still be alive—had we
been weak and cowardly or just stupid and afraid. As with Alexis,
the extent of our betrayal would go unsurveyed. I didn't blame
La Canaria for her ability to turn from these questions, a move
made of velvet and without ripples, I just wished I had the ability
in my spine to bend as fast and far as she did.

"What fun to be with such Bohemians," Jean-Paul said, opening another bottle of red wine. He'd brought roasted chicken,

mayonnaise, mustard, olives, bread, and cheese. We nodded at him, chewing slowly, trying not to act like this was the first warm, real meal we'd had in months. "One of my maids said she thought she'd seen a woman climbing in and out of my apartment fire escape—it wasn't until a nosy country neighbor called me in Paris that I even began to dream it would be you!" He looked a bit like a *facha*, clean-shaven and starched, but one who thought himself to have an artistic temperament—his hair a little long, a weave of pink thread in his vest. "But why are you here?" he continued. "Why not be back in your country, where the action is?"

Marco finished chewing first. La Canaria and I looked at him to speak.

"We were where the action was," Marco said. "And it almost got us killed."

Jean-Paul's eyes widened on cue, and he took a slow sip of wine.

"We were staying with these artists in an old factory in Madrid," Marco said, staring into his glass of wine. "They were doing protests, political art, that sort of thing. There was also an arms deal with a group of militants. We'd collected the guns and were going to give them to our contact, but the *fachas* broke us up. I was the lookout, but they were already there, they knew we were coming. The problem was"—he flitted his eyes up at me—"Mosca had this package. And we couldn't let the police get ahold of it."

Marco told his story without pause or fumbling, as if he'd rehearsed it several times. As if such substitutions were easy and possible.

Jean-Paul nodded slowly as if he, too, of course, had crossed paths with people like that and he, too, knew how to act when you were in real trouble.

"What was it—this package?" he asked.

"We figured the less we knew . . ."

"I understand. But you couldn't just drop it?"

"All we knew was that it was important." Marco leaned back in his chair and spread his arms. "No one we were with would help us. Those artists, they acted like they were part of the movement, but when we asked for help, they wouldn't."

"They were pinkies," La Canaria said. "Only half-red. In it for the look." She blushed as if she'd been rude and cared. "I'm sorry, but it's true."

"If you're not willing to risk your neck, then you don't really care," Marco said to Jean-Paul, who smiled a comradely smile.

La Canaria raised her glass to them. She'd joined in Marco's lie flawlessly.

"What did you do?" Jean-Paul asked. He pushed his dish away and leaned closer to La Canaria.

"Someone set fire to an old factory we were staying in. We just left, left the package, and started heading north, out of there. La Canaria had told us so much about you, I thought we could stay here for a while."

Jean-Paul's arm around La Canaria stiffened into a hook. "It was your idea?"

Marco knew he'd misspoken. It was better if Jean-Paul thought La Canaria had brought us here.

"No, it was mine," La Canaria said. "I knew we could trust you."

"You should have told me you were here."

"I didn't want to worry you. And I couldn't risk anyone else finding out, *cariño*." She leaned in close to him and stroked his cheek, cheery and demure.

"Was there anyone else with you?" Jean-Paul directed this

at Marco, though we all knew whom it was for. Marco kept silent. La Canaria should be the one to say it, whatever she was going to say.

"No," she said. "No one else was with us." Inside the lie Marco had told, Grito's body—already white with water decay—faded and was never there.

"I would have rather known," Jean-Paul said to La Canaria. "Then I could have helped."

"You are helping."

"I hadn't gotten a letter from you in so long."

Marco rose to clear the dishes and I went to join him.

"Sit with us, Mosca," Jean-Paul said. "I think Marco is man enough to handle a few plates."

"Jean-Paul's a forward thinker," La Canaria said, snuggling into his shoulder.

"About some things." He ran his fingers through her hair and slowly down the length of her spine. He whispered in her ear and she giggled. The second time I'd ever heard her do that.

"Are you worried you'll be followed?" Jean-Paul whispered into La Canaria's ear but loudly enough for all of us.

"We're kind of low on the rung," Marco said.

"Even a small fish can muddy the water," Jean-Paul said. "In the papers, it's the tiniest bit of evidence that links a name to a deed, even tangentially. I've been following your country's situation. It's cost lives before."

Marco was about to speak but didn't; instead he leaned toward the sink, his hand tightening around the fine china, definitely not looking at me.

"All this talk of danger is making me tired." Jean-Paul rose from the table, and so did La Canaria. They walked up the stairs but turned at the landing. "Mosca, why don't you come upstairs with us?"

Marco stepped away from the sink and put his hand on my shoulder. I knew there were two options. I could walk out the door with Marco and never come back to the mill. Or I could walk upstairs with La Canaria and Jean-Paul. But I wasn't thinking of that; I was thinking of the story he'd told Jean-Paul.

"Is it true?" I whispered to Marco.

"Come on, Mosca, I just made something up so he'd lay off of us. I didn't mean it."

"But is it true that you were the lookout?"

"Yeah," he said. "I was."

It wasn't for failing at the job I was supposed to do. Marco had never spoken to me about that night. I'd never asked. I realized then that he'd had the possibility to play the scene over in his mind, to edit and erase his actions, layer script on script, and I had only a blank blood-black sky. I couldn't ask about that night because then I'd have to admit the full extent of my betrayal, the part even Marco didn't know. That I'd refused the package Alexis carried. I'd rather Marco thought I knew nothing than have him know my most damning shred.

I looked at Marco and saw a ghost. A ghost and someone who could have told me more. Who could have been alive to me in a way that he refused.

Marco wasn't lying. He'd just mixed two stories together. He'd slipped me in as a fiction and let me live there but left me paralyzed in this stretch of life. For Alexis, he'd substituted me. I couldn't forgive him that.

I walked up the stairs behind La Canaria and Jean-Paul.

Marco was gone in the morning. I figured he'd headed back home to beg, and that wasn't where I wanted to be. I had to keep searching for the shadows. For a way to get to Alexis. Marco would probably have a better chance with his parents without me, anyway.

I looped slowly around the mill, then headed outside of town, keeping to empty streets, catching the worst of the wind. Sleet started to fall. I'd been waking up with headaches that got worse each day. I couldn't see clearly; my skin had this strange tinge. Patches of time were dropping out from under me, like when I couldn't remember that we'd decided to move to the mill. But there was less to mark these disappearances. More and more, the life I walked through felt like that little room when I'd climbed into it from the rain to find it empty. Emptier and smaller for all it once contained.

Edging around an abandoned schoolhouse, the last building before the brambles and oak saplings took over the sidewalk, I felt something following me. I knew not to turn but kept walking, more slowly, hoping to catch the shadows once they stilled. Usually then I could see them, but I had to be patient and wait for them to stop moving. I smelled rot and I saw a different shape, clearly a man's figure, neatly dressed and ducking behind an abandoned woodpile, just inside my peripheral vision. It was the ducking that frightened me. The figure was comfortable in his skin, rigid and regimental in bearing yet agile in movements, but ducked slowly enough that I could see. It wanted to be seen.

I changed directions and crossed into the street with the bakery. My feet skidded slightly on the forming ice.

The rotting smell stayed with me—the scent of something wrapped in salt and left out too long. The figure had disappeared into shadow when I turned to it, like smoke among the rotting wood, and when I tried to name the shape, I saw only a cloud moving over a black ocean, shades of a different dark. If I saw a hand or a face in the cloud, there wasn't any I recognized, or it was a hand that couldn't be there, layered memories—the man's hand on Alexis's shoulder by the bridge, the policeman handing my abuela his medallion. I didn't know if this figure was different from the shadowy openings I'd been looking for. Now both frightened me.

La Canaria and Jean-Paul were fighting. I could hear La Canaria shouting through the thick stone and plaster. It comforted me because at least it was La Canaria and not this creature she'd slipped into when Jean-Paul walked in the door. I heard glass shattering and a heavy scrape across the floor. I didn't know if I should go up there. La Canaria was strong, stronger than I was, but probably not stronger than Jean-Paul.

A door slammed and I could hear her walking down the steps. She held an open bottle of white wine to her cheek. The chilled glass sweated from the heat of her hand. Through the glass I could see a bruise blooming.

"*Qué idiota,*" she said, knowing I'd heard it all. She took a slug of the wine and walked out of the mill. It was raining slightly, the air cold. I could see her walking to the dam and leaning over the rail. The water must have been below freezing, but it was moving too fast to solidify into ice.

Jean-Paul walked down the stairs, and I moved toward the door. He sat down at the farm table and started speaking as if I would care what he had to say. He looked split in half, so I stayed to watch.

"She told me on the islands that she was a virgin," he said.

I almost burst out laughing. If I'd had something in my mouth, it would have unleashed in a spray across his face like a scene from a telenovela. Instead I bit my lip.

"I really believed her," he said. "She said she'd been waiting for me." The lavender scarf he wore hung limp and tangled at his neck. He had two deep gashes on his cheek. It was a tes-

tament to La Canaria that even a lie she didn't want anyone
to believe would bloom into something far larger than she'd
imagined when she tossed it into the air.

I shrugged and struggled not to laugh.

"You can't stay here," he said, and walked out the door. He
met La Canaria at the bridge and moved close to her. I couldn't
hear what they said. After a few moments he turned and walked
back to his car, reversed quickly down the gravel, tires shooting
up small stones. La Canaria stayed where she was, staring out
over the bridge.

*I don't see anything I want to here. There are people I should
see. When we were kids, our fights meant so much, stupid
kids tormenting each other, always over nothing, but Mosca
knew how to end them. You wouldn't know our parents if
they walked right up to you, she'd say. You'd run away from
Mamá and Papá like they were strangers. I'd deny it and
cry until Abuela came and comforted me. Really, I always
won, because Mosca knew what she said wasn't allowed,
wasn't something Abuela could hear. But Mosca was right.
I might pass them every day. The photo doesn't do much. It's
blurred here. I can't just hold it up to everyone I pass. I tried
that and it didn't work. They might be the only people here,
and I still don't know them. But I don't think so. I can't
see them, it's true. But I don't think they're here. I can't ask
them to help me. And I'm not the one who needs protecting.*

La Canaria woke me in the dark. We'd spent all day waiting for
Jean-Paul to return and kick us out. Finally I'd curled up by the
fire to try to sleep.

"Mosca," she whispered, her hair lit by the moon through the lead-glass windows. Her skin was pale.

"Stop it," I said. "I'm sleeping."

"Mosca, wake up." She pushed me off the pile of blankets and found my hands between my knees, where I kept them warm.

"Canaria, leave me alone—"

"Please, *mija*. Come with me."

Her back was stooped; holding my dry palm, calling me her child. The only person I could remember calling me that was my abuela. I rolled onto the wood floor and let her pull me up. Let her lead me, almost weightless, up the stairs, through halls I still couldn't recognize, shafts of moon mimicking our white breath in the dark. She opened a door with keys I didn't know she had, pulling them out from under her sweaters, hiding them underneath again. She stood in front of a door and said, "Close your eyes," but she didn't need to. The door opened to darkness. My eyes couldn't adjust. She brought my hand up to graze something. A cloth hung behind the door, enclosing a room within the room, made of scraps and cardboard. I lifted the fabric opening and stepped inside. A sort of glow in there from light I couldn't trace—perhaps a window covered by blankets, the moonlight turned yellow through wool. Shades of brown and cardboard as padding, with polished stones from the banks of the dam in the corners. The room outside it—the shell room—wasn't large, a maid's quarters or a place for brooms. The space she'd made inside it was even smaller. Neither of us could stand up, and we couldn't go far from each other. Our heat mixed involuntarily. I was still almost asleep. I dropped down and found the floor as soft as the walls. So soft, the room felt like it was floating, a hanging chrysalis inside an endless house. La Canaria knelt and placed a blanket over me. Climbed underneath and pulled off her layers of sweaters.

"We can stay here," she whispered into my ear. "You don't get hungry."

I nodded, and with my eyes still shut, my hand found the way to her stomach. I tried to cup what was growing there, but it was too big for my hand to hold. It had been for a long time.

I could almost sleep in the cocoon La Canaria had built, heated by her body and what it was growing. Grito and Marco lopped off from me. Even lying beside her, the sinews that connected La Canaria to my tissue were shredding. I had only what had happened, my refusal, my betrayal, what had brought me there. I watched the memory fill the cocoon and wondered if La Canaria could see it. If she could dream my thoughts, and would she hate me for them more than she already did.

Jean-Paul's headlights hit the gravel drive and curved around the mill. I crossed the bridge before he could speak to me, and I watched from a distance. He didn't look angry. He slunk back into the mill, tail tucked, waiting to be told what to do. He had brought another roast chicken and the evening paper. The sounds that came from their room were soft and muffled. But he left before dawn, and I found La Canaria sleeping again in her cocoon. I crawled in beside her.

She was getting bigger. I noticed the change as if I'd been away for months instead of a few hours.

"How can you sleep in here?" I asked. It was suddenly too hot in the cocoon. Her own heat, because that night had brought an even more insistent frost than the last. I stretched as far from her as the cocoon would let us. She was barely awake.

"It keeps me warm," she said.

"Did you see the paper Jean-Paul brought?"

"I can't read French," she mumbled.

The front-page article said two students were found dead outside their apartment in Madrid, in the same style as the attorney months before. The article even mentioned the attorney by name, not afraid in this country to make the obvious associations.

"It said the students were part of an anti-fascist group," I said.

"Uh-huh."

"And it said someone's targeting people who have information about the old guard, who can prove the crimes they committed, just like Marco said—"

"So what?" she snapped, fully awake. "What's it got to do with you?"

I didn't speak.

Soon I could hear her breathing heavily, sleeping or faking well enough.

In that floating world the objects she'd collected buried light within them, creating a live and pulsing cadence. I thought I could hear notes, though they never linked to a melody. The city I walked through with my eyes closed was dimmer there, and I was happy for it because the city had become full of shadows like the one I'd seen by the woodpile, figures I didn't want to see.

I write all over the thin floors and walls of this city, hoping it will seep into wherever you are. This is a scroll inscrutable.

This is ink that can be read only as it washes away. These aren't my words. That's not how I speak. I trace the words in the dirt anyway. I lick them again and again with my dry tongue, a sad dog licking the broken paws she thinks are her pups. When I can find a way to write, the words are as dry as my tongue and deader, but I write them anyway. I write on a white floor with charcoal from something's fire. The words go up the walls, but when I look at them, I wonder if they're like the notes the others write. Do they look like that because I killed them with my tongue, or is that how my words have always looked? All my words turn into one word, my name, but you know that one already, what will it do to you? Mosca, I am no good with them.

I must have fallen asleep, because she woke me. The layers of cardboard and cloth filtered the streetlight like a candle through a cat's ear, warm and full of blood. She moved my hand slowly to her stomach.

"It's Alexis's," she said.

"What?"

"The baby, it's Alexis's baby."

"That's not possible," I said, still groggy.

Her lips tightened into a cruel, filigree smile. "You've been looking for him, right? Maybe I found him first."

Fully awake, I pushed away from her. My hands landed hard on her chest, and her breath caught there. I shoved my way out of the cocoon, tearing the fabric and cardboard, my arms flailing.

Outside on the bridge, I stumbled over the moss-slick stones. On my fingers, I counted the months since Alexis had disappeared. I kept losing track. But he'd been gone two years when we burned our clothes in the mountains outside Casasrojas.

The first time I saw Alexis and La Canaria together at El Chico, I'd thought they were the same. Not just the way they linked into each other, driving out all other sound; it was more than that. A quality of visibly false bravado, like a kid boxing with his shadow. There was an uncrouched attitude about La Canaria that Alexis had, too. It drew us all to her. She might break, but it would be something to see.

The months bled when I tried to count them, but it had been too long, too long to be possible. All I could remember was that La Canaria wasn't around those days we were waiting for Alexis to not be dead, to come up the stairs, and she wasn't around the days after the police brought his medallion, the days after the Mass. When I resurfaced from my abuela's weeping, she and Grito were sitting together at El Chico, his hand on her thigh, and I couldn't say a word. She didn't speak about Alexis then and hadn't since.

It was cold outside the mill, and I didn't have a coat. I just had on old sweaters, picking up dust and the thin sweat of a bad sleep.

La Canaria was cruel. She'd take what she wanted, but usually her actions were like the wavering air before a gas stove lights. I could understand them, see right through them. Throw a match and it was gone. This I couldn't see through.

Maybe I'd misheard her. She'd said Marco or Jean-Paul or Grito. Maybe Alexis's and Grito's bodies were blending in her mind, both unfound, both forming anew. Maybe she'd said Alexis because it was the closest she could get to saying Grito. Or the other way around. But I replayed her words in my mind, and I could see her shaping the long *A,* her tongue hissing through the complicated *x* and *s.*

By the dam was a pile of hand-rolled cigarettes, one of them still burning. I picked it up and held the ember cupped against my palm to protect it from the splashing water. La Canaria slid up to me slowly, becoming visible piece by murky piece.

"It's funny, isn't it, what Marco said?" she said. She looked over me to the green water, mostly covered by shadow. Her eyes rested on a pocket of froth where the current stilled and trash and leaves collected. The cigarette kept burning in my hand. Tobacco ash dropped onto the wrought-iron railing. I could feel the ember on the tip of my forefinger.

"What's funny?"

"That story Marco told Jean-Paul about you and him being big revolutionaries."

"He was making something up to cover your ass."

"But it's true, isn't it?"

"No," I said, and started walking away. One more word and I couldn't control what I would do next.

"It is true," she said, moving closer to me, smiling, making me turn involuntarily. "You *were* gonna be big revolutionaries, but you backed out. You had to save your own ass. You and Marco left him to die."

She stood close to me. Even though we were outside the cocoon and in the wet night air, she felt closer to me than anyone had ever been.

"You have no idea," I whispered.

"Don't I?" She brought her lips to my ear. "Alexis told me everything." Her stomach pressed into mine, harder than I'd imagine it would be. She leaned back a few centimeters. "Actually, he didn't tell me anything. He thought I was too stupid to figure it out—how he was trying to play resistance fighter but was having trouble finding the supporting roles."

"It can't be his," I said.

"Of course it can't! Alexis is dead in a ditch or a river. Long dead. Even if someone did find the body, there'd be no way to even tell it was his." She wrapped her arm around my neck and grabbed my ear like she had at the bar in Casasrojas. "So why do you keep looking for him?"

"Shut up, *puta*." I pushed her back and punched her in the stomach where she was largest, right below her navel. She doubled over but then grabbed my hair and twisted it around her hand until I was pinned to her cheek. I elbowed her in one of her massive tits, and she fell back on the cold stones. The turbine was on and its roar echoed over the stones. For a second I saw Alexis standing by the red door, head thrown back in laughter.

I had to get away from the mill. I didn't even recognize Alexis. He was an impostor, the seams showing, a creature poorly wrought.

It was raining slightly, a fine mist. I left La Canaria staring up at me and crossed the bridge, running away from the mill. I ran over to the fields that had been full of birds when we came, dipping toward the ground like fighter pilots, skimming over our heads and calling out. The brown grass wet and matted, caught in mangy clumps on the barbed-wire fence. I could see a figure walking into the fields. I ran and tore my jacket crossing the fence.

"Alexis! Stay there!" I shouted. "Just stay there!"

I ran but could barely see him against the trees on the far side of the field. I moved through the air, becoming water, swimming farther away from the lights of the town. He was a bird or a crucifix, shadow against darker dark. He didn't turn around.

"Where are you going? Tell me!"

He stopped then and turned around. "You want to know? Ask your good friend Marco, you chicken," he said.

Another figure, taller than he was, came out from the trees. I yelled at Alexis, though I knew it was too late. They were gone, and I couldn't be sure where that man came from or if he was really there, but I saw him and I had to get to Alexis before he did.

Mosca, you brought something with you. Because you can see the shadows, I can see something else, too. Someone is following me. I know him, and his face doesn't change how everyone else's does. I can't see his face, but I know it doesn't change. I'm bleeding, a sepia tone, that's not my word. I've been collecting them. Dead tongues are hard to shape, but they bounce back with new words splattered on them. I wonder if he made me bleed, why would he? The time blurs, but all the moments are open-eyed and watchful. I don't know how he could've slipped in. Maybe I'm trailing something else. Not blood but a scent, lit on the striking surface of this city. I try to wash the trail. Nothing can be cleaned.

He is getting closer and Mosca is, too. He knows I see him and he knows I know he follows me, but we haven't acknowledged each other. We're playing, flirting, pretending we're really into the beer and the loud music, but instead of a bar and music, it's gray concrete and wax paper and receipts in the wind. I told you not to come, Mosca. He is following me, but he is following you, too. He can do far more damage to you.

I search for phones. I write all over the city, but the

only words that matter are the ones I know will never get through:

   Mosca, it's not me you're following.
   Mosca, I would never lead you here.

I woke up the next morning on a part of the road where I'd never been, wet, cold, and surrounded by dew. I hitched to Paris on the back of a truck packed with boxes of winter pears and headed toward Jean-Paul's apartment. The city felt orderly, its streets open wide to any invading army, the houses far apart.

I passed a brightly lit art gallery hung with paintings made from collaged newspapers and comic books, posters that looked like the covers of punk albums. Inside, young women in jumpsuits and David Bowie hairstyles sipped white wine. A group of students walking in front of me tossed a half-full paper envelope of roasted chestnuts onto the sidewalk, and I grabbed it when they turned the corner. The chestnuts were still hot; their wrinkled flesh puckered my mouth.

I found the apartment. I shouldn't have worried; it was impossible for my feet not to carry me there. Four perfect walls rose up out of the slick gray cobblestones. The glass of the windows was black against heavy, drawn curtains. Above the door was a carved marble face, scowling lopsidedly, its lips pierced into an *o*. I turned into the alley and found the fire escape we'd first climbed months ago. Our window had slid shut but wasn't locked. I shoved it open. No one had been there since we'd left. The air hung heavy with our bodies and our thoughts of those silent, hungry months. Thicker than dust, a weight skirted around every object in the room. It circled my feet, trying to ease up my legs.

The chestnut and mulberry trees that had partially blocked

the view to the Tuileries stretched bare arms. Below them, the plane trees' branches ended in swollen stumps, hunched around themselves, displaying only black lichen and brown moss. The sidewalks were emptied of the calls of students going out, children running home, old people pecking at sunflower seeds. Somewhere below me, the muffled sounds of a family eating, the measured squeal of silver on antique porcelain. I lay down on the mattress and tried to coax the remnants of the chestnuts from my teeth. When the family spoke, the sound was so filtered through plaster and pipes that the language could have been my own. I closed my eyes and tried to sleep, but the other city swirled in front of me, refusing to dissipate into blankness. I saw Alexis alone, walking down a street I hadn't tried yet, down an alley I couldn't find, someone at his back.

> *I find ringing phones. I see the city as sound, the phones a constellation of sound, some dimmer, visible only out of the corners of my eyes. I close my eyes and sound becomes light, a whole city of phones ringing. Voices speaking, or trying to speak, through water. They dug phone lines under the ocean. They are more reliable than stars that shift when you move south. What keeps me from Mosca is very thin. I can almost push through it. The whole city is lit with the sound.*

The sound started in my dreams and I didn't want it but when it woke me I could hardly move. The old rotary phone was ringing close to my head. It had been collecting dust, untouched, and now it was ringing, almost bouncing in its cradle. I closed my eyes to make the sound stop.

> *Eyes half closed and walking, I find the phones, hear the light and heat they give off. Light and heat, enough of it,*

makes sound. That's true, that's not true, that's true here.
I have stopped writing. I wonder what you brought here,
Mosca. It won't be satisfied just following me. I pick up the
phone and wait for the sound before the sound. The sound
that travels through water and I will catch it.

Pink dawn light catching breath gray and cold. Making light
and air heavy, too much polished stone flecked off by heels,
hands, and cat paws. Inside my stomach, I felt another type of
light. Underwater, but winning out. Turning into a pressing
mass, and it wasn't soft. It wasn't dawn. The light from my
stomach fused into sound. I knocked the still-ringing phone
off the hook and pushed away from it, pushed the mattress
across the floor, and felt the warmth from where I had been
sleeping condense into a voice I knew coming out of the tele-
phone.

It was Marco.

I sat up, suddenly awake, and grabbed the phone.

"Mosca?" he said. "Are you there?"

The line was clear, as if his chin and not the plastic receiver
were cupped gently between my ear and the wood floor.

"Marco?" I whispered. "How did you know I'd be here?"

"I didn't. I just—I've been calling and calling. I can't believe you picked up. Are you safe?" My eyes stayed fixed on
the corners of the room. It was full of shadows as it had never
been before. Unsought, they frightened me. "Mosca? Are you
there?"

The shadows couldn't move if I kept my eyes on them.

"Mosca, I'm in Cádiz."

"Why?" I remembered, a thousand years ago, Marco talking
about Cádiz and Carnival.

"I'm in Cádiz. You need to come."

"Why?"

"I bought you a ticket—it's in the apartment, under the mattress."

"Where'd you get the money?"

He paused. "Mosca, there's something I need to tell you."

CÁDIZ
February, Carnival

Marco wouldn't speak when I got to Cádiz. Not of anything that warranted the trip, the call, the ticket waiting for me. And what I needed to ask, I couldn't, not yet. He met me at the station in Cádiz, and we walked through the dawn-lit streets. It was cold, but because of Carnival, the streets were never empty. People were sleeping on the sidewalks or carrying each other out of makeshift bars, singing balefully. We talked about Carnival, about the smell that the city carried, or we didn't talk at all. The smell was different than just trash and ocean, spilled beer and rotting fish; it was a body being dredged up and stronger by the shore. It was a potion, a hypnosis I could feel working within, drawing me toward it.

Marco had enough money to rent a room in a boarding-house with a shared bathroom down the hall and two twin beds. He had enough to buy us sandwiches and refill a bottle of wine. I didn't know if it was from his parents or if he had kept a bit to himself those months in Paris. I didn't ask how long we had. I didn't ask what he wanted to tell me.

The sun was just rising when we got to the boarding-house, but instead of going back to bed, Marco took me to the very top of the building. The door to the roof was closed with a tiny rusted padlock, like the kind on girls' diaries that you can open with your fingernail. I was tempted to take the lock off, hook it onto my neck with the medallion and the bullet, but Marco slipped it in his pocket. No one else came up those stairs. The rest of the lodgers were old, widowers and rag sellers, barely making it to their second- and third-floor apartments. You could see the whole city there, unraveling itself.

The sunlight eased itself over the white stucco buildings, and I turned my face from it. I spent all day up there, though I hadn't slept since getting on the train. The weather had turned suddenly warmer, and it was hot on the white roof in the middle of the reflected light. The white stucco buildings surrounding us were almost brighter than the sun. To the west, the sea obscured itself, each wave catching the light and blocking what was to be found there. I wondered how many people were looking at the sea at that moment, if it added up, if their eyes weighed anything, created an opening, at least.

"We could have saved him," Marco said, looking out over the rippling body of red tile roofs. He was shirtless and his skin was slightly cool when I accidentally brushed against it. The sun was directly above us, ruining any shade. It must have been siesta, people sleeping for the longest time the city would allow. "We could have at least looked for his body."

"Who are you talking about?" I said, though I didn't want to hear any names. Two hawks circled in the sky, backlit into black silhouettes of whatever colors they might have been. Each hunting for the same kill in the same place, neither acknowledging the other.

"You're right."

He got up and returned in a few minutes with beers. We didn't search for shade. He handed me a beer, and we let the sun seep into our skulls, dizzying us beyond words, beyond

names, beyond rivers and whatever was or was not found on
their shores.

The *chirigotas* started in the morning, as soon as everyone had
enough espresso to forget they hadn't slept the night before.
Men in brightly colored wigs rode through the city, stopping
whenever there was a crowd to sing to. They were out of tune,
still drinking, not having stopped. The daylight was a tonic that
made the night not have happened. The sun turned the buildings pink, then purple until they disappeared and all that was
left was what was under them, an ocean of unmarked graves. I
felt I could see them.

That night Marco and I walked through the Carnival crowds.
There were no punks on the street or disappearing into underground bars. Marco said that even before Carnival, all he saw
were people getting ready for the big party or kids walking to
school with their grandparents. We could feel the presence of
the old guard, men in starched shirts climbing into American
cars with tinted glass windows. They weren't retreating. A bear
climbing into its winter cave isn't retreating. Along the beach,
the iron supports for huge new high-rises were being raised,
luxury apartments for the new generation of executives, luxury
hotels for the new tourists. In the papers were more photos of
dead students. The articles blamed it on sectarian violence, labor
feuds, or the newly organized anarchists, but the deaths were all
the same, a line so thin and neat across their throats, it seemed
easy to put back together.

Even walking beside Marco, the shadows found me. At
first I didn't recognize them. They blended with the living and
didn't look so strange. But the shadows made the Carnival cos-

tumes real. The dancing young women dressed as pregnant nuns became scared and skinny things with nothing but gruel and another body needing all they could give. The singing priests covered up the garters they were displaying so proudly a moment before, took off their wigs, and disappeared into the crowd, quiet and ashamed. It was not the shadow's shape that was important; it was what it could do and where it proved I was. The spoiled scent—I recognized it, each time both familiar and like nothing I'd ever encountered, each time terrifying.

I forgot Marco beside me. Before, I had to search for the shadows, but in Carnival they showed themselves freely. I wondered that no one else could see them. I wondered that no one else shivered to be wading at the edge of where the dead live. I couldn't see Alexis, but the dead were all around me. I was getting closer to him.

Mosca wakes up screaming and sweating, and she should, because the room is full of much more than just me and Marco. He gets up from his bed and tries to calm her, but he's sweating, too, and she pushes him away. She can feel me press up against her window. She sees the living and the dead in the Carnival crowd. She can't tell them apart. She's waded far enough that there are more dead than living. Marco can feel me, too, and he puts his arm around her when he does. I want to kill him for touching her. He knows I come at night and he waits up for me and he talks to me but he's already started whispering when I come into the room. I know he can't tell when I'm there or not. Just that I come. All he can say is that he's sorry and he'll keep Mosca safe. The first, I don't care about. The second, I know he can't.

"Mosca, look at me, look here." Marco shook me awake. It was almost dawn and I could still feel my dream around me. The shadows shaping into figures pressing against the glass, trying to crawl down my throat. Marco's fingers pressed into my arm, accidentally separating the thin ropes of muscle. The dreams pressed back. I knew he didn't sleep well, either, and not just because of me.

"Why did you come here?" I asked him, staring at the wall of our rented room, trying to fix anything solid in my sight. Dirty clothes and paper from old sandwiches covered the bureau, the only piece of furniture in the room except the bed. The wallpaper had given up on most of the wall, revealing strips of newspaper from before the war. This part of the city was old, the buildings left to decompose on their own. I hadn't asked Marco before: Why this city? Why had he come here, where he knew no one, a city so far from our own, jutting out into the sea, as far as you could get while staying on land?

"Why did you come back?" I said, an easy question but getting closer to what I needed to ask. "Why here? Why Cádiz?"

He didn't speak. I should know the answer, his look told me. I shouldn't dare to ask it out loud.

"I thought you knew," he said. "Isn't that why you came?"

"I came because you were here."

"You left La Canaria."

Someone shouted beneath our window and the shadows faded.

"I told you, she left me. I woke up one morning and she wasn't there."

"I don't believe you," he said.

"I can't sleep. I'm going out."

The crowds were larger than before, growing as we approached the final night of Carnival. People had arrived from all over the country. But all I could see were children. Not students in swarms, massing on the street and calling out, spraying cava and beer, but skinny kids in the shadowy alcoves near mosques and synagogues converted to churches centuries ago. They moved slowly in pairs or alone. They were dressed in long shirts, black hair shorn close, the dark skin of their skulls covered by round hats. The smell strengthened. It was coming off the people at the edges of the crowds—the wandering children, the men dressed as monks who were too solemn to be a part of the revelers. The shadows walking among the living. They weren't just shadows anymore. They had form and heft. I was closer to the city I walked through in my half-sleep, on the outskirts, where the dead and the living mixed. The city's shape was coming to me. I felt I was remembering it.

An old woman was standing in front of the boardinghouse when I got back. I recognized her from the hallway outside our room, passing on the way to the toilet, or when she disappeared behind her door. She was a widow born into mourning, covered at birth in her dark lace mantilla, her skin stained blue by decades of cheap black dye. But she looked different in the doorway. It was almost dawn, and she was lit by the fading stars. The streetlights were off. Under real light she looked less solid. She might have been a creation of the boardinghouse— the mansion she'd probably grown up in and seen the rooms rented out one by one until she lived in a partitioned hovel with papery walls. She had stepped out of the shadows when I approached, but when she knew that I'd seen her, she receded back into them.

"This is an old city," she said when I was almost past her.

"I know, Señora."

"You came here for Carnival?"

"Yes."

"No, you did not," she said. "You came for the water."

"For the beach," I said.

"It's too cold for the beach."

I don't know why I didn't move past her. That salty scent clung to her and coated my mouth when I breathed in. Her tiny figure blocked the door.

The Carnival crowds were thinning a bit with the daylight, and people passed us, using the alley as a shortcut to their apartments. A group of men in crusaders' costumes of cheap polyester, the silver crosses on the front of their shirts already peeling off, dragged one another down the alley. They paused behind me, but the old woman ignored them, as if she couldn't hear their vomit splattering on the cobblestones.

"It's an old city," she said again.

"Yes, Señora." The men stood up and kept walking. I turned back to her, drawn in by her voice.

"This is the country's greatest harbor. All the rivers flow into it and out to the sea." When she spoke, spit formed in the corners of her mouth and stretched between her lips like blades of grass. "In the water are the wrecks of ships that tried to take the city long ago."

Past the door, in the hallway behind her, I heard the hollow clatter of a wheeled grocery basket. The baskets sounded every morning outside our door, the rubber wheels sticking on the worn tile, like there was an army gathering to hoard up all the chorizo and dried garbanzo beans in the world. I moved aside to let the woman and her basket through, but she stopped the cart in front of me and whispered to the woman in the doorway. She stepped closer and drifted into her shoulder, her dark coat merging with the older woman's shawl. They were distinct figures despite the shadows, but they blended at the shoulders. This new woman, I hadn't seen before, but

I could tell she was only slightly younger than the other. Her face had the same transparent quality that seemed solid only in the shadow from the doorway. The light rose and strengthened behind me, but the doorway was cool.

"This little girl, she doesn't know," the first woman said to the newcomer. They spoke quickly and mostly to themselves.

"No, the young people, they don't."

"Beneath the water is all the gold of the great ones of the city."

"Oh yes, they dropped it there when they could not stop their city from being taken—"

"Then they climbed in after it."

"There is more buried in the harbor than in the whole city."

"These young people, they think this is the place to be." The old woman arched her arm up and out grandly, though her wrist could barely reach her forehead. "This is not it."

"But the other city is all around," the other woman broke in. "This girl knows that much, at least." She held up her hand as if pressing gently against a gauzy curtain or the cheek of someone she loved.

"Yes," the old woman said. "But there is a difference. Beneath the water, the dead can speak."

I heard the soft pad of bare feet on stone in the hallway behind the door, and my shoulders twitched involuntarily.

"You are right to be careful," the one with the shawl whispered. "But you should be much more careful. Looking is very dangerous. You have to leave everything behind when you enter the city. And you need someone very strong to bring you back."

Marco's head emerged from the doorway. "Mosca, I was worried about you." He was only wearing his undershorts, no shirt or shoes.

The women clucked at the impropriety of it all, shifting into the light and off the step. I turned away from them and followed Marco up the stairs, wondering how two old women, a grocery cart, and I could have fit in that tiny doorway. As if they were no larger than birds.

That night, the final night of Carnival, I asked Marco again. I woke to the shadows at the window, and I knew if I didn't speak, they would break through, they would crawl across the room and paw into my throat. I spoke because I had to.

"Why did you come here?" I said. "To this city, why now?"

He got out of bed and picked through the sandwich wrappers on the bureau, folding them with tight creases like my abuela always did. Marco could have been anywhere then, in any cheap room with torn wallpaper. He could have been a continent away, not speaking to me, not known to me at all.

"I thought I'd find him here," he said.

From the particular way he didn't look at me, I knew he was talking about Alexis. "I mean, I knew I wouldn't find him. But ever since Grito—I had this feeling." He turned back to the wrappers. He stacked them in a neat pile, lining their edges up with his index finger. "I thought there'd be some part of him here that I could bring back to you."

"*Pendejo,*" I said quietly. "You left me alone and with no money."

"And you fucked that asshole."

"Paco?" I said, almost laughing. "What do you care?"

"You know just how much I care." He paused, waiting, but I didn't say anything. "Whatever—this isn't about that, it's about them. Grito and Alexis. I couldn't have them on my back. Not both of them."

"What happened that night?" I said.

"What night?" Marco turned away again.

"When we were supposed to meet the militants. What happened?"

"Same as I told Jean-Paul—the police showed up. We ran, but they had seen us."

"But why did you come here?" I asked. I wanted him to look at me, though I knew he wouldn't until I stopped speaking and let him find the words. I held my breath until he spoke.

"Alexis said he'd come here. Some contact—I don't know who. When you said no."

"Said no to what?" I got up off the bed. Marco was still facing away from me. The air was suddenly thicker, catching in my throat, becoming visible and coated.

"You know—to keep the package for him." He looked at me then, his hand on the sandwich wrappers.

"He told you that? He told you I said no?" I couldn't keep the knowledge in my head, that Marco had known my worst secret. What I thought I'd kept hidden from everyone, he'd known all along.

"I thought at first he was lying that you didn't have it. That he just said that to protect you—from me."

"How could he tell you? You've known all along it was my fault?"

"Listen to me, Mosca," he whispered. "You have to just listen to me."

Shadows were filling the room all around us, bringing with them the chemical water that transforms light. All the names that had been spoken catching on fire.

"He said they didn't see you. Did he ask you to keep it? Did you?"

"Mosca, please, please. He didn't ask me. He couldn't."

Marco stepped toward me, and later I saw what that meant. "Mosca, just listen, I need to. It wouldn't have mattered if you were the lookout, whatever you did. The police—they knew what was happening."

"What do you mean?"

"It's my fault. They were following me. Keeping tabs on me for my father. I didn't know, I swear. I led them right to him."

I punched Marco in the mouth. My knuckles split across his teeth. But the pain was like Marco's words, distant and unconnected to me. I'd already known the truth of what he'd just said, the part he'd played; in some way it didn't surprise me. Perhaps I'd known since his parents' villa, perhaps I'd known for years.

Marco pushed me down onto the bed and held me there; the blood from his split lip dropped onto my cheek. I tried to get my hands out from under his body, but he wouldn't let me move. "Let me just talk to you, Mosca. Let me just say what I have to."

"I don't want to hear it," I said.

"He made me promise to take care of you, Mosca. Promise to never touch you and to take care of you."

"Well, you didn't listen, did you?" I spat, trying to move beneath him.

"I promised him," Marco said.

"When?"

"What?" he said, his breath clouding my ear.

"When did you promise?"

"After. Later."

"Later, when?" I knew Alexis was nearby, if only I could reach him. "Is he here?" I said. "Marco, do you know where Alexis is?"

Marco looked at me, and he was so sad. Because I said what we both hoped, and he was the one who had to answer.

He let go of me and I sat up straight and fast, expecting resistance and receiving only air, like trying to force open a door you think is locked but isn't even there.

"The package," Marco said. "It wasn't just information about your parents. There was a lot more. He'd put it all together—gotten it from other people, all those different trips he went on. Names and dates that linked a lot of important people back to what they did. That's what he was protecting—that he couldn't let them get."

I could feel Alexis by us. I couldn't see him, but I could feel him. It wasn't Marco that was the door—I could feel a door inside me open wide and close. Alexis walking away and shutting the door. I leaned into it, but it wouldn't open. The cities had been a lie. There were no steps to trace that the two of us hadn't already planted. Everything that had happened that night was a trap Marco and I had laid for him. We had set it and we had turned away so we wouldn't have to watch him fall in.

"But you said you thought you'd find him here." I was grasping for anything that might be left.

"We all tell ourselves lies," Marco said. "But he didn't. He knew."

"What? What did he know?"

Marco pressed a dirty sock to his lip. The red caked to brown on the gray cotton. "I'd betrayed him. But he knew I wouldn't betray you too."

I covered my face. My hand ached. "Even if it didn't matter about being the lookout, I still wouldn't hide the box. That's why he died."

"I don't know—"

I dropped my hands from my face. Marco's expression was

the same as when he was on his horse in the olive grove. But it wasn't a smile. It was something else. He was terrified, he was so sorry, but just for one second he wasn't either. He didn't give a shit about either. He had said everything he could say. He had laid his burdens at my feet and he was weightless, blank. Marco was waiting, his face the stillness before action, but an action based not in fear or in the past, in only what he saw before him at that moment. His face open, looking only at me.

I kissed him gently, on the side of his mouth I hadn't hit.

"I have to bring him back."

If I could touch Mosca, I would do it now. Touch her softly on the top of her head. I'd say she's come far enough, she knows enough secrets now. I would touch Marco, too, on the shoulder. To tell him the same. The other shadows are gone. The room is empty except for me, and it's all right. I want to be a priest and touch them and lift a weight off of them. But it's me I want to lift. My own body ground into fine silt and spread over the length of their skin. It catches light like mica. I have settled, grown into their bodies, shaped them. A tree letting barbed wire curl into its heart. It would take years, a fine chisel, patience I do not have, to unwind it. It is me that I need to lift. But that is not a job I can do.

I reach out to them anyway, step toward them, my arms open wide. I know it won't be enough.

I left Marco standing with his bloody sock in his hands and ran down the boardinghouse stairs. At the entryway, I passed the old woman who had told me about the city under the harbor. She nodded as if she knew where I was going and why. I nodded, too, certain. I pushed through the crowds. Carnival was at its peak, but I shoved anyone who got too close, dead or alive, no matter how big. I caught sight of my reflection in a store window—a sight I hadn't seen in months. I was thin, my flesh a screen my bones were trying to push through. My skin cast off a light like the moon but more taut. A light ready to snap and launch. I got to the water quicker than I thought I could.

The dancing crowds were thick right up to the shore, then stopped just short of the sand. The scent was strongest on the sand, the ocean blending to black at the edge of the horizon. I thought of ancient artifacts, women who never bathed and instead coated themselves in scented oils. Women with coins slipped over their closed eyes who could read messages written in the fumes coming from the water. The Carnival lights flamed over the harbor. There were no birds, few in the whole city, and the only sound was the water inviting me in. The scent from the water was pleasant, like an opiate bath, or I was used to it and no longer noticed the other note, of uncovering, of thawing. I knew what I would see if I looked behind me. The breaker wall, crumbling from the force of decades of waves, lifetimes of tides. Scrawled over the length of it, in loping serifs and proud curves, was Alexis's signature, the trailing *x* visible for miles.

On the edge of the crowds I saw the man who had been following me. But he was many men, the police who brought the medallion, the old guards on street corners, the man who put his arm on Alexis's shoulder, the body that stalked me through the shadow city. He was wearing a Carnival death mask, grinning white bones over a black background, pulled halfway over his face. The other half was shadow, hollow and blank. He broke away from the crowds and edged toward the sand. I couldn't let him see me, I had to get to the water first. Marco had made me certain that Alexis wasn't in any living city. If I wanted to find him, I would have to go where he was. I waded into the ocean until I was knee-deep in kelp, took off my boots and sweater, and dove in.

PART III

THE CITY OF
THE DEAD

Beneath the water, at first all I felt was tightness, my chest unable to expand. The water dark and freezing. I could see nothing and my limbs were numb. But then I saw another city stretching out low and long, larger than the white one with the Carnival parades and crowds in costumes drinking all night. My limbs glowed and my air bubbles turned to gold medallions—one for each of the saints, all protectors of hopeless prayers in their way. I swam through branches and the water turned into snow and sound ringing as light, over and over. I swam into the city beneath the water, but it was not just a city or a fixed place. Each death made it grow, added buildings and terrains, split rooms, each room already containing a whole world. The city above the water lit the water on fire. There was no way I could go back up.

Beneath the water, I swam into a hunting shack surrounded by mountains. A tree was breaking through the wooden shutters. The limb sneaked through the window, splintering the wood fiber by fiber. The sun through the broken shutters glinted on spilled bullets and pheasant feathers ground into the floorboards. I could smell the scent of a boy who would not hunt with his abuelo, who cooed like a fox beneath the kitchen table. His hand stretched out to me like the tree limb. But something else coalesced in the opening in the shutters, forming from a branch into an arm, not a child's but a man's, capable of dragging me down.

Beneath the water, I swam into a countryside of mountains, following a stream of snowmelt that cut through fern-covered hills. A shadow drifted over the hills, moving closer to me. I circled a pool where spring water tore out of the rock like a tongue. The rocks in the pool were green and slick with all that lived on them. But there was something white circling in the water. It was the color of life drained, a child sucking red from strawberry ice and dropping it in the sand. The white thing swayed and I moved closer. A scrap of cotton. An arm, thin as a branch, emerged from it. Grito's black hair circled beneath his arm, moved gently by the water. I reached out my hand to touch him and was pulled deeper.

Beneath the water, I saw all the ways I could have accepted the box from Alexis, all the frames that had repeated endlessly in my mind since I refused. I crossed the ocean with it. I threw it into the river and left Casasrojas. I carried the package with me to every exam and every class. I still carried it, and every day Alexis asked if it was safe and I said yes, because he could still ask. But these were fabrications no different from what kept me up at night—all the ways I could have and did not.

I kept swimming. The fire the Carnival lights made on the water was no longer visible. I doubted that this was really a city and not just water taking away all my air and leaving me unable to break through ice. I knew I was being followed. The man was getting closer. He didn't need a mask. There were others with him, circling me. The scents I'd caught while looking for Alexis, the shadows behind me and exiting his mouth when he spoke. They were getting closer and I was running out of air.

Above the water, La Canaria turned on the turbine to make the mill shake. She thought of those pictures of fish getting chased by bigger fish. Something was inside her and she was inside something big and loud. She went outside and stood at the bridge overlooking the dam. The water was green. It was the only real green thing. It foamed and caught glass bottles that once held hard cider and silver tins of pickled fish. The containers swirled in the water. They were like her, except what they carried had already been eaten. She leaned against the bridge. The baby was eating her up. She didn't have enough to give. The mill was cold. The cocoon she built was colder than the rest of the house because of the hole Mosca had punched in it. She thought she should have gone somewhere where everyone would hate her so much they couldn't touch her, not so much they wanted to touch her all the time. The baby made her tired. It made her remember everything she'd lost. Alexis and then Grito, she was all alone but for the wreck inside her. The baby was eating her right up and she was going to get skinny, skinny, and the baby was going to be huge. She wanted to disappear like everyone else. She wanted to leave, but she didn't know where to go. She didn't want any of them, not Mosca, or Marco, or Grito, not even Alexis. But they were growing inside her. They wouldn't leave her alone.

Beneath the water, the man who had been following, the shadow in death's mask, found me.

He closed his hand around my arm, tugging me into a cement room with only a bare bulb and the scent of sweat tortured out. I turned in the water, nothing to propel off but a fading catalyst within, nothing to kick against but the air exiting me. I bit his fingers and my mouth exploded with salt. He was nothing. Nothing other than the one room I wouldn't go into. The one room that held the one way I could have saved Alexis. The light swung from a bare bulb into the yellow streetlamps of my abuela's apartment on Calle Grillo, and the silence into the sound of the garbage truck backing up the night Alexis asked me for help and I wouldn't. I closed my eyes because I knew who I would see next if I didn't. I heard the door open and Alexis walk in. I didn't want to see him beneath the water. If I looked at him, then he couldn't come back with me. I knew that much.

Like he had above the water, Alexis asked me to keep the package, and again I refused and fell asleep. All this was the same. All this was the reel in my head I could not stop, that, since he disappeared, would spin me into and out of an endless half-sleep.

I pulled myself up, out of the memory, and into the water. I kept my eyes closed, but I yelled after him. "I'll take it," I said. "Please, I will keep you safe."

But beneath the water, Alexis hadn't left my room.

My eyes shut, I could hear him walk slowly up to my bed, quietly, as if I were still sleeping. He slipped the package beneath my bed, behind books and old clothes, beside the boxes of my parents' belongings, left it there, to gather dust.

This wasn't a dream. This wasn't part of the reel. This was the sight the water gave me. Alexis stood by my bed, and this time, beneath the water, he woke me. My eyes opened when he put his hand on my arm, and I couldn't stop them from seeing him. He wanted me to see him there, beneath the water, where only the dead live.

"You have it," he said, almost laughing. "Under your bed with all that other fucking junk."

He held on to my arm, gripping it tightly. His hand was a carbon wire used to cut through metal. It was cutting through my skin, but I didn't want him to let go. Even if his hand were a wire, it was still his hand. It was still him. I looked at him and looked at him and looked at him and I didn't look away. My looking meant he had to stay there. It meant I could go back.

He knelt down, reached under the bed, and pushed aside the old boxes knotted in twine. He pulled out a small cardboard box, about the size of a bag of flour. "It wasn't me you saw," he said. "I didn't lead you here."

He set the box, battered and covered in shredded packing tape, on my lap. I opened it. He grabbed hold of my arm again. The box was full of papers and photos like the one Alexis had shown me of our parents; there were notes of recorded conversations, there were memos that ordered death as casually as an afternoon espresso, there were names. In the photos, the mouths were open, calling me.

Each photo I pulled from the box floated out of my hand

and up through the water. I plucked them one by one until there was only one left—completely black and undeveloped. Yet when I touched it, a face slowly surfaced: Alexis. Blackness behind him, his face the only object the flash could catch clearly in the dark. The shadow of the river just a smudge on the film. The sand a cushion beneath his knees. I stared at the photo until I knew his features were layered on mine, an endless series of exposures, until I saw out of his eyes.

On the sand that final night, Alexis could just see the outline of the bridge where we played years ago. We would race to the edge and dare to take one step farther out onto the crumbling wood, the river rushing brown and black beneath us. If Alexis looked hard enough, he could see my silhouette when I was still taller than he was, putting my hand on his shoulder and pulling him away from the edge of the bridge. It might have been something he imagined, that never happened, but even though it was dark and he was on his knees and men's legs surrounded him, blocking everything but the sand and their black boots shifting in it, he could see it anyway, me catching him.

But it was no longer the bridge he saw. It was sand, it was rock, it was a leather heel at his neck, and a gun. He tried to explain, he knew nothing, had done nothing, would say nothing, but the men didn't speak. There was nothing to explain. No questions to ask. It was the cold of the gun making a perfect circle at his temple, but it was not the gun. It was the hand pulling his hair and his neck stretched back, mirroring the river curving, and a knife above him and moving across. They pulled his head farther back, he could see the bridge and the cathedral golden with floodlights and the river black and finally, finally the stars. What had been following him found him after so long. But he looked through it straight into my eyes, my face lit with water.

I opened my mouth to speak, as I knew he had, to say the words I'd come to say, to beg him for forgiveness. But there was no air left. Instead I pressed into his hand gripping my arm, letting it vise to my skin, welding me to him in a way that could never be undone, anchoring me, forever.

Above the water, Mosca's abuela knelt before her shrine. She stared up at the carved faces of Saint Judas Tadeo, for helpless causes, Saint Juan de Sahagún, for the city that was still Mosca's home, and Saint Teresa de Ávila, protector of writers, those with headaches, and those who feel God press down on their skin to wake with bruises. On the shrine was a wooden box that had once held nuns' marzipan, filled with stacks of funeral cards—a saint on the front, the dead's dates and a chosen prayer on the back. The box was full of cards: the abuela's children, her husband, her grandson. On the shrine was Mosca's penknife that her abuela had found on the kitchen table the night she didn't return. Every week she dusted Mosca's room, wiped down the desk, and straightened the blanket. Though no one had slept there in months, there was still old skin drifting down through the air to cover and re-cover the surfaces of the room. Mosca had once told her that dust is mostly that, human skin. Though it made her shiver and think she'd gone mad, Mosca's abuela collected the dust on her rag and shook it into the marzipan box. She used the same cloth to dust her saints as to clean Mosca's room because she believed that the saints, too, were not really dead. Beneath Mosca's bed was a box she would not touch for the same reasons she polished her saints with the rag from Mosca's room, for the same reasons she believed that dead wood would bring life to dead skin. She believed her prayers could bring Mosca back.

Beneath the water, objects floated by me. But I no longer saw divided rooms and mountain pools. Just wires, trash, metal rusting whole. I passed something dead—a body whitened by salt. It didn't look how Alexis had looked, unmarred, speaking, and showing me what I could not see above the water. The body was drifting with the current, skin glowing green, fish trailing its eyes and too-wide mouth. I should not be here. I followed a thick brown cloud to a slash on my arm. The blood billowed into the water like squid ink. But I didn't have those tendril legs that can move without effort, that seem to be made of air. I should not be here. I clasped my arm to slow the blood and headed toward the lights reflecting on the surface of the water. But the surface was too far. I was paper weighted only in names and faces. No matter how I flailed, I could no longer stop my descent. I was sinking.

Above the water, La Canaria whispered and her breath fogged white around her. She said, Marco is a chicken and Grito is a weasel and Mosca is a fucking pussy. She said, I am not a bird or an island but a fish getting eaten from the inside and the out. She didn't know why she'd lied to Mosca except that Mosca deserved a lie for all of hers. Betrayal is not so easy as what you didn't do or a weight growing inside you don't want. Betrayal is something else. It runs you red.

La Canaria feared her baby would be only air. Air would be enough or a total lack of it, boiling up from the inside. If she had to guess, she'd say it was Grito. Drowning inside her for months. She lied only because it was the words Mosca needed. It was the words that Marco wouldn't say, that Grito slipping under the water had let loose inside of them. And they might have been true. Alexis had been growing inside her, too, for so long, growing larger each day she refused to name the lack he occupied. Name him a loss she could not forget.

La Canaria leaned against the bridge overlooking the dam. There was no one beside her. She wanted to watch something burn. She had sent everyone away. There were no bodies to be found. She would get on a boat or a plane and go to a new land, and this thing inside her would burst from the pressure. Seep out in rolls of paper ribbons yellow and black or fade into steam. Or it would be solid and squirming. And because it was hers and only hers, she would love it.

But no, it would not wait. There was water beneath her, water not from the dam but from deep inside her. It was coming. They were all hers. Grito and Marco and Mosca and Alexis. They were all growing inside her, and she made them hers. La Canaria pulled them out of her wet body one by one, out of the red of her dark room. She reached down to pull Mosca from the water and brought the rest behind her. She held them up to the light.

She could go anywhere she wanted.

Above the water, Marco stood on the sand, looking for a break in the waves. Behind him, the Carnival crowds screamed and cheered, making up new words to old songs, forgetting and remembering in one breath, throwing their heads back to dance against the stars. He saw letters he recognized on the breaker wall, though they had faded. He reached his hand to touch the spray-painted tag: *A L X S*. His fingertips traced the long tail of the *X* until it broke off where the wall ended and he touched only air. Then he sat on the edge of the water, dug his hands into the sand until they were drenched, and repeated Mosca's name. He didn't know how long he had been sitting, his voice rubbed raw into a whisper, when he saw something break through the water.

He swam out to it and saw Mosca, dark hair trailing, skin reflecting the moonlight, body limp but buoyed somehow. He saw that her mouth was just above the surface of the water and she was gasping for air. Marco wrapped his arm around her and swam toward the shore.

CASASROJAS, CASTILE-LEÓN
1978

Spring again, just before dawn, and the plaza is full of students. Though the night is almost over, they are still celebrating passing their exams and still spilling cava on the cobblestones to toast those who've graduated. We skirt the plaza and walk straight toward the philology library. The windows are dark. It's closed, but what I want right now is not inside. I find the spot on the wall of the library where I was going to write my initials when I graduated. The same spot I pointed out to Alexis when we were young, the spot that is visible from the train leaving the city. I climb up the huge slabs of golden stone, turning pink with the sunrise. The cut on my arm still aches. It is healing into bright pink slashes, the memory of a hand printed deep into my skin. It smells of salt and washed-up kelp. I prick my finger with a piece of glass I found by the shore. Then I press hard into the slash on my arm. I want the blood from the scar to be the blood that comes out of my finger. I press my hand down next to all the other signatures. But I don't write. The blood courses out of me and settles deep in the stone, wetting what was once dirt, marking it as long as it can.

Marco helps me down from the library's walls and we walk through Casasrojas. The students stumble out of bars, lift their bottles to the men sweeping the cobblestones and fixing the flickering lights underneath the bridges. Calle Grillo is packed. Men and women too old to be out this late walk arm in arm.

The stones are wet from someone's laundry. Soap bubbles circle the sewage pipes. Marco will go to Grito's abuela. He will not be able to explain, but he will speak. For now, he stays outside and I climb the stairs to my abuela's apartment.

The elections have come and gone, and they are writing a constitution. The price of democracy is that there will be no trials and everyone will forget: the piles of bodies, the disappeared, what both sides did in a war that wouldn't end.

We went to the bridge beside the cathedral. The water rushed in dark shapes. The sand was littered with plastic bags and drowned milk cartons. Broken gold chain-links glittered up through the sand. At the edge of the bridge, my toes curled around the decaying railroad tracks. I took off Alexis's medallion and the rope necklace wrapped around La Canaria's bullet. As they fell, the water reflected them back at me, larger and larger, until they disappeared, intertwined, into its depths. The river will keep them safer than I can.

At the bridge, I took Marco's hand. We'd both failed. The betrayal complete. A body fully formed and buried in the waters beneath our skin, moving through us, whole and breathing. What we'd done is big enough to live in. It is big enough to hold us both.

In my room is the box Alexis hid, what I once refused. I will pull it out from under my bed. I will place the photo of my parents on my abuela's shrine. And the rest, the others, their strained necks and bound hands, the lists of names, murdered and murderer, Marco and I will take to the print shop beneath the philology library. There, where I studied for hours, where I learned that anyone can die, we will strike up the machines and make the names repeat. The grays and blacks will spark to yellow and orange, a river of faces, tongues alive and crackling, blazing through the city—because I have done my forgetting. I don't want to anymore.

I come to the top of the stairs. Through the door, I hear my abuela moving, her hands already turning the lock. I will not need to speak when she opens the door. The water is written on me, its baptism soaking everything I touch. It says I know who's alive and who isn't. I know just who I am bringing home.

Acknowledgments

Massive, planet-imploding thanks:

To Reginald McKnight, for believing passionately in this book and for continuing to strengthen my trust in my work.

To Elisabeth Sheffield, for being one of the earliest and deepest readers.

To my wonderful agent, Ethan Bassoff, for making the book better and for fighting for me.

To everyone at Touchstone, especially my editor, Etinosa Agbonlahor, for your keen eye, intelligence, and brilliant problem-solving skills.

To my friends and readers in Boulder, the Sunday Salon, especially: Caroline Davidson, Nick Kimbro, Shannon Douglas Kimbro, Vanessa Angelica Villareal, and Rachel Levy. For the support I received from the University of Colorado-Boulder, and a huge thanks to my teachers there, especially: Stephen Graham Jones, Jeffrey DeShell, Karen Jacobs, and Julie Carr.

To my artist family in Athens, in you I've found friendship and home, especially Magdalena Zurawski, Shamala Gallagher, Lindsay Tigue, Gina Abelkop, Adam Gardner, Kristen Gleason, Jenny Gropp, and Prosper Hedges. Thank you to the University of Georgia for the support I received while editing this book.

ACKNOWLEDGMENTS

To all the kind people I stayed with in Europe, who bear no resemblance to any unpleasant characters found here, though they might recognize their homes and surroundings. To my teachers and mentors, especially at Brown and Interlochen.

To my dear friends stretched across the time zones, to Jason, and to the ladies of 168 Williams.

To my family in Wisconsin and Miami: I love you deeply and keep you close to my heart.

To my parents, for everything.

To Thibault, for the Church of Art and Love.

And to Daniel, who I am always looking for, and always finding.

Gabrielle Lucille Fuentes has received fellowships from Yaddo, the Millay Colony, and the Blue Mountain Center, and was a Bernard O'Keefe Scholar in Fiction at Bread Loaf. Her work has appeared in *One Story*, *Slice*, *Pank*, and elsewhere. She is Cuban American, was born in Wisconsin, and has lived in Spain and France.

TOUCHSTONE READING GROUP GUIDE

THE
SLEEPING
WORLD

Gabrielle Lucille Fuentes

For Discussion

1. Discuss your theories about the significance of the title *The Sleeping World*. Why do you think the author chose it?

2. Mosca and her friends love punk music such as Patti Smith and the Ramones. Why do you think they are drawn to punk?

3. Reflecting on her abuela's experiences after the war and the teachings of those who have come before her, Mosca declares: "Our tongue the tongues of murderers. The general didn't come from nowhere." Do you agree with Mosca that Franco's regime of oppression was inevitable and that it was fostered by Spain's history of genocide and imperialism toward other nations?

4. Each of the main characters has a defining nickname: Mosca (Fly), La Canaria (the Canary), Grito (Scream). Discuss the author's choice in giving nontraditional, distinctive names, and the symbolism behind them.

5. Why do you think Mosca is so intent on hiding her true reason for wanting to go to Paris? How do you think Marco and La Canaria would have reacted had she been open with them?

6. Mosca's abuela remembers the devastation of the war. She recalls that "their means of breaking you [were] very specific." How does that time of upheaval compare to Mosca's generation's?

7. How does Fuentes's retelling of student activism and unrest in Spain in 1977 compare to the political unrest among young people today? How much is universal in these upheavals throughout history?

8. Mosca asserts that it is "better to stay numb than to know the details of your frostbite." Do you agree with this sentiment?

9. What do you think La Canaria wants and how does that change throughout her journey with the others?

10. The final pages of the novel contain several passages that repeat the imagery of being "beneath the water," with several references to purification, the tide, waves, sinking, drowning, and baptism. Why did the author make this choice? Consider other places where water is significant in the narrative.

A Conversation with Gabrielle Lucille Fuentes

What inspired you to write about this time and place?
I wanted to study abroad in Cuba, where my father was born, but at the time it wasn't possible. Any other Latin American country felt like a betrayal and I've always been a Europhile (for mixed and dubious reasons) so I chose Spain. The rest wasn't really a choice. The first chapter came years later and almost whole cloth—complete with setting and time period. When I slow down my own intuition, I think Spain during the transition was the perfect mix of close and far. The time was separate enough from me to imagine a new narrative into it and yet it spoke of both current political realities and my own emotional landscape. My younger brother had just passed away. Mosca's journey was, of course, my

own: through numbness and fear, into the deep recesses of longing. I wrote into my grief as the only way I could experience or imagine it. I wrote to keep both him and myself alive.

The Sleeping World **is filled with strong, distinctive young characters. Why did you choose Mosca's point of view to tell this story in particular?**

The Sleeping World is Mosca's story. It wouldn't be possible from any other perspective. She is the character most connected to me emotionally and a way for me to move into grief. I can't imagine the novel from any other perspective than a woman's perspective. The only other character who could narrate would be La Canaria. That would be an entirely different book. A very interesting one.

How much research went into your process, and was it difficult to divide time between analytical research and more creative inspiration?

Luckily much of the research had happened years before the writing started so there was time for the information and facts used to structure the narrative to sink in and become less conscious. I studied at the University of Salamanca in 2007—and what became research for *The Sleeping World* was at the time just me living and going to school: staying up late, drinking wine in parks, camping in sheep pastures, and not doing much actual studying for the first time in my life. I read different pre- and postwar Spanish authors [and] Spanish history, and met people who had lived through the transition. Many of the young Spaniards I hung out with then were similar aesthetically and politically to Mosca's friends. They had a punk sense of fashion, organized freegan potlucks, were frustrated by the older conservative citizens, drank cheap beer, etc. They had a wildness and desperation to them that I was attracted to—perhaps I'm romanticizing, but that's how it felt. I drew on my actual experience for much of the texture of the novel.

So much of writing a novel is problem solving, and so much of problem solving is movement into instinct. Especially with a character like Mosca, who is so guarded and thoughtful—she's very careful with her words—I have to balance letting her speak alongside my own sense of the narrative, the symbolism, the politics. The more official research came after the first draft but was also a creative act—I was following hunches, snatches of sentences, moods, and trusting I would find that the things I'd written had in fact happened, or something that bore an emotional resemblance to them had.

What is the first thing you like to tell students in your creative writing classes?
It changes from semester to semester. I like to teach contemporary work—or what I'm currently excited by. There's a freedom with creative writing courses in that the texts can be modeled after one's own (shifting) artistic practice. Something that I've used in the past to start the course and want to repeat is Sister Corita Kent's Rules, which are part art object/part list. The Rules are easily available online and often misattributed to John Cage—who was the more famous male in the equation. They are a simple list that she posted outside of her art classes: how to be an artist/student/teacher. The Rules focus on work, on messing up, on a sort of uncreative push that feels very catholic (little *c*) to me. They make creative work more possible without removing its mystery.

How much resonance do you see between the upheaval Mosca and her friends faced compared to the political unrest in the world today?

Writing about Spain in the 1970s was definitely a way for me to write slant about several different histories as well as my own present. In a way, Mosca's generation is similar to my own. There's a deep sense of betrayal and mistrust—that those who were supposed to be leading us were in fact destroying any hopes of a livable future. I wrote the first draft of *The Sleeping World* alongside the Arab Spring and Occupy movements and as I kept writing, the abuse of power by our political and police forces (whether by kidnapping Mexican students or murdering black citizens across the U.S.) became ever more visible. I think of this as an American book, as it is informed by the injustices and struggles happening in the U.S. and Latin America. This all sounds generalizing, which is why I write fiction. With fiction, with a novel, I can speak specifically and deeply about a certain place and time, and, like a case study, as Chris Kraus writes, my writing can be used as a paradigm for the reader. What the reader applies the case study to is her own choice.

The last few pages of the book are ambiguous, almost surreal, filled with poetry and symbolism. Were you influenced by the magical realism of Latin American writers? What other writers have inspired you?
For me, those final pages are absolutely real. All through the book, Mosca has been running from the reality of her past, refusing to recognize the truth of her haunting. Then she finally stops and yes, everything falls apart, including the language, but it was absolutely necessary. A sort of sense had to break down to express her emotional reality and for her to continue in the world of the living. I'm definitely influenced by Gabriel García Márquez and Jorge Luis Borges but for me, *magical realism* is a mistranslation that never quite fit those writers and doesn't fit me. I believe in mystery on many levels: I make these events real

in my writing; I need them to accurately express lived experience and emotions; and, most important, I know they were real long before me and will continue to be long after me.

Toni Morrison—in both her critical writing and her novels—has shaped me more than perhaps any other single writer. She is the greatest, but of course needs none of my praise. In terms of other influences, for *The Sleeping World* I drew on many books, especially: Kazim Ali's *Bright Felon*, Cristina García's *Dreaming in Cuban*, Laird Hunt's *Ray of the Star*, Simone de Beauvoir's *The Mandarins*, Jennifer Egan's *A Visit from the Goon Squad*, Selah Saterstrom's *The Meat and Spirit Plan*, and of course, Federico García Lorca's plays and poems and Carmen Laforet's *Nada*. Music and film were extremely important: Pedro Almodovar's films, especially his early ones; Albert Camus's *Black Orpheus*; the Clash; the Ramones; Patti Smith; and I doubt this particular book would exist without many repeated revolutions of the National's *High Violet*.

As a debut novelist, what advice would you give to other aspiring writers?

Read extensively and strangely. Read books from before you were born by people different from you. I love Tove Jansson, Tarjei Vesaas, Halldór Laxness, Sei Shōnagon. Find people whose writing/thinking/spirit you respect and see if you can trick them into reading your work. Find people who write and make art and figure out how they do it. And spend just so much time writing. Writing isn't conceptual; it's only possible in its own practice. Only in the actual writing will you find out what you believe and what kind of writer you are, which is, of course, the only writer you can possibly be.

Enhance Your Book Club

1. Do some research with your group about Spain in 1977. How does Fuentes bring the time and place to life? How much did you know about this time period before reading the book, and what did you learn while reading that surprised you?

2. Create a playlist based on the songs mentioned throughout the novel and listen to it during your discussion. How does the music affect you when you think about the political atmosphere of Mosca's time?